8TH GRADE SUPER ZERO

OLUGBEMISOLA RHUDAY-PERKOVICH

8TH GRADE SUPER ZERO

SCHOLASTIC INC.
New York Toronto London Auckland
Sydney Mexico City New Delhi Hong Kong

ISBN 978-0-545-09725-3

Arthur A. Levine Books hardcover edition designed by Christopher Stengel, published by Arthur A. Levine Books, an imprint of Scholastic Inc., January 2010.

12 11 10 9 8 7 6 5 4 3 2 1   11 12 13 14 15 16/0

Printed in the U.S.A.   40

First paperback printing, June 2011

"Speech to the Young: Speech to the Progress-Toward" by Gwendolyn Brooks reprinted by consent of Brooks Permissions.

For all those who pick up their teaspoons to do a little bit wherever they are.

Everyone knows what's up, because it's the first day of school and I set the tone.

Donovan's opened his stupid mouth one too many times. He's too much of a coward to say anything to my face, and the punk takes pleasure in harassing people when I'm not around. I've tried to cut him some slack, because I know he's insecure . . . but now he's done it and I'm walking down the hall toward him, past everyone at their lockers, and the silence is so heavy that I feel like I have to hold it up with my own two hands. One of the security guards moves in my direction, but Principal Blaylock holds him back.

Even Blaylock knows.

It's my time now.

A little boy wants to run with me, and I stop to tie his shoelaces so he won't trip. I pat him on the back and toss him an autographed copy of Night Man: Under Pressure, Underground. First edition. Hands trembling, he slips it into a plastic bag right away.

I'm getting closer now, and Donovan's up against the wall and breathing hard.

I'm almost there. I can see the fear in his eyes.

And suddenly —

He bolts.

The entire school gasps as Donovan Greene scurries out of the school building, tripping over his own feet as he stumbles through the doors.

That's right.

You better run, punk.

I stop and turn slowly, scanning the crowd that has gathered to see the great Reggie McKnight, Night Man creator, superhero simulator, triumph yet again without even lifting a finger.

Mialonie Davis, who's been working everything she's got to get next to me, is smiling, eyes sparkling. Justin Walker, the second-coolest boy in school, starts a slow, solid clap that echoes and resonates. It's like a movie; soon everyone joins in.

The applause is thunderous.

And they're clapping for me.

Again.

I saved the day.

Again.

The school TV show asks if they can profile me, and I'm fine with that, as long as we feature the Green Team environmental club and the Peace Is the Word discussion circle — we are all stars at Clarke Junior School. Joe C. starts the chant of my name: "Reg-gie! Reg-gie! Reg-gie!" and I nod and smile as even Blaylock and Ms. A get into it. Ruthie starts people doing the wave.

This never gets old.

I am Reggie McKnight.

I am King of Clarke Junior School.

I am —

OCTOBER 5
8:08 A.M.

"Hey, Pukey, got a pen?" Hector Vega jabs me in the back. He does this every day. Mostly so he can write "The Villain Vega" — his future pro wrestling name — all over his notebooks. I hand a blue ballpoint over my shoulder without looking, then Hector taps me so I can turn around and see him stick the pen down his throat and fake gag.

Almost a month of this. Every. Single. Day. And he still cracks himself up.

"Ignore him," whispers my best friend Ruthie. "You will need so much therapy when you're forty," she tells Hector, her braids swinging. She turns back to me and mutters, "Reggie, you really should —"

She stops when Ms. Anderson shoots a look our way. Ms. A's cool, but she's no joke. She's also Dean of Students, which is basically Dean of Detention. I hope she didn't see me sleeping a minute ago. Ruthie usually pokes me if I'm about to get busted, so I figure I'm okay.

Hector's still snickering. And if Sean Glanville weren't up front doing his current events report right now, he'd be back here laughing it up too, like Hector was some kind of joke conquistador. Clarke Junior is a smart kids' school that's supposed to have high standards; I don't know how Hector and Sean got in. I just hope they end up at Future Leaders Alternative School next year, with my big sister Monica and other jerks with "suppressed promise," as her principal says in his letters home.

Sean sits down and Ruthie volunteers to deliver her report next. She marches up to the front with her usual mountain of papers.

"Ruth," says Ms. A, "we don't have a lot of time and I'd like to give others a chance. That looks . . . extensive."

"Because of the American media's obvious bias, I used seventeen different global news sources — including the *Madagascar Weekly* — to put my report together." Ruthie tries to stare Ms. A down.

"You have three minutes," says Ms. A.

Ruthie loses the stare-down. My other best friend, Joe C., laughs. Ms. A growls at him, "Mr. Castiglione, feel free to Close. Your. Mouth. Now." Definitely not a good day when she calls him "Mr. Castiglione" instead of Joe C.

Ruthie's titled her environmental racism report "Closer to Death with Every Breath," and it has a whole apocalyptic you're-going-to-DIE-TODAY! factor that wakes us up for a few minutes. But it's not enough to run out the clock. I keep my head down; the last thing I want to hear is Ms. A trilling "Reginaaald? What news do you have for us today?" Then I'd have to walk up to the front and somebody would try to trip me or something.

Donovan Greene tosses Justin Walker a note, and Justin smiles as he reads it. Donovan makes me sick the way he sucks up to Justin. He acts like he didn't used to come over to my house every day after school.

"Ruth, thank you very much for that extensive report. Let's get some more in. . . ."

"Sorry for this brief interruption," says Principal Blaylock from the doorway. "Time for a little Clarke community booster shot!" He tries to strut into the room, but gets tripped from behind by Assistant Principal Gordon, who's walking his hunched-over, prehistoric man walk as usual.

"I have a very special announcement," Blaylock says. "The mayor has just announced a new program called the Young People Participate Project, which will award grants to New York City schools that exemplify the spirit of community partnership and student leadership. Clarke, with its proud tradition of student involvement, would be a shining candidate for this honor — except, as you know, we were left, rather unpleasantly, without a school president this year. Thus, after much deliberation and examination of the budget, I am most pleased to announce that a new presidential campaign season has officially begun! And we're going to do it right this time." He glares at us. "We will have REAL candidates, REAL campaigning, and REAL rallies, and the winner will be announced at the Holiday Jam. This is a big opportunity for a member of the eighth grade to step up and be a Clarke School Power Broker! Leader of Tomorrow, I know you're out there!"

Yeah, I guess, since our elected Leader of Tomorrow decided that the school presidency was too Yesterday. Last June Brian Allerton resigned the day after the election and called it subversive. Blaylock held an emergency assembly to yell at us for forty-five minutes about responsibility and respect, but no one cared. Blaylock sounds like he's on a mission this time — I guess this money thing makes it a whole new ball game.

"Perhaps," says Ms. A, standing, "this is an appropriate time for a meaningful discussion about leadership: what is important at Clarke, why we celebrate the Clarke Pledge of Proactive Community Service every year, what a Clarke leader should be."

Blaylock looks confused, like Ms. A is something that's not supposed to happen. I guess standing around and doing nothing all the time is pretty taxing, because Gordon uses his Assistant Principal status to slip into Ms. A's seat. He pretends not to notice her glare.

Vicky Ross coughs loudly and sits up so straight she's about six inches taller.

Blaylock clears his throat. "I'm glad to hear you agree with me, Ms. Anderson. Civic responsibility and democratic principles are embedded in Clarke's collective consciousness." He switches to Suspension Voice. "Some of you may not realize this, but somehow the election process has a tendency to DEGENERATE into a POPULARITY contest. This is not about who's COOL or who's a NERD. . . ."

He blowhards on and on, and a few kids start checking their text messages. Elections have always been a joke here. We only elect a president, no other officers, and the only thing the president does is plan class competition night, when we have three-legged races and a cheesecake-eating contest. That's it. For the whole year. The campaign is all about big lies ("I will change everything!"), big speeches at the big assemblies ("I will change everything! Repeat after me: woo hoo!"), and a vote that crowns someone Most Popular of the Year. Clarke's motto is "For the students, by the students, and of the students . . . with a little help from their friends."

I think we need more help or more friends.

Ms. A tries again. "Perhaps we should address that. Popularity does seem to be the primary qualification when it comes to the Clarke presidency. Can that change? Do you want it to change? Are we ready to see this election as a challenge to upset the status quo?"

"Yeah," says Ruthie. "Are we finally ready for a revolution?"

Yeah, right. Now that Brian's gone, Justin is destined to be president. He's the guy every girl wants and every guy wants to be. Even me. Back in third grade I was hall monitor for two weeks and thought I was destined for political greatness. But sixth grade and reality struck hard, and I realized that I was lucky just to have the right to vote. Guys like me who are *thisclose* to last pick for teams do not become president except on TV or in some dumb movie. Guys like me focus on how to get through the rest of the year under the radar and on the sidelines. We save the fantasy life for our fantasies.

I should write down the dream I was having before Hector woke me up. The best part was when Donovan punked out. And Clarke was a place where people cared.

Blaylock stops blabbing for a second, and Vicky Ross jumps in. "Ahem. I have a few words that I'd like to say on the subject of the election."

Blaylock closes his eyes for a minute, and gives Vicky a quick nod.

"As Principal Blaylock said," starts Vicky, "we need to have a meaningful discussion about leadership." She pauses, and holds her head so high you can see up her nose.

"Principal Blaylock didn't say that," says Ruthie. "Ms. A did."

"Our school newspaper is supposed to be the voice of the people," Vicky continues. "We're the people, yet the issues that concern us are ignored. I feel that the paper should include regular profiles of high-achieving students, the ones who show leadership and inspire the rest of you — er, us," she finishes, like she's just made the Emancipation Proclamation.

"I feel that there shouldn't be a newspaper at all," mutters Hector. "Maybe if we paid less attention to current events, we could focus on real life."

Ruthie doesn't even raise her hand. "Are you for real, Vicky? You're focusing on how to position yourself for the Ivy League when sub-Saharan Africa is about to implode?"

A few people groan. "Please don't let her take that map out again," whispers Veronica Cruz.

Vicky plows ahead. "I'm talking about real leadership," she says. "We saw what happened last year. It was a complete popularity contest and a waste of time." A few people are nodding. "We need to cultivate an elite team of leaders at Clarke."

"That doesn't sound very community-oriented," says Mialonie Davis. That voice. Is singing to me. "Clarke is supposed to be one big happy family, helping hands, and all that stuff the Pledge says." A few people snort, and Sean Glanville laughs out loud.

This is so stupid. No one's answering Ms. A's questions, and most people don't even want to. I feel Ms. A's eyes on me, like she knows what I'm thinking and wants me to say something, but she's crazy if she thinks I'm about to put myself out there. This place is hopeless.

Isobel Sirrett raises her hand. "I have a question about the reading assignment from yesterday. Is it going to be on the test?"

Yep, that's the *real* Clarke.

Ms. A holds up a hand. "Does anyone else want to add to our discussion about civic responsibility?" Vicky opens her mouth, but Ms. A switches to "talk to the hand" by keeping her hand up and turning her head.

Justin looks up. "Clarke isn't that bad. We all work hard, and we're good people. Why do we have to be so negative all of the time?"

"Yeah," chimes in Donovan. "A president should be somebody who brings positive energy."

It's not negative to want to make things better, I think.

"That's not the point," says Joe C. "Anyway, if we're having a do-over, it would be nice if the candidates talked about real issues. Like the cafeteria food. Like the bathrooms."

"Like the losers who create more work for the janitors on the first day of school," says Donovan, snickering.

I won't look at him.

"He's talking about you, Pukey," whispers Hector.

Yeah, I got that.

"Leadership should certainly inspire," says Blaylock, who has been standing there like he's wondering who he is. "And also present the most attractive face of the Clarke community to the, um, community."

"Attractive?" says Ruthie. "What does that mean?"

"Well, uh," mumbles Blaylock, "my dear, I'm saying that a leader . . . looks and sounds like a leader!" He's all triumphant, like he won something.

Ruthie's getting geared up, but Ms. Anderson speaks first. "Well, thank you so much, Principal Blaylock, for spearheading that . . . illuminating and inspiring discussion. You most certainly exemplify the type of leader you've described."

A preschooler would have recognized the sarcasm in Ms. A's voice, but Blaylock just puffs up a little more. "Er, yes. Well. Dr. Gordon, on to our next classroom community circle! Thank you, Ms. Anderson, for your time."

Gordon and Blaylock leave; Blaylock turns around to give the class a double thumbs-up.

Ms. A shakes her head a little. "Back to work."

Two minutes to go. Ms. A looks around the room. I cross my fingers and look down at my desk.

"Reginaaald? What news do you have for us today?"

11:07 A.M.

Cafeteria food is usually puke-worthy (tuna fish tacos — with barbecue sauce), but today is pizza day, so I'm taking my chances. I hold my breath while I'm in line; no matter what's for lunch, it's funky — like hot dogs cooking in bleach.

Me and Joe C. wind our way through the crowd to our table in the corner. He gives me the apple juice from his tray and takes three bottles of Juiced! out of his backpack. "Uh, my mom said she had some new leads that your dad might be interested in," he says without looking at me. I don't know why he's embarrassed; his father's not the one out of a job. I don't respond, and he leaves it alone.

Hector and his crowd are at the next table and they're laughing. Is something on my back? I hope I didn't sit on anything. I bite into my pizza and wish it were one of the peanut butter and plantain sandwiches that my mom made for me every day of second grade. She called it the "Jamerican."

Joe C. cracks his Juiced! open and reads the trivia inside the bottle cap. "'Did you know that when doctors drilled holes into the heads of dead boxers, their liquefied brains just oozed out of their skulls?'"

"Having you tell me stupid trivia like 'a rabbit likes to snack on its own poop' is really getting old. Nobody wants to hear that stuff. I know girls don't."

"Then they're not the girls for me. Besides, I have Maria. You keep forgetting."

I wonder why. Joe C.'s my boy and all, but he allegedly has this *thing* with a girl named Maria Salvucci from his old neighborhood. He says they have an *understanding* and they hang out when he goes to his dad's house. No one's ever seen her, not even me.

"So what do you think about this election do-over thing?" I say. "All that stuff Ms. A was saying about change; I wish it could happen. I wish people like Donovan weren't the ones who set the tone."

Joe C. wipes a little Juiced! from his mouth. "Whatever. Blaylock just wants that money and to get on TV. Vicky is obviously going to run this time, no one will care. So she gets to plan toilet-paper tree-wrapping races. Woo. Hoo. And forget Donovan. I mean, I know it's hard, since, um, you know, but . . . I keep telling you, keep a low profile and it'll all blow over." He hands me some paper. "Some Night Man panels for you to look over."

"You've been working a lot," I say, scanning the pages.

He shrugs. "You come up with good stories," he says. "I liked that thing with Night Man and Valkyryna; it's hot. Just don't make it all mushy."

When I was in kindergarten I created this Night Man character — a busted-looking homeless man by day, vigilante for justice by night. Night Man is the kind of guy I want to be. Well, not the homeless part. The hero. People ignore him because they think he's just a dirty street guy, and then *BAM!* — he's the one saving the world.

He doesn't puke in public.

I turned Night Man into a series of graphic novels; I focus on the story, Joe C. does the art. When I started writing, Donovan liked to draw a little, so he covered that. But when Joe C. came along with his three years of illustration classes, we took it to another level. Donovan stopped helping pretty fast.

We've put together *Night Man* Volumes I through VI already, and I tried to write the Big Finish all summer, because my sister Monica told me that eighth grade is your last chance to cement a positive image. I was going to present *Night Man*, like *BAM!* at the first day of school assembly — but something else ended up on display.

"These are good," I say, handing back his drawings. "I need to get inspired; I want the ending to be really big."

"You'll come up with something," Joe C. says. "You always do."

Ruthie plops down next to me, almost knocking down Joe

C.'s row of Juiced! bottles. I'm afraid to look at her lunch. Last week she made a vow to "effectively utilize nutritional resources" because of all the people starving in the world, so she mixes different leftovers and calls it a meal. She says her usual quick prayer and pulls out slices of beets and cheese on an end piece of whole wheat bread. Ruthie's been my best friend ever since kindergarten, when we were both in the West Indian American Day Junior Parade and she said I wasn't a real Jamaican. Yeah, I was born right here in Brooklyn so I'm more "Yankee" than "Yardie," but she came here when she was three, so whatever.

"I may get the New World Order Collective going again," says Ruthie. "I can't be the only person who cares about thinking globally."

"Maybe you should start another petition," says Joe C., elbowing me.

"I already have. Cristina Rodriguez was in the library. She was my first signee."

"Hey," I say. "I bet if you add up all of the signatures on all of your petitions, Ruthie, you'd have, like . . . tens of names!" Joe C. and I laugh. Ruthie does too. Ruthie's okay. Even though she takes a bite of my pizza.

"I'm sorry that I don't concentrate on more important things, like comic books," she says, rolling her eyes. Not okay. She grabs some of my chips.

"Can I offer you something to eat?" I ask. "Something of yours?" She takes more of my pizza. I grab it back from her just as "Sparrow" Barrow and Vijay Chandra come by our table. Sparrow's chattering as usual, and Vijay's carrying a camcorder. They do the school TV show, *Talkin' Trash*, which comes on during homeroom. Sparrow got her nickname because she has the skinniest legs and the chirpiest voice ever.

"Uh . . . Roger?" says Vijay. Everybody used to call him The Terrorist, especially during the annual Tolerance Week activities, but then he grew a hundred feet last summer and now he thinks he's all that. A lot of girls do too.

"It's Reggie," I say.

"Yeah, right," he says, not looking at me. He turns a little so he can face the girls' table next to us; it looks like he's filming their legs. A couple of them are wearing skirts, so knowing Vijay, he's probably aiming a little bit higher.

Sparrow clears her throat. "So, um, Reggie, we're doing an exposé on cafeteria food, and we have a proposal for you." (Giggles.) "You're . . . a *celebrity*," she says (giggle), "and you can put that to good use. We want to do on-air taste tests of cafeteria food. You can be our Puke-O-Meter."

Ruthie snorts. "And you think we can't hit new lows," she says. "I salute you, Erica."

"Thanks," chirps Sparrow. Then she thinks about it for a minute. "Whatever." She turns her back on Ruthie while Vijay lines his camera up with Ruthie's chest area.

"I'm not interested," I say. "At all."

Sparrow starts to say more, but she gets distracted by something a few tables away. "Come on, Vijay, it looks like there might be a food fight." She scampers off on her little bird legs. Why she wears miniskirts every day and Mialonie Davis doesn't is one of the world's great mysteries.

Justin walks into the cafeteria; half the girls start giggling and the other half touch their hair. Donovan runs over to him and I see that the back of Donovan's shirt says Booty Hunter. I hope Blaylock busts him.

It used to be the four of us: me, Donovan, Ruthie, and Joe C. We sat together at lunch. We'd play two-on-two chess in Underwood Park. Donovan taught us poker. Then one day he just didn't show up. We went over to his house to see what was up, and his mom was all, "He's out with his friends." I thought *we* were his friends.

"It would be nice if those two didn't rule the school this year," I say. "If we were all about looking out for one another instead of hierarchy."

"Yuck, 'rule the school,'" says Ruthie. "That's so . . . Western, so imperialistic."

"Whatever, Secretary-General," I say. She's gotten worse since we did Model UN. "This is school. Someone is always at the bottom of the food chain. I just don't want it to be me anymore."

"Nobody likes people who spend their time wanting to be liked," she says. "That's one of the laws of . . . humanity or whatever."

"Easy for you to say. You *like* being weird." I duck and say "Remember Dr. King!" as Ruthie lunges for me.

"Make change, be change," she says, eating one of my peach halves.

"Why don't you run for president?" I shoot back. "You're all about Change with a capital *C*."

"Ha! A revolutionary like me do something so . . . mainstream? Besides, you people are not ready for me full-strength." Ruthie's parents have a storage room full of posters that say things like "End Poverty Now," "No Justice, No Peace," and "They LIED." They use them every six months or so when the whole family marches on Washington for one of the many things they march and yell and write letters about.

"You could pull a Brian Allerton," I say. "If another candidate gets all subversive, people might pay attention."

"That is *not* what being subversive is about." Ruthie pulls out a bag of homemade chocolate chip cookies and hands it to me. "What did that do for Clarke anyway? And where's Brian now? Total establishment." Blaylock came down hard on Brian, and word is that his parents paid a boatload of money to get him into private school.

"Did you bake these cookies, or did your mom?" I ask.

She gives me a look and mutters, "My mom."

I wolf them down.

"I gotta pee," says Joe C.

"Thanks for letting us know," shoots back Ruthie. "Here, take some of this stuff with you," she adds, giving him some of our lunch trash. "And you know I'll be watching you."

"Yeah, yeah, yeah. Recycle, reuse, *repetitive*," he says, getting up. "See you guys later." He turns to me. "Low-pro. You know, just let it go." He smiles and shakes his head. "Poet and didn't know it! I could kiss myself." Ruthie and I both groan, and he leaves.

"Is youth group on Saturday or Sunday this week?" Ruthie asks. "Where are we meeting?"

"I don't know," I reply. "I'll e-mail Dave." Dave is the congregation librarian and youth group leader. Youth group is basically a few of us hanging out and talking about churchy stuff, but it's not boring like church. We're supposed to meet in the library during services on Sundays, but sometimes we have to move the meetings when the bishop bogarts the library for "meditation on the Word." That word is usually "nap."

Lunch is almost over and I can hear girls screeching and squealing as Hector does his grand finale cafeteria trick — shooting milk out of his nose. I see Justin standing next to Mialonie's table, and she's smiling up at him like he's a movie star or something. Donovan is talking to her friend Josie, who's cute, but not as cute as Mialonie.

"Give me that," I say to Ruthie, pointing to the empty milk carton. She hands it to me, and I stand up and toss it into the trash. Two points.

"Woo hoo!" Ruthie yells, but nobody hears.

3:47 P.M.

I make it home just in time to grab a new bag of plantain chips and a Coke before big sister Snuffleupagus gets back and sucks down all the food in sight. I think Pops is around, but he doesn't come out, so I just head upstairs, skipping over the creaky steps. Who knows what kind of mood he's in; sometimes it's worse when he's all fake happy, like a morning show host. He watches a lot of TV while he waits for job phone calls that never come. When I was little, I used to hate it when he'd work late, but now I'm praying for him to have a meeting to go to or something.

There's a Post-it from Mom stuck to my door about the mess in my room. She never gets that I know where everything is, and that's what matters, right? Right. I don't hear any roaring, so

Monica must be out on the courts trying to dunk on some old guys. She spends hours out there, challenging anyone who shows up. She and Pops have been doing extra drills together so she can get ready for community-league tryouts in a few weeks. Guess there's a Big Scary She-Male division.

I step over the books on the floor and turn on my Mac. There's an e-mail from Reverend Coles — he sends out these corny form letters to all the kids that supposedly belong to our church. I guess their parents don't make them go as much as mine do. The subject line of his e-mail is "WAZZUP from a member of the God Squad!" I press delete. Mom and Pops are always pushing me to go see Reverend Coles to talk about spiritual things. They actually want me to open up to someone who says to call him "Reverend *Cools*."

Sometimes I talk to Dave; he does God-talk without preaching. I never say anything to him about the whole Pukey deal, but I think he knows. I hope that's not because he can smell it on me, like Loser Funk or something. I shoot him an e-mail and try to be kind of casual and jokey, like a guy who says "hey" instead of "hi" and gets hugs from all the girls.

I log out and check out the rest of the Night Man ideas that Joe C. gave me. I pick up my notebook and a pen, but I've got nothing.

"Reginald!" Uh-oh. It's Pops.

"Coming." I wipe the crumbs off my face and run downstairs. Pops is in the kitchen.

"I just bought some plantain chips. . . . You haven't happened to have seen them, have you?" Uh-oh. That "have/haven't happened" stuff — he's in a bad mood.

"Uh, yeah, sorry . . . I'll go get them." I start to run back upstairs.

"Forget it. Let's just figure out dinner so your mother doesn't have to come home and cook." He sighs. "So, what's new at school, son?" he says in this real hearty TV dad voice.

"Nothing," I say. He keeps looking at me, so I add, "Oh — we're having a special election do-over . . . for school president. . . ."

The danger with talking about the election is that he's always telling me the same old story about how he was elected Head Boy or Top Dog (or whatever it was called in old-time Jamaica) by a unanimous vote because he had the respect of his peers.

"Now that's something to get involved in — leadership! You know, I was the first boy at St. Joseph's to be elected —" he starts.

"Yeah, I remember, Pops. I'm not running for anything." I wait for him to say I should be a leader, blah blah, but he just sighs as he takes a huge package of free-range chicken from the top refrigerator shelf.

"I don't know why your mother keeps shopping at that Whole Foods," he says. "We can't afford this eco-eating anymore. Chop up the onions and garlic and let's get this started."

I get a couple of red onions from under the sink and pull out the Big Knife. The front door slams. The Monster's home.

"Be careful with the door, Monica!" Pops yells.

"Whatever," says my sister Monica, stomping into the kitchen. "My day sucked. What's Little Lord Suckyboy doing — ruining dinner again?"

"Monica, watch your mouth."

We all have to, Pops, I think. *With her hair pulled back like that, all we see is her big mouth.* I start chopping, hard. I have to squint to keep from tearing up.

"Sorry," Monica says sarcastically. "I forgot we live like we're on the Family Channel."

"Don't start. Not today," Pops says as he rinses the chicken. "I had two interviews canceled. They hired other people before they even saw me."

Monica and I look at each other. Truce for now.

"Maybe you need a new look, Pops," she says.

"They didn't *see* me, Monica," snaps Pops. "That's the point."

"I know, but in general, I mean, maybe you could get a whole makeover, like your look, your attitude, the way you talk and everything . . . maybe be a little less, um, old-school?"

Pops drops the meat, washes his hands, and walks out.

"Good job, hobgoblin," I say.

"Shut up, hobbit." Monica starts rubbing spices onto the chicken pieces.

"Don't mess it up like you did last time," I warn. "That was nasty."

Monica shoves me, then washes *her* hands and walks out. Looks like I'm making dinner. I'm an okay cook. I get the chicken simmering and head to my room to tackle my mountain of homework. As I go up the stairs, I pause in front of the office and catch a glimpse of Pops mumbling to himself as he types on his computer. Probably working on another cover letter.

. . .

Dinner's pretty good, if I do say so myself. And I might as well, because no one else is saying anything. Mom made a rule that we have to eat together at least three times a week. She says it gives us time to savor the flavor of family life, cherish the big moments. We actually used to have fun at dinner, playing word games and stuff; now we usually mutter a little, shovel the food down, and run away. I say grace, even though it's Monica's turn. That's about it for table talk.

We have lemon pound cake for dessert. Mom has been getting up in the middle of the night to bake. It's kind of weird, but I'm not gonna say anything, because the results are all good. Dessert cheers things up a little, so I try out a little meaningful conversation for us to savor later.

"I've been thinking," I say through a mouthful of cake. "I need a new image at school."

"When are you going to give it up?" Monica says. "You're a lost cause."

"Go eat some babies, Voldemort," I say.

"Shut it, Bulimic Boy."

"Both of you, stop," says Mom. She runs a community health center in the Bronx, so she's usually all motivational ("Like a cheerleader mom, but in a fierce way," Ruthie said once), but she's been working overtime and lately her main contributions to dinner conversations are yawns.

"What are your goals right now? High school is coming soon. This is an important time, time to buckle down," says Pops. "Not time to be worrying about image."

"Well, I was thinking —"

"And don't think we're going to spend money on new clothes, if that's where this is going," he adds.

Oh, well. "Who said anything about new clothes?" I ask. "I just thought it would be cool if I —"

"What do you mean, cool? Reggie, you've got to be focused on how you spend your time, decide you want something and go for it. . . ." Blah blah blah.

"Pops, he's in eighth grade. It's not exactly a life-or-death situation," says Monica, getting up for more cake. I am shocked that she says something almost nice. But she still eats the last piece of cake without asking if anyone else wants some.

"Monica, everything we do in life has eternal consequences. Maybe if you thought more about your spiritual life . . ." Even worse. When Pops gets in preachy mode, even God must cover His ears. Next he'll come home with some dumb book like *God Speaks to Preteens 2!* that has nothing about real life, like why doesn't God do something about war, drugs, and poor people.

But then *we're* the poor people now, so he won't be buying any more of those books. Thanks, God, I guess.

"Maybe I could try a new activity," I say. "There's a steel drum ensemble starting up."

"Steel pans, yeah?" says Pops. "You know, I played for a while, back in the day, but your grandmother didn't like my practicing."

"Never thought I'd say this," says Mom, "but your mother was right. Don't bring all that noise up in this house, Reggie."

"But I could drop piano," I continue. "I know that costs money, and the steel drum thing is free." That should score some points.

"There is always money for the important things," Pops says quickly. "We're not paupers."

Monica jumps in. "Can I go to Sephora with Tatia and Renee?" she says. "There's going to be an event tonight."

"What's Sephora?" asks Pops. "I thought we were going to work out a little. Those tryouts are coming up."

"Whatever, Pops. It's makeup and stuff. You see what I mean about being out of it?"

"What kind of event would a makeup shop be having?" asks Mom.

Wait, are we done talking about me?

"Tatia and Renee said —"

"I am tired of hearing about Tatia and Renee," Mom continues. "Those two girls are not serious." I saw Monica with Tatia and Renee at Starbucks once. Monica had a foam mustache and they looked like they had just stepped out of the club scene in a hip-hop video.

"Where's Asha?" asks Pops. "You don't bring her around anymore. Now, that's a nice girl. A Trini, but still very nice." Trinidad is above Barbados and Guyana in Pops's personal Caribbean Country Rankings, but nowhere near Jamaica, "the crown jewel." Don't get him started on Haiti. "Asha has her head on straight — I'm sure she's not talking this kind of nonsense."

"I can't even be bothered with this right now," says Mom, standing up. "It's a school night, Monica, so you will not be going to any 'event' at a makeup shop. You can do your basketball, and then —"

"I'm not working out tonight," mumbles Monica. "I don't feel like it." Pops starts to say something, but Mom puts up her hand.

Then it's quiet for a while except for the sound of Mom scraping the plates.

"Why don't you guys both go and finish your homework," says Mom. "I'll come check on you in an hour or so."

And that's it. Mom starts on the dishes, Pops goes into his study, Monica stomps off, and I'm left alone at the table.

That went well. I'll cherish it.

Maybe homework only took "an hour or so" in the olden days when Mom and Pops were in school, but even though I work for a while, I know I'll never be done by bedtime. I'll just get up early and finish before school. I got an e-mail back from Dave. He's all positive and says how life is about taking risks and growing, and he tells me to pray and be true to myself. He also tells me to look at Jeremiah 29:11–14. Dave says you can always find stuff in the Bible that relates to real life. I don't know about all that. Maybe it's because Dave prays a lot. I try to pray sometimes, but I don't know if I do it right, because I mess up all the time. I mean, if He's all the things we say in those prayers, why can't God just zap things into shape? Or at least just me?

OCTOBER 6
3:02 P.M.

"Still waiting for your encore, Pukey!" yells Donovan. "That last performance was . . . puke-tacular!"

I walk fast, pretending not to see the plastic blobs of fake vomit everywhere, like a yellow brick road. I keep my head down all the way to my locker, where Joe C.'s waiting. While I'm packing my backpack, a little boy runs up and yelps "Pukey-Pukey-Pukey!" real fast and then runs away. This from someone who hasn't even graduated from Velcro to laces on his sneakers.

"I guess this nickname is better than . . . the other one," says Joe C. after a minute. For a while last year, Donovan got people calling *me* "Whiteboy" for hanging out with Joe C. so much. Clarke Junior is known for being one of the most "ethnically and culturally diverse" schools in New York City, but we still keep things pretty separate but equal when you get right down to it, so "Whiteboy" wasn't exactly a compliment. "And I still think they'll just forget about it eventually."

"Whatever," I say. "Should we go to the library to work on *Night Man*?"

"You need to get to the office, Reginald. You have a Big Buddy check-in," says Ms. A, practically sending me through the ceiling. Where did *she* come from? Silent but deadly.

"I don't have a Little Buddy, Ms. A," I remind her. "I signed up, but I never got assigned." Eighth graders can be paired up as "Big Buddies" with kindergarten kids, and Ruthie's parents and my parents fell all over themselves signing us up to be "positive role models." Joe C. doesn't have to do the activity thing the way we do. Whenever I say that to my mom, she just says, "White folks have that luxury."

"You do now," Ms. A says, peering into my locker. "New student. Get going. Main office. The meeting started ten minutes ago. You're late." She leaves.

I look at Joe C. "Sorry."

He shrugs. "Go do permanent damage to impressionable youth. Don't forget to tell them that cockroaches can live nine days without their heads before they starve to death." He hands me a few sheets of paper. "More art to talk about later."

"Thanks." I walk to the elevator, then decide to take the stairs after I see the crazy long line. I catch a glimpse of Isobel Sirrett in her wheelchair at the end.

When I get to the office, it's packed. A lot of people sign up to be Big Buddies just so they can boss the little kids around. Ruthie comes over to me, trailed by a little girl with huge Afro puffs. "What are you doing here? Are you a Big Buddy now?"

I shrug. "I don't know what's up. Ms. A ordered me here." I look around the room. Vicky's here, of course; she's been collecting extracurriculars for her college applications since second grade. And Justin, with Donovan glued to him, is surrounded by kids. Mialonie and Josie are perched on the secretary's desk. I don't look at Mialonie directly, but I smile at the desk. I think she smiles back. Out of the corner of my eye, I see Josie whispering in her ear.

"This is Jamila," says Ruthie, pointing to Lil' Afro Puff, who frowns at me. "The little ones are so cute," Ruthie whispers.

"Yeah, right. Remember how *we* were in kindergarten?" My parents have a picture of us on the first day. Ruthie had just punched me because I didn't know what divestment was, so I'm crying and holding my stomach.

"I don't know what you're talking about. *I* was cute."

"So I don't get it, then — what happened?" I say.

"You mean, how did I go from cute to spectacular in such a short time? I know, right? It's amazing!" We both laugh. Jamila pulls Ruthie away as the secretary jams a sheet of paper in my hands and leaves to answer the phone. I glance at the bubble letters across the top: "Tips for Being a Top Big Buddy!"

One of the little kids is crying so hard there's a long rope of snot hanging out of his nose. The secretary goes to get a tissue but the kid rubs it on the back of his hand before she gets back. Then Blaylock leads the snotty kid over to me — my new Little Buddy. Why am I not surprised? His pants and socks are both way too short; his ashy legs are straight and skinny like stilts. He's at that post-crying/gasping-for-air stage. I hope he doesn't die on me. Blaylock, who is not known for his emergency response skills or his compassion, frowns and leaves.

"What's your name, little man?" I say.

No response.

Cryboy and I stand there while the other Buddy pairs talk and laugh. Looks like we'll need the whole box of tissues. I look at the wall clock. I shift, my backpack unzips, and my Night Man notebook falls out. The kid checks out the cover that Joe C. designed.

"Is — is — that yours?" he whimpers.

"Uh . . . maybe, but tell me your name first."

"Ch-Charlie Calloway."

"Okay, Ch-Charlie. I'm Reggie."

He giggles. "Not *Ch*-Charlie. Just Charlie!"

"Okay, Just Charlie."

He giggles again. Maybe this won't be so bad. "*No*, Charlie Calloway." He giggles some more. "That looks like a superhero."

Okay, I've got him laughing. Good sign. "Oh! Sorry, Charlie!" I grin. "He *is* a superhero. I'll tell you a secret — I made him up when I was the same age as you." Charlie's eyes get big and he looks at me like *I'm* Night Man. I feel like a cheat, since he's really impressed by the drawing Joe C. did. "I have a whole bunch of stories that I'll show you one day. Anyway, I'm going to be your Big Buddy. So I can help you with stuff . . . and, um . . ."

What are Big Buddies supposed to do anyway? I eavesdrop on Ruthie's conversation.

". . . because we don't realize that the American government supports the oppression of children worldwide. Maybe next time I'll read to you from UNICEF's Convention on Rights of the Child."

"I have new markers at home," Jamila replies. "And my cat is going to have kittens!"

I try the "Tips" sheet instead. "Um, what's your favorite color?"

"Blue," he answers right away. "And green."

"Oh, I like —"

"And black too," he finishes.

"Do you have a favorite TV show or activity?"

He just looks at me.

"What about a favorite book? I used to like Dr. Seuss. *The Cat in the Hat*? *Green Eggs and Ham*?"

More looking.

I clear my throat. "Would you, could you, talk to me?" He almost smiles, and I continue. "We would . . . um . . . we would have some fun, you see!"

Now I can tell he's trying hard not to smile.

"Yeah, fun . . . in a boat, on a float . . . lots of fun, Charlie, you and me!" I pretend to wipe sweat from my forehead. "Whew!" I mutter. "Tough crowd. Those were some of my finest rhymes."

He's looking at me like he's half hoping, half afraid I'm going to start tap dancing or something. I look back at my "Tips" sheet. "Uh, do you like school?"

His face breaks open in a smile. "Yeah!" he says. "Lunch is really good! And we get waffles at breakfast." He stops smiling and glares at me. "Are you gonna be my friend?"

"Uh, yeah, sure. That's what Big Buddy means."

"Like best friends? Do you live in an apartment?"

"A brownstone. It's like a house."

"A house! Can I come over? I'll bring toys."

"Yeah, sure, one day. We're friends now, so we can do a lot of things together. Maybe go to the zoo or something."

He starts to hug me, then he stops and holds out his hand for a high (for him) five instead. Even in kindergarten, you've got to be smooth.

"Um, so it looks like it's time for you guys to line up," I say, giving him a little fist bump. "It was nice to meet you, Charlie. I'll see you soon. In a car, on the moon . . ."

"Bye, Reggie!" He's got a big grin on his face.

Someone thinks I'm cool.

OCTOBER 7
8:00 A.M.

There are red postcards with big purple *V*s on them stuck in all of the lockers. There are also a lot on the floor. I pull out the one in my locker; it's a scary close-up photo of Vicky over the words "Vote Vicky!" "Oh," I say. "Vicky Ross."

Joe C. nods. "She just shook my hand and smiled so big I thought that she was going to eat me alive."

"The Grin Reaper," I say as I throw the postcard inside my locker.

"I'm not looking forward to weeks of Vicky Ross in my face," adds Joe C.

We get to class before the last bell rings for once, and Blaylock is standing up front and Mr. Gordon is already sitting at Ms. A's desk. Ms. A is standing by the door; she keeps track of who's late because "promptness accounts for a significant portion of your final grade."

"Just a little election check-in!" says Blaylock. He's not giving up. "I may have mentioned those grants to schools that exemplify the spirit of community partnership, as Clarke certainly does, and our first annual Step Up And Lead rally in December will celebrate that. I am confident that there is someone here who is the perfect representative of the Clarke Pledge of Proactive Community Service." He leans forward as though he's looking for someone in particular.

Vicky stands up and Blaylock frowns, like he didn't want to find *her*. "As some of you may know," she starts, "I am running for president." She pauses, and some people fill it up with groans, which Blaylock doesn't stop. Vicky raises her voice. "I am running for president because I have a duty to this school —"

"*Doody*," whispers Hector, snickering.

"— and I want to make it better. I want to make *changes*."

She's talking pretty strong. Maybe I'm not giving Vicky enough credit.

"I was inspired by our classroom discussion on Tuesday to make a commitment, and that commitment is to you." She's fired up, and it feels like the whole room is holding its breath. Has Vicky Ross become a human being?

Ruthie stands up. "Yeah, right, Vicky. You have a long history of a complete lack of regard for anything that doesn't benefit *you*. I mean, let's talk reality; let's talk about what's happening right now across the Atlantic in —"

"Let's talk about doing something right here at Clarke," I say under my breath.

Ms. A jumps down my throat. "What was that, Reginald? I didn't quite catch what you said."

"Uh, nothing," I say, wishing for the millionth time that I had that Harry Potter invisibility cloak. "Talking to myself. Sorry."

"I'm sure it was more than 'nothing,' Reginald. Speak up." She's not going to let me slide.

"Um . . . okay. Not that there's anything wrong with celebrating our achievements," I start, "or that it's not important to pay attention to the global, uh . . . landscape," I add, with a quick glance at Ruthie. "But I just wonder if . . . if civic responsibility could mean making changes right here." I look at my desk. "Right now." I hear a gagging sound, but I don't look Hector's way.

"Interesting," says Ms. A. "Elaborate."

Why did I open my mouth? I'm not trying to be on some platform. "I don't know," I say, wishing Ms. A's laser beam eyes weren't burning a hole in my face. "I mean, there's that saying: Think global, act local. I guess I'm thinking that there are ways we could, um, show civic responsibility by working on our community and going from there." Blaylock looks at me like he doesn't recognize me with words coming out of my mouth. This is the most I've spoken in class without being called on since last year. It might have a little to do with the fact that Donovan's absent today, but there's another reason too. I'm sick of this. "Right now it's like nobody cares." It feels good to speak up, like taking a deep breath at the beach.

No one laughs! In fact, a few people, not just Ruthie, are nodding their heads.

Then the door bursts open and music blares into the classroom. Real heavy bass and a thumping beat. An older guy with a portable turntable is leading a crowd of kids into the room. Donovan comes in, chanting through some kind of electronic voice machine, "JW's house! It's Justin time! You're 'Justin time' to party outside with the next prez!" Then Justin walks in, arms raised like he's already won.

Is this really happening? A few kids get up and start dancing. Blaylock bangs on the blackboard. "What is going on here?" He has to shout over the beats.

Justin makes a "cut it" gesture to the older guy, who shuts off the music. Donovan starts handing out Vicky's postcards, except now her face is covered with a big red X. Justin goes over to Blaylock as his party train disperses and the DJ leaves. "Sorry, sir, it's my fault. We got a little carried away about the election, giving back to the school and everything. I'm very anxious to do my part to sustain and improve our wonderful community."

Did he steal a memo off of Blaylock's desk? Why does it sound so smooth when he says that stuff?

Blaylock smiles a little under his frown. "I take it that you are running for president then?" he asks.

Justin nods, and Donovan says, "And I'm his campaign manager. We will *rule* this school this year!"

Blaylock pats Justin on the back. "That's great, but this is still an educational institution, so you'll have to keep it after school, and outside."

"Right, sir," says Justin. "I apologize again."

Blaylock actually waits for Justin and Donovan to take their seats. Justin gets a couple of high fives and takes his sweet time settling in. A few people clap.

Unreal.

Vicky stands up again. "As I was saying, let's take this opportunity to transform our community." She looks at Justin. "Let's reject *more of the same*."

Justin just smiles at her.

"So, er, we're in business!" says Blaylock. "Justin, thank you for stepping up. I am confident that you'll run an effective, inspirational, award-winning campaign." He pats Justin on the shoulder a few times. "Vicky . . . thank you too, of course."

"Are Justin and Vicky the sole candidates from this class?" Ms. A looks around the room.

Vicky clears her throat. "Ahem," she says.

"Yes, Vicky?" say Blaylock and Ms. A at the same time, with the same sigh.

"I just want to say that at least I'm trying to do something, I'm not just sitting around throwing parties all the time, or complaining." She stands up and looks around the room. "Does anyone want to help out? We can work together on this. Who's with me?"

No one will look at her. That's not unusual because Vicky is pretty much as heinous in appearance as she is in personality, but still.

A couple of kids make a point of sitting on their hands.

Mr. Gordon makes a paper clip chain.

"Anyone?" asks Vicky.

Blaylock looks at his watch.

This is brutal.

Vicky speaks up again. "I was thinking that, um, Pu — Reginald had some valuable insights in our last discussion. I'd like to publicly invite him to be my campaign manager."

Huh?

Donovan snorts. "I guess it's a good idea to have a loser help you lose," he mutters. Ms. A shushes the giggles.

I clamp my lips together and look at my desk.

Donovan is drawing a mustache on one of his anti-Vicky flyers, and I know that this is just the beginning. He will decimate her, just because he feels like it. I don't want to be associated with the Grin Reaper's lame campaign, but she's in for Donovan the Destroyer.

I know how that feels.

Ms. A's about to speak when Vicky says softly, her voice cracking a little, "Reginald? Can I count on you?"

"I'll do it," I say, because I can't say anything else. I try to look managerial and not like I want to run away. I glance at Vicky. She's not looking at me.

Ms. A shakes her head just a little before she tells us to take out *Native Son*. Gordon and Blaylock leave; Blaylock turns around to give the class a double thumbs-up.

I have to look at Donovan. He grins and makes the universal sign for throat-slitting.

Ruthie hits me with her math textbook as soon as we get to our lockers after class. "Ow!" I say. "Stop the violence!"

"What is wrong with you?" she asks. "I was so proud of you for a minute there. I mean, you're better off doing nothing than shilling for that bloodsucker."

"Going over to the Dark Side," says Joe C. "I'll pray for you, my son."

Ruthie glares at him. "The dark/light thing. Don't get me started."

"Oh, yeah, sorry," says Joe C. I pat him on the back.

"Listen, I'll probably just give her a few suggestions and that's it," I say. "I couldn't just leave her hanging like that in front of everybody. And you know how Donovan is. He's going to play so dirty. Maybe I can keep her from suffering the same fate I did."

"Maybe you should focus on keeping yourself from that fate again," says Joe C., shaking his head. "This is not what I meant by 'low profile.'"

"I'm not going to be the one out front; I'm not going to be the one making speeches onstage and all that," I say. I turn to Ruthie. "You're the one always telling me to get involved, to be change."

Ruthie sighs. "That's sweet and all, but she's such a user. Vicky just knows you'll work hard because you're nice. Do you really think she cares anything about helping Clarke?"

"Maybe I can help," I say. "Maybe this will help me."

There's a tap on my shoulder. It hurts. I turn; it's Vicky.

"Welcome aboard," she says, dumping an overstuffed accordion folder into my hands. "The V Team is happy to have you."

I look around for the rest of the "V Team." Vicky glances at Ruthie and Joe C. "Are you two —" she starts.

They almost fall on their butts, they back away so fast. Ruthie gets busy in her locker and Joe C. holds a notebook in front of his face.

"Uh, Vicky," I say. "Maybe we should talk about what we're going to do, have a meeting or something."

"Great idea! This is going to work out so well. Tomorrow morning, 7:30, on the steps. Don't be late. And thanks again!" She walks away.

"You didn't say 'thanks' the first time," mutters Joe C.

She turns back and slows down a little, but she doesn't stop walking. "That folder is a chronological listing of all of my achievements since preschool. Please read up tonight so we can focus in the morning on what I need you to do. Learn it, live it, love it. And get every last one of Donovan's defacements out of people's hands. You've got to be on top of these things." She stops to flash a big, scary grin at a couple of little kids. "Hi! I'm Vicky! I'm running for president! I'll walk you to class!" She grabs their hands and pulls them away, in the direction opposite to the one they were going.

"Still feel sorry for her?" asks Ruthie.

"Good luck with that," says Joe C.

OCTOBER 8
7:28 A.M.

At least I'm a little early, I think as I turn the corner toward school. I even wrote down a few ideas in case Vicky really wants to make a difference. But my heart still drops when I see her standing on the steps, another accordion folder cradled in her arms like some kind of crazy Vickybaby.

"You're a little late," she says, scary-smiling. She's practically blocking the school entrance. "Timeliness is essential to a successful campaign."

"It's 7:30," I say, looking at my watch. "And hi."

"I was here at 7:15," she says. "Anyway, it's okay. I don't know anyone else who's able to start the day with as much alacrity as I do."

Alacrity? "Right. So Vicky, I picked up the School Leadership Team's guidelines from the office yesterday — did you know the president is supposed to be the 'student voice' at School Leadership Team meetings? We never hear about that happening."

Vicky shrugs. "That's boring, a lot of people standing up to talk about nothing. Listen, I don't see you around after school, so I guess you have a lot of time on your hands. I mapped out all of the 'hot spots' for posting flyers so that you can start right away."

She smiles as she hands me a laminated color printout. "It's color coded. You don't have to thank me."

"Okay," I say slowly. "What are the colors for?"

"You know, where the different groups hang out, the vulnerable voters. The Veronica Cruz-ers — total clones who've never had an original thought in their lives. The future drug dealers, the future drug users, the drama queens, video game freaks, basic nobody losers . . ."

"I get it," I cut in. "But we probably don't want to label people like that." *At least, not out loud.*

She starts to frown, then grins. "You are so right. It's easier my way, but it could get tricky. That's exactly why I'm glad to have you on the V Team. Here, I got two thousand flyers printed last night; we can start posting them now. First floor's done, I'll do the second and third floors, you do the basement and fourth."

I see Joe C. coming toward us. *Thank you, God.* I can escape soon. "We should talk about our platform," I say.

"*Our* platform?" She raises her eyebrows almost off her head. "Is someone trying to take over? Is someone not a team player?"

Is someone crazy? *Yes, and I think it was me.*

"Sorry. *Your* campaign, which you asked me to manage. Anyway. Maybe we should start surveying the students, find out what the people want."

"That's so cute," she says, smiling. "And old-fashioned."

"Okay, yeah, it's not that innovative or, um, exciting, but we're supposed to be all about community here. A campaign should be about bringing us together. The whole popularity contest thing just makes the divisions worse. You could show that you're the candidate who's going to finally make it happen."

"Sure, I'll give it some thought," she says. "You're an ideas guy, I like that. Great meeting! This is going to work out really well." She heads inside, turning around to wave a flyer at me. "Get those flyers up! We'll talk about that School Leadership Team thing too — sounds very interesting! Thanks!"

"Don't you feel a chill whenever she's around?" says Joe C. as he climbs the stairs toward me. "How are you going to keep from killing yourself? Listen, you want to run over to the bank with me?" he asks without pausing. "We've still got a few minutes, and I've got to get some cash for lunch."

"Yeah," I say, and we head toward the bank. Joe C. has his own debit card — he says it's one of the perks of divorce. He uses his card to open the door, and I wait outside.

A cop walks over. "Yo," he says, like he doesn't care much. "Keep moving."

"I'm waiting for my friend," I mutter, looking at his badge. Name: Tucciarone. Brown hair, brown eyes. My parents taught me to do quick "police scans" when I was five, just in case I got hassled. I look in the bank window and see Joe C. still in line. The cop follows my gaze, and then looks toward me, somewhere in the vicinity of my neck. He stares so hard it hurts. Usually they ask for ID at this point. Does he think I'm going to jump Joe C. in broad daylight? Or maybe I'm scamming folks on their way out of the bank, raising money for "basketball team uniforms"?

"What are you doing?" he asks.

Standing in a free country, I think. I stand straighter.

Joe C. looks up, sees us, and waves me in. I shake my head, and the cop gives me some extra glare and moves on. I look straight ahead. Joe C. comes out, and I start walking right away so that we don't have to talk about it.

"Hey, I have to visit my dad this weekend. Do you want to come?" he asks after a while. "There's this guy who rented the basement apartment who's pretty cool. He's a DJ."

"Like on the radio?"

"No, a real DJ, at a club. He said he would show me how to spin records."

"Spin records?" I ask. "Don't DJs use digital equipment now?"

"Yeah, but Gunnar is old-school. He says we have to respect the past before we tackle the future."

Joe C. sounds like a Black History Month public service announcement. Since when does he care about DJ-ing anyway?

"Maybe not," I say. Mr. Castiglione always invites me in like he wishes I'd use the back door. "I need to work on *Night Man*. I guess we can do stuff on our own and compare notes."

We don't talk too much as we head into school. Science lab instead of homeroom today, so I have to race to the fourth floor to beat the last bell. Hector, my lab partner this week, is already there, and he's eaten the sulfur that we're supposed to use for our experiment. Mrs. Rostawanik sends him to wash his mouth out and I start working alone.

When Hector comes back, he acts like he won something. "I don't think you'd be able to handle the sulfur, Pukey," he says. I don't bother to respond. There's not much time left, so we just work. I'm surprised at how fast and efficient he is during the experiment. He doesn't even look at my notes; he never takes any of his own. I don't know what he uses my pens for. He does most of the work and we finish early.

"So you're friends with Ruthie Robertson," he says slowly, as though that hasn't been obvious for years. I just look at him. "Are you guys going out?"

"Going out where?" I ask.

"Going *out*, you vomitocious fool," he snarls. "Is she your girl?"

"What are you talking about?" I ask. "That sulfur is rotting your brain."

"You don't even realize how badocious she is," he mutters, shaking his head.

"Don't you mean 'bodacious'?" I say.

"No, I mean 'badocious.' Better than bodacious. Don't you know anything? How did you even get into this school?"

I open my mouth, and then close it.

"Forget it, Pukey. I forgot that you wouldn't know what to do with a girl. Except maybe spill your guts." He starts laughing so hard at his "joke" that he knocks over our experiment. Mrs. Rostawanik immediately sends him to the office and I'm left to clean up. The bell rings before I'm done.

"How's the campaign going, loser?" Donovan "bumps" into me as I leave class.

"Leave me alone," I mutter. Great comeback, Reggie.

"Oooh, I'm intimidated," he says. "Like that ugly skank wouldn't have lost it on her own. Now I get to crush you too. This is going to be so much fun. I love politics."

Even though my next class is right down the hall, I make a sharp left and take the stairs up two flights. I can still hear him as I go upstairs.

"*V* is for *venereal disease*," he calls. "Have fun with Vicky the Virus, punk. I know you're desperate. . . ."

OCTOBER 9
11:00 A.M.

"Okay, okay people," says Dave. "Let's just get to the meat of the sammich." That's one of his favorite sayings, along with "If you think you know everything about God, you know nothing about God." He bangs his fist on a table, making a little coffee spill. Tiffany Parker, his unofficial youth groupie, wipes it up.

The cashier behind the counter frowns. Javalove Café doesn't love our youth group all that much. Saturdays are pretty quiet here, but sometimes they act like that's our fault.

"What's the point of this story?" Dave continues. Nobody says anything. He looks at me. "C'mon. Reggie? Jesus. Walking on water. What's the point?"

I look back at Dave; this is one I know. "You know, it's like Peter was fine when he was looking at Jesus, but he got scared and that's when he sank," I say. "It's the whole thing of letting fear mess with your head."

"It's kind of stupid that he got scared of the wind. Life was easier in Bible times," says Jeff Gibson. "They didn't have all the things to worry about that we have now."

"Uh, yeah, Jeff. Just *survival*," I say. Everybody laughs. I smile. I wish we could meet more often. Ruthie and Mialonie are the only youth group kids who go to my school. Most of these kids don't know the real me.

"What this is saying to me is that we can do great things if we focus on Him," Dave starts.

("Or Her," mutters Gabriella Munson, as usual.)

Dave continues. "He can lead us to participate in miracles!"

"So all I gotta do is think of Jesus and I can walk on water? Or fly?" asks Jeff with a snort. "Come on, man. What about fate? Or working hard and getting results? That makes sense. How do you know when it's God?"

We all just sit there for a couple of minutes. Silence is okay in this group. Dave isn't just waiting for you to stop talking so he can start, like most adults, and you feel like you can say any stupid thing (Jeff) and it's all good. But sometimes I *want* someone to tell me the right answer, and Dave is not about to be that person. Eventually he sighs and points to his washed-out T-shirt, which has a picture of Malcolm X on it and says THINK: IT AIN'T ILLEGAL YET! in big white letters. Another favorite saying.

"Okay. We'll leave that alone for a minute. We've got a project," he says, rubbing his hands together like he's starting in on Thanksgiving dinner. "A service project."

"Oooh!" says Ruthie. "What is it?" Jeff mimics her and I give him a quick kick under the table.

A cool wind blows in when the door opens; it's Mialonie. She slides into the booth next to Jeff, looking just like the girl on the cover of this magazine Sean was passing around last week. I put my chin in my hands and narrow my eyes, trying to look simultaneously spiritual and sexy.

"We're going to be working with the Olive Branch Shelter," Dave says. "It's a temporary housing facility on Ryerson Street."

"Oh, yeah, Ryerson," says Precious Walters. She frowns. "Where's that?"

"It's right in the neighborhood," says Ruthie. "About five blocks from your house."

"I'm excited about this," says Dave. "It's the Listening Ears Project — you may have heard about this, it's been featured on National Public Radio, NPR." We all look back at him blankly, except Ruthie, who smiles. "Well, NPR has teamed up with a bunch of community-based organizations that serve the homeless to record and document the life stories of the people they help. We'll interview residents at Olive Branch, and the whole thing is going to be put together into a book and documentary project."

"Sounds depressing," says Jeff. "Why don't we just wait until Christmas and sing carols for the old people again?"

We ignore him. "Residents?" I say. "I thought you said it was a temporary facility."

"Olive Branch was just a soup kitchen with a few beds, but now there are people, families, kids who stay there long-term," says Dave. "The reality is that the homeless population has exploded. If a family is lucky, they get a shelter locker the size of a shoebox to store their entire lives in. If they're really lucky, six or seven of them get to live in a room that was designed for one. The kids get bounced around from school to school, sometimes into foster care and group homes. And if a shelter gets too crowded or dangerous, or gets too costly for the city, it can just get shut down."

Everyone's quiet for a minute. I think of this guy who's always at the subway station by our house. He's been there for as long as I can remember. Most of the time he's asleep and looks like a pile of old rags, but sometimes he's awake and screaming and cursing at everyone who walks by. Once in a while, usually during the holidays, I see the cops shoo him away, but I never think about where he goes. And he always comes back.

"I don't get it," says Jeff. "Why does God let there be homeless people? I mean, some of them look okay, like that guy who plays the guitar in Fulton Mall — he even has CDs. But it just seems wrong. Not like the God you're always talking about."

I'm glad he asked it. Even here, I feel like a jerk for asking those questions, like I'm challenging God. And I don't know if I'm up for that.

"Well, why does He?" asks Dave in his usual I-am-now-going-to-be-provocative way of answering a question with a question. He looks around. "Or why do we, for that matter? Why do we let there be homeless people?"

"It's about what God would have us do," says Ruthie. "That's all up in the Scriptures, how we're supposed to take care of the poor and old people and kids and stuff."

Mialonie nods. "My parents always say that's what sharing the Gospel is about. Justice, humility, serving . . ." Her voice is like a late night DJ's.

"But why doesn't God just eliminate the bad stuff?" I ask. "Why do some people have to suffer? It just doesn't seem fair." I look at Dave. "And I know God is just."

"Do you?" shoots back Dave.

I'm confused. "Are you saying He isn't?"

"Or She," mutters Gabriella.

"I'm asking *you*, Reggie. Do *you* know that God is just? How do you know that?"

I look over to Ruthie for help, but she's flipping through her Bible. "Uh," I stammer. "I don't know how to answer that."

Dave looks at all of us. "Don't just be parrots. Think about what you say. Are you saying God is good, God is just, only because that's what you've heard?"

Nobody answers, and Jeff grabs another muffin. Dave lets the silence settle, then he writes something down in his little notebook.

"All right, y'all," he says as he writes. "Think about this question: If God is so good, why are so many things so bad? Come back with some Scripture and some real thoughts. I don't want simplistic catechism-type answers — and I'm not even saying that this question has a 'right' answer." He glances at Ruthie as he says that. "So don't feel like you have to come back with one. Just do some thinking."

"When is this due? When is the next meeting?" Precious Walters asks.

"I'll e-mail you. It's not school. Just chew on this for a while, and we'll talk about it. It could be tomorrow, it could be next month. You don't know the hour or the day. . . ." He trails off, laughing. Only Dave laughs at his Bible jokes.

"I don't even know where to start," I say.

"That's good," Dave replies. "If you think you know God . . ."

"Yeah, yeah, then you know nothing about God," I finish, smiling.

"Back to the project," says Dave. "We're looking at a tight

schedule, just a few weeks. All this has to be done by Thanksgiving. We need a leader, someone in the group to help put together some questions, transcribe the interviews, and so on. Any volunteers?"

Quiet.

"This is an opportunity for someone to step up," Dave continues. "And I'll be working with you, so don't worry about carrying a heavy load by yourself."

This is not Clarke, I remind myself. I'm not a joke here. And for all of Blaylock's blustering, I'm feeling the whole community service thing. It matters.

I raise my hand. "I'll do it," I say. "Am I going to Heaven now?" Everybody laughs, but with me, not at me.

"I'll help out," pipes up Gabriella.

"Maybe we can go to the NPR people," I say. "They can give us a few tips, maybe even lend us equipment."

Dave nods. "That's what I'm talking about. Let's meet for a few minutes after this meeting, guys." Tiffany looks disappointed. I guess she's realizing that she's missing extra opportunities to snuggle up to Dave.

"I've, uh, been doing some research on homeless people," I say, thinking of Night Man. I remember those "Tips for Being a Top Big Buddy." "And I'll get started on interview questions."

This is good. Maybe working with real homeless people will help me finish *Night Man* at last. Maybe I can be the Justin of youth group. Eighth grade isn't all there is to life. Maybe now things will change. With a capital *C*.

OCTOBER 12

2:55 P.M.

Vicky bombarded me with e-mails the entire weekend. I made some more suggestions for the platform, like cleaner bathrooms or a fund-raiser for a community organization, but she just ordered me to hand stuff out after school. Which is what I'm doing right now, shoving a couple postcards into kids' hands and mumbling, "Vote Vicky, please."

Mialonie is standing across from me, in front of the office, and she's alone. She looks like royalty. This is A Moment, and I know I should say something to her, and I'm looking at her, and I'm like, *Look at me, look at me,* but I chicken out and turn away. Okay, deep breath. Maybe I'll even say "hi." No, "hey." I turn back around. Josie is with her now, so it's too late. Again. Oh, well.

When I get to the lockers, Ruthie's sitting in front of hers, humming and writing in her journal.

"I was so inspired by *FRONTLINE* last night," she says. "Lots of ideas for the New World Order Collective." Ruthie isn't allowed to watch TV, except for as much PBS as she wants. Her family sits down together every morning and has newspapers for breakfast. Our parents share a subscription to the *Jamaican Weekly Gleaner*, and Ruthie actually reads it.

"Did you write a little something about your boyfriend Reggie, King of the Wedgie?" says a voice over my shoulder. I turn around to Donovan cackling, Justin a little behind him, not smiling. I keep my eyes away from Donovan's so that I don't have to look away first.

"Or maybe you can come up with things to rhyme with Pukey," he continues, looking at Justin. "You're good at corny stuff like that."

"Come on, D," Justin says. "We're gonna be late for practice." He looks at me. "You know he's just playing," he says. He gives Donovan a light shove and they head down the hall.

Ruthie stands, shaking her head. "I don't believe Justin even likes Donovan. He just likes having a lackey around, I guess. How insecure. I'm disappointed."

"Justin doesn't have anything to be insecure about," I say. "And since when did you expect a lot from Justin? I thought you said he was hollow."

"Everyone has something to be insecure about," says Ruthie. "It all depends on how they deal with it." She puts an arm around my shoulder. "You're worth an infinite number of Donovans. He's not even in the same dimension as you."

"Thanks," I say. "You always have my back." I point to a yellow "Save the Date!" flyer taped to the wall. "Speaking of having my back . . . you know our parents are going to want us to go to the Holiday Jam together, right?"

Ruthie grins. "Of course. That way it's not a real date and they don't get all crazy."

"Exactly," I say. "Maybe Joe C. will even bring mythical Maria and it can be a double non-date."

Mialonie and Josie walk by.

"Hey, Reggie," says Mialonie. "See you." A book falls from her stack, and I jump out from under Ruthie's arm to pick it up.

"See you," I say, handing her the book. I watch her walk away. When I turn back to Ruthie, she's pulling some books down from her locker.

"'See you'?" I say. "Did you hear that? What do you think that means?"

Ruthie shrugs and rolls her eyes. "Do you have to be such a sheep?" she says. "What was I saying a minute ago? Must've had a brain leak."

Whatever.

Joe C. walks up to the lockers. "So, today, right?" he asks, opening his locker and pulling out his portfolio.

"Today is the day Mialonie Davis spoke to me," I say, grinning. Joe C. high-fives me.

"Sweet. Pretty soon you guys will be double-dating with me and Maria." He goes on: "Anyway, I meant, are you coming with me today? Or do you have to do stuff with Vicky?"

"Sounds good," I say. I'm remembering how Mialonie's eyes look like chocolate.

"Hello? Earth to Reggie," says Joe C.

"Huh? Yeah, um . . . what?"

He laughs. "You said you would let me know about going over to the mall, remember? Or do you have to do some campaign managing?"

Ruthie snorts.

"The mall sounds good," I say. "I want to stop by the public radio offices first, though, since they're right next door. They told me that I could pick up some equipment for the homeless shelter thing." I look up and down the halls. "Come on, let's get out of here before Vicky tracks me down."

4:00 P.M.

When I brought my cousin Grace to our neighborhood mall, she almost fell down the escalator stairs, she was laughing so hard. The malls up where she lives in Westchester are like palaces, with giant fountains and free samples everywhere you turn. Our perpetually broken escalators and Not-Even-Close-to-Super Target can't compare. But we're happy to have a place to hang out, and there's McDonald's. My uncle Terrence says that mall fast food offerings are part of "the White man's genocidic plan to oppress us." Sometimes Uncle Terrence is like an adult Ruthie on drugs, and I guess that's not too far off. Pops is always telling him how he is such a disappointment to the family, but then he tells Mom that the Ivy League and the Navy killed Uncle Terrence's spirit. He seems pretty spirited to me; every time I tell him that I looked up one of his words, like "genocidic," and couldn't find it in a dictionary, he says I shouldn't be conned by the wordplay of the White man. Uncle Terrence is pretty cool, though, if slightly scary.

Joe C. needs to buy dog food at Target, but we stop for some school supplies first. I pick up a giant three-ring binder. We had a Very Special Health Class last week where we got divided up and the guys went to the gym with Coach Conners (we have no teams at our school, but still, it's "Coach"). He told us that "strong" guys who are "secure in who they are" don't need to "engage in, er,

um . . . sexual activity before the, er, um . . . appropriate time."
But if we're inappropriately weak, we should "protect ourselves
responsibly." He also said the binders were good to carry around
for those "unexpected moments of spontaneous excitation —
even when there's absolutely no discernible cause." His exact
words. I feel stupid getting the binder, but I don't want to get
caught out there. Joe C. gets one too. I don't say anything, and
neither does he.

As we weave around shopping carts and escaping toddlers,
we enter the world of grooming. I stop to get some deodorant.

"Have you ever tried this stuff?" I say, picking up a black
spray can.

"Perfume for men?" says Joe C., raising his eyebrows, which
always seems like a lot of work because they're so bushy. "Are you
kidding me?"

"What, you never heard of guys wearing cologne?" I say.

"Yeah, but that's different," he says, and then before I even
have to ask how, he picks up a can himself. "Let me take a look at
this . . . 'Get your freak on'?" He laughs. "Good thing I've already
got my mojo. I'm a strong man, secure in who I am."

"Don't act like you don't need help," I say. Maybe this stuff is
like a magic potion: spray on sex appeal and self-confidence.
Nobody else is around, so I take the cap off and spray a little into
the air. We cough and sniff.

"Not bad," says Joe C.

"You think girls really like this?" I wrinkle my nose.

"Girls are always into smells and scented everything. Maria
wears this watermelon lip gloss that you can smell a block away."
Joe C. makes a face. "And it's all sticky."

"Yeah, okay," I say. I get ready to spray a little body spray over my head when I see Monica with Tatia and Renee. She looks like their bodyguard. "Let's get your dog food," I say to Joe C. "We can hit up McDonald's and then go to the comic shop."

The lines at the registers are all long and barely moving. Joe C. points to a magazine with a cover story about the latest celebrity cause — homelessness.

"Those public radio people were sure happy you're doing that project," he says.

"Uh-huh," I say. "I guess most people aren't really checking for the homeless."

"Are you scared?" he asks.

"Of what?"

"You know, the whole shelter thing," he says. "I mean, those homeless people. They're not . . . My dad wouldn't let me get near a place like that."

He says "a place like that" like it's another planet, full of living nightmares too horrible to describe. And "they're not . . ." what? Most of the homeless people that I see have skin closer to mine than his, and I wonder if he would talk about me the same way. I say, "A place like what? What are you talking about?"

"Forget it," he mutters, picking up the magazine.

Good. Because we need to leave this conversation alone.

I feel a tug on my jacket. It's my Little Buddy Charlie.

"Hi, Big Buddy Reggie!" he says, grinning so hard it must hurt. I've been looking out for him at school, but I guess I keep missing him. "I got a new Thomas train! And a coal car!"

"That sounds great," I say. A woman in the next line waves Charlie over. "You can just call me Reggie. Is that your mom? I think she's calling you."

"Do you want me to bring the train to your house today?" he asks. "You can be my first friend to play with it."

"Um, yeah, well . . . maybe another time." It's like I just told him that I was canceling Christmas and birthdays forever; his whole body droops. "I promise, another day real soon, okay? So, um, how's it going?"

"Okay," he mutters. His mom comes over.

"Hello, Reggie," she says, smiling. "I'm Beverly Calloway. Charlie spotted you right away. He said you were the really tall, smart guy in line."

I shrug and smile and try to look responsible.

"Did he tell you about the trouble he's having at school?" she says, looking at Charlie.

"No," I say. We both wait; Charlie concentrates on his Cookie Monster sneakers.

"Charlie, Reggie might be able to give you some advice," his mom says.

Yeah, maybe, if he wants How-to-Be-Humiliated lessons. Charlie doesn't say anything, and his mom gives him one of those little hugs I remember. "I really appreciate what you're doing," she says to me. "You must be quite a student to get picked for this program."

"Uh, my parents signed me up."

"Well," she says. "I'm sure we're fortunate to have you as Charlie's buddy. Our boys need positive role models more than ever. Our people need to work together to rebuild our communities." She looks at Joe C., who's looking around for another magazine.

"Oh, sorry — this is my friend Joe C.," I say. For a minute, I want to add, *Don't worry, he's my only White friend. I'm still rebuilding and keeping it real.*

"Hey," he says.

"Hello," she nods.

"I want to go play with Reggie, Mommy," says Charlie. "He lives in a house!" Mrs. Calloway stops smiling for a minute.

"Uh . . . yeah, maybe one day soon, Charlie," I say. "We have to plan it . . . or maybe I can come to your house."

"I don't live in a house," says Charlie, looking down. "I've never even been in one."

"Okay, your apartment, then," I say.

"I'm sure Reggie has a lot to do, honey," says Mrs. Calloway.

I jump into the pause before it becomes significant. "Or hey, why don't you sit with me at lunch one day. With us," I say, pointing to Joe C.

Charlie opens his mouth so wide that I can see his uvula. "Will you show me more of those comic books you made?" His mom's eyebrows rise; my role model status may have slipped with the mention of the *C* word.

"Sure. You know, Joe C. is the artist. He does all of the drawings." Charlie looks at Joe C. in awe and I add, "But I made the whole thing up."

There's another pause, and then Charlie's mom picks up her bags. "It was nice to meet you, Reggie, and thank you. Nice meeting you too, Joe-see," she says, like she's wondering what kind of name that is. We mumble back, and she takes Charlie's hand and leaves. Charlie keeps turning back to wave.

We finally check out and head downstairs. We're still planning to hop the train to the comic shop for *Night Man* inspiration after we get our fries, even though I've got three tests to study for and a report on Larry Doby that I haven't even started. But from the escalator, I can see the huge crowd of kids in McDonald's. There's no music playing, but it seems like there is; it's bubbling over with energy and laughter and girls' shrieks. More kids squeeze in as we get closer and everyone looks happy to see everyone else, but when we get off of the escalator I turn to Joe C. and say, "Forget it. Let's just go."

OCTOBER 17
12:33 P.M.

At church on Sunday, I try to listen to Reverend Coles, but licking my room clean would be more fun. I flip through *The Book of Common Prayer*, but then I drop it and Pops gives me a Look. Yeah, okay, Pops. Like I didn't see you roll your eyes a few minutes ago. Monica brought Nana's old giant Bible with her; I can see her looking at skirts in the catalog she has tucked inside. Mom snores a little, and Reverend Coles's wife (who used to try to make kids call her "Mother" Coles) stares hard and long. I don't think I'm holy enough to go up for Communion, but I don't want to be the person everyone's wondering about, like, "Oooh, look at that McKnight boy, got himself into trouble. Can't even take the bread and wine." Then I'd have to get some Cools Counseling, and my descent into Hell would be complete. So I whisper "sorry, God" three times and shuffle up with everyone else.

After the service, while Mom and Pops are telling Reverend Coles how great he was, Vicky comes over.

"Hi, Vicky," I say. "I thought you didn't go here anymore."

"I don't really," she says, "but, you know . . . we have to show our faces a few times before the holidays so we look good, blah blah blah."

"You should come to youth group sometime," I say. "It's not bad."

"Yeah?" she says. "It seems like a . . . tight-knit group. I don't really know that many people here."

"Everyone's cool. I'm sure the group would welcome you." *Please God, forgive me for lying in church.*

"Yeah, right," she says softly. We stand there for a few seconds. "So I thought we could talk about the campaign."

"Now?"

"Nothing else to do," she says, looking around. "And while it may seem like a long time till the election, remember, there's a lot of business to take care of. We need to start working on plans for that rally with the mayor. I've *got* to make a good impression on him; if I can win us that grant money, I don't have to worry about Harvard."

"I think you don't have to worry about Harvard until at least next year," I say.

She laughs. "I bet you do. Anyway. Have you handed out all of the flyers I gave you? I have some new postcards that I'd like you to laminate and turn into magnets. Hot idea, right?" She smiles.

"Um," I say, and leave it at that. "Remember what I was talking about in homeroom that day? About the community stuff?"

She looks at me without blinking. Or smiling, which is a relief.

"My cousin Grace gets school credit for volunteering at a children's hospital. Maybe our campaign can support an organization in the neighborhood or something and get Clarke to give volunteers extra credit."

"Extra credit!" she crows. "I can work with that." She smiles like I'm a puppy. "You have such cute ideas." She pulls out a stack of postcards. "But first. The office supply store in the mall is slow, so you should get started on the laminating now."

"Don't you think we need to do a little more than laminate, Vicky? Did you hear about this shelter project we're starting? I didn't know there were people living like that right in our neighborhood. If you like the community service idea, we should talk more about it."

"Actually, we should talk more about your postcard distribution strategy," she snaps. She moves a little closer to me and lowers her voice. "Listen . . . I have to win this. I have six brothers and sisters, and they've all won every single election they've ever entered. I was going to try something different, but my mom . . . Anyway, do you get it? I'm a legacy."

"Whoa," I say. "That must be a lot of pressure." I know about pressure, but Vicky's family must take it to the next level.

She shrugs. "I've just got to be a winner, you know? So if you do your job right, everything will be fine." As Reverend Coles starts to approach, she hands me the postcards and slips away.

Looking around for my own escape, I spy Monica trying to chat it up with John Wilkins. He lives on our block and he's a big-time basketball player at her school. The Sephora face paint plot thickens. My parents tell me to drag Monica away from Mr. NBA.

I jog over to them. "We gotta go, Fright Face," I say without thinking. John laughs. Uh-oh. For a second, Monica looks like she wants to cry, but that's not possible because she's not human.

"Oh, did you wet your pants again, Weggie? Do you need to get home to change your diaper?" She smiles at John. "My little brother has a big bladder problem."

"Yeah?" says John. "I heard you got a lot of problems, son."

John and Monica start laughing and I try to think of a comeback that won't get me stomped. His Nikes are huge.

"Later, John," says Monica, pulling me away by my neck. "You'll pay for that, you bridge troll," she whispers to me as we head over to Mom and Pops.

Dave walks over. "Reggie, what's up? Monica, long time no see. . . ."

"Hey, Dave," I say, rubbing my neck.

"Hello, Dave, good to see you," says Pops. "Monica, Reggie, we've got to get going. I know Monica's probably dying to eat." He looks surprised at Monica's responding glare. Takes the heat off me, at least.

"I've been thinking about that suffering stuff," I tell Dave. "You know, why do things suck so bad if God is so good?"

Oops, didn't mean to say *suck*. My parents frown and Monica smirks.

Dave smiles. "I knew you would. So, what did you come up with?"

I shrug. "I have no idea." Dave laughs, and I add, "But I want to keep thinking about it, okay?"

"That's the first step in the right direction," he says.

"The public radio people gave me a lot of ideas for our visit to the shelter," I say. "I made a list of sample interview questions for the homeless, like what their childhoods were like and what are some things about homelessness that people don't realize." I remember Joe C.'s comments. "I think a lot of people might not relate to them so well."

"Fantastic," says Dave. "We're well prepared for Wednesday. Reggie, thank you for being on top of things. I appreciate it. And I'm not surprised."

"I didn't really do anything," I say.

"Reggie, you did your thing. Thank you. Take the grace with graciousness."

I nod even though I'm not sure I know what he's talking about. That's nothing new.

"I'm looking forward to our relationship with the Olive Branch community," he adds. "It's going to be great."

I wonder what it's like to have that much faith all of the time. In *anything*.

"Yeah, okay," I say. "It's going to be sweet."

OCTOBER 20
4:00 P.M.

The stench almost takes me out as soon as I walk into the room. I thought bleach and hot dogs were a bad combination; bleach and homeless people take funk to a whole new level. I have to work hard to keep my face fixed. Jeff is wrinkling his nose and covering his mouth just in case we don't get that it smells. The place looks old and gray, and the people do too, even the kids. I look around, then I look down fast; I'm embarrassed and I don't know why.

"This way, guys. There's Wilma," says Dave, sounding all cheery like we just walked into Disney World. There's a very tall woman waving us over to a long table. She looks like Valkyryna, Night Man's occasional partner in crime-fighting (and, as Joe C. now calls her, "his lady friend"), but when we get closer I revise that to Valkyryna's mom, or grandmother. She's pretty old, but she's big, and even her hair looks like it could beat me down. We all shuffle over to the table and sit down at the bench.

"Welcome to Olive Branch," starts Wilma. "I'm glad to see so many young people willing to help out and give back to the community. This is an exciting project and many of our guests are enthusiastic about participating. Before you begin, I want to tell you a little more about the shelter. We meet the basic needs of over two hundred people every day, and as the weather gets colder, that number could double. . . ."

As she talks, I look around some more. Most of the "guests" are sitting in folding chairs, watching the news on a little TV. A couple of old guys are playing an intense game of dominoes and a bunch of little kids are running around like they really *are* in Disney World. There are only a couple of kids who look around my age; they're staring at us. I feel like they hate me, and I feel like they should.

Ruthie raises her hand. "Excuse me, but, um . . . I don't know how to say this."

"Why, is it in another language?" says Wilma. "If it's in English, then spit it out."

"Well, okay." Ruthie takes a deep breath. "I feel kind of silly, us doing this whole interview thing. Just talking. Especially now that we're here, I feel like we should be doing something more, something real."

"What do you mean?" asks Wilma, in a voice that sounds like she knows exactly what Ruthie means.

"Like food. Like finding real housing, Habitat for Humanity kind of stuff."

"Like showers," mutters Jeff.

Wilma sits down, and as soon as she does she looks less like Valkyryna and more like my nana who makes the best fried dumplings ever and won't move out of her house in Kingston even though the roof will probably blow off in the next hurricane.

"I understand where you're coming from, hon," she says to Ruthie. "You too," she adds, glancing at Jeff. "Even though you have an ignorant way of expressing yourself." Dave doesn't hide his smile, but she glares at him too. "It's not pretty, is it? These could be your friends, your family . . . you. This is a temporary shelter facility, but we have people who have basically been living here for close to a year. There was a baby born right over there last week. Mr. Tilden, whose first name I never knew, died last month, just before celebrating his eighty-fifth birthday and six months here. We have to confiscate weapons daily, and we don't always get them all. This is real. Maybe too real for some of you."

Ruthie raises her hand, but Wilma puts her own up and keeps going. "What you came here to do may seem unimportant or silly or a waste of time, but be clear: It's precious. Listening, really listening, is precious. Preserving someone's story is precious."

"I'm Precious," says Precious Walters, smiling. We all laugh, even Wilma, and it's like a giant balloon releasing air. I glance at Mialonie, who gives me a quick smile before turning back to Wilma. Dave is nodding like a bobblehead.

"No one listens to these people. Our society doesn't even see them. You probably don't see them when you walk down the street past that pile of clothes in a church doorway, or in the corners of the subway stations." She sounds like the first Night Man book. "It's vital to meet basic needs, to provide food, shelter, health care, and so on — even when it's just a Band-Aid; but the stories are important too. Our stories are our identities."

"So, we're giving a voice to the voiceless?" I ask.

"Everyone has a voice," cuts in Dave, sounding a little annoyed. "You are acting as an instrument, helping them to share it."

Everyone's quiet for a moment. Some little kids run by, and one of them, a boy, trips. I look to see if he's hurt, and . . . it's Charlie.

No wonder he was so excited about my house.

I don't know if he's seen me, or if I should go up and say hi. I wonder where his mom is? I think about them at the mall. They didn't look homeless. I mean, she was buying him toys. I figured homeless people just buy bread and milk and stuff if they get money.

Charlie's looking right at me, and he's not smiling. I raise my hand and wave. He waves back and looks away.

"Enough preaching," says Wilma, standing up. "We've all got work to do." She looks at Dave. "You okay?" Dave nods, and as she walks away, she gives us a bigger grin than I would have thought she could do. We mumble thank-yous and then nobody else moves.

Dave claps his hands. "All right, y'all, you know the guidelines so I won't go over them again. Reggie, start handing out equipment."

I try a motivating smile as I give out digital recorders, microcassette players, notepads, and pencils. I take a closer look at Jeff and I can see he's freaking out, so I murmur, "You got this," as I give him a digital recorder.

He smiles. "Thanks."

Dave continues: "We'll regroup for a quick meeting in forty-five minutes. I'm sure you'll all have something to share about this experience. Now: All of the guests here who signed up for this got a number, so I'll give you numbers and that's how you'll get your match. Any questions?"

No one has a question, not out loud at least. I wonder if I'll be matched up with Charlie, but we're only talking to adults. Then I wonder if I'll get his mom; that would be awkward. While I'm trying to figure out what to do, I get number seven. When Dave calls it out, nobody responds until the third time, when a guy sitting with his back to us raises his hand. I look at Dave, who nods and smiles, and I go over and sit in the chair next to the guy.

He turns and looks at me. He's pretty old, like forty or something. His hair is cut low but could use a trim, and his forehead is smooth except for one deep line in the middle. He reminds me of Pops. Maybe this is a sign of the future, like if Pops doesn't find a job. The guy just stares at me. He looks tired, and he looks serious, to put it mildly. If I were to put it less mildly, I'd say he looks furious.

"Uh, I'm Reggie," I mumble, putting out my hand.

"George," he spits back, not taking it. *Furious George*, I think, which makes me smile.

"Something funny about my name?" His eyes get all slitty.

"No! Definitely not. I was just . . . smiling at . . . nothing. You . . . I . . . No, definitely nothing funny." I look over at Dave for help, but he's having a talk with Jeff, who looks like he's about to walk. I see Ruthie chatting up an old lady who's wearing a church hat and clutching a shiny black purse, her coat all buttoned up to her neck. Mialonie is right next to them, gifting a tall skinny woman with her smile.

I turn back to George. "Uh, thank you for doing this," I start, remembering what Dave told us to say. I wish I had a tips sheet now. "Where were you born?" I ask.

"In a hospital," he replies.

"Okay, thanks." I pretend to write that down. "So . . . how old are you?"

"Old enough to know you aren't supposed to ask grown folks their age," he says, raising his voice a little.

Oh-kay. "Excuse me for a second." I get up and go over to Wilma.

"I don't think this is working," I say to her. She's watching the little kids play with blocks. Charlie's on the edge of the group; he keeps looking at the door.

"Then make it work," she says, not looking at me.

I point to Charlie. "I know that kid," I say.

"Good for you."

"Um, is his mom around?" I ask, still not sure of what I'll do if she is.

"She's at work," says Wilma, finally looking at me. "And don't you have some to do, number seven?"

Obviously she's one of those doesn't-miss-a-trick types. She walks away to check on a delivery from a van full of books and toys, and Charlie is so excited as he watches them unload, I wish I could put that look on his face every day.

I walk back to George and clear my throat. "Uh, sorry . . . okay . . . So, I'm Reggie. . . ."

"I know." His lids shut completely. He doesn't look angry anymore, just bored.

"Yeah, so." I take a deep breath and sit up straight. That helps a little. "So let's get started. First, I'd like to thank you for participating in this project. It's a privilege —"

"You don't have to go into the whole routine, Regina. Just do the job you came here to do." He points to the recorder. "You want me to use that?"

"Yeah," I say. I clear my throat again. "And my name is Reggie."

He opens his eyes all the way. "And I'm George. So are we straight?" He smiles a little, and I nod. "Let's do this, then." We look at each other for a minute. He shifts in his chair. "Isn't this supposed to be an interview? Do you have more questions prepared? Some notes, maybe?"

"Oh, yeah. Okay, um . . ." I look at my list, thinking of how Dave told us to let the conversation flow naturally, not to just read from a list of questions. "Don't interrogate," he'd said. I read the next question word for word: "Where are you originally from?" *And how did you get here?* I think.

And when I look at him I can tell he knows what I'm thinking, and he's not mad. Not that much, anyway. He sits back in his chair, and so do I.

6:30 P.M.

When I get home from the session at Olive Branch, no one's around. Normally that means I can guzzle some chocolate milk straight from the carton and watch some music videos that my mom would call "less than empowering." Instead I grab an apple and some chips, then head straight to my room and sit on my bed with my voice recorder. I remember everything George said, and nothing. What he told me sounded like a story I read by mistake. I need to listen to that growly voice again, right away, because it was real and I don't want to let him down.

There's some scratching, and me saying, "Testing . . . test," like a jerk, and then: "I had it pretty good," says George in his rough voice that got less scary as he went on. "I was a quiet Carolina kid. Grew up in Raleigh with lots of fresh air and high hopes. My parents took us on vacations every summer. I was one of those honor roll guys too. Woulda topped your class, smart boy. Always standing up in front of the church to get some certificate or medal. My sister was a baller, got a scholarship to Chapel Hill. I had two years of college myself right here in Brooklyn." Then he squeezes out a laugh, and I know it was in response to the surprised look that I couldn't keep off of my face. "Yeah, college. I was going to be an engineer. I used to walk over the Brooklyn Bridge, man, and read all that stuff about how they built it. I had lots of ideas, and I was talented too. Damn, I'm *still* talented. I had dreams, you know, like I'm sure you do. . . . I was dreaming big. Living big too."

I can't picture the man I just met getting medals in church or going to college. I can't even picture him having a family. I don't get it; he sounds like he used to be me. I sit there and forget to eat and listen to George talk about pressure, and dreaming, and being scared, and being a Black man. I don't even open my notebook to transcribe everything like I'm supposed to. His voice gets oily and soft when he talks about drinking, and drugs I never heard of; it's like he misses it at the same time he's telling me how bad it all is. I listen to myself saying "yeah" and "uh-huh" and "um" in a squeaky voice like I'm four years old, and right now I *do* wish I were four years old and playing with my train set and thinking Super Grover might actually come to my house. I even wish I only knew about people like

George, not that I actually knew them. Then I wish I didn't wish that.

There's a knock on my door. I don't answer, so of course Pops just walks in.

"You okay, son?" he asks. He's wearing his good suit, and I notice that it doesn't look so good anymore. "I left you some dinner on the stove, but it looks like you didn't touch it."

"How poor are we, Pops?" I ask, stuffing the tape recorder under my pillow.

"Yes, sir, I'm fine, and it's good to see you too," says Pops.

"Sorry," I say. "So . . . are we going to stay in our house? What will we do if . . . if we run out of money?" *And if you don't get a new job?*

He laughs, which I guess is a good sign. "We'll be fine, by God's grace," he says. "You don't need to worry about those things. Your job is —"

"I know, I know, keep up my grades and stay out of trouble. But . . . sometimes things happen, right?"

Pops stops smiling. "Is there something you need to tell me?"

"No, Pops," I say. "But I need you to tell me some things . . . please."

After a while, he answers. "Your mother and I have been prudent, we have savings. And her income is keeping us afloat. I know that . . . it's been difficult, with my layoff and everything. But it's temporary. Nothing for you to worry about." He looks like he's wishing he'd never walked in. "Er, but if you still want to drop your piano lessons . . ."

"I do," I say quickly. "That would be great." I've never liked piano anyway. He pats my shoulder and half-smiles. "Dave has us doing some work at a shelter," I start. "With homeless people. They all just looked like . . . like they used to be regular people, Pops. Some of them probably had savings too, right? And jobs. And lives. And now . . ."

I hear George's angry voice. *I thought that I was going places, man. And I was going to take people with me. I had a girl, real cute. Was going to start up a company with my little brother. I haven't talked to him in ten years.*

"I thought it was going to be different, somehow. Not so . . . scary. I mean, there were all these people, and kids, and whole families . . . and I talked to this man, and he was kind of harsh, and . . ." I stop. I can't say *and I'm scared that that's who you'll become.*

"And?" says Pops.

"I want . . . I feel guilty or something. There was even a kid there that I . . . know. It's like I'm about to mess up, and I don't want to. I just want to know what I should do." My throat hurts. This is more than I've talked to Pops since forever. "What should I do?"

"I don't know, son," he says. And he hugs me. Longer than he's hugged me in a long, long time.

OCTOBER 21
7:42 A.M.

I walk to school thinking of those people at the shelter looking like they've got no reason to keep going . . . but they were still moving forward. By the end of our interview, George was talking about going back to school to get a master's degree. In our meeting at the end of the session, Jeff said his partner wanted to build birdhouses, and I watched this little girl pretending to be an astronaut. That takes a kind of faith that I've never even thought about before.

Donovan is sitting on the school steps eating what looks like a bacon sandwich. I try to slip by, but he sees me and jumps up.

"Pukey!" he yells. "Good to see you. It's always nice to encounter lower life-forms. Reminds me of how lucky I am."

"Whatever," I say. I don't know what I'd do without that word. I head over to the folding table set up by the front door for campaign activities and pull the stack of Vicky flyers out of my backpack. I'm giving up on Vicky too quickly. I bet there's a way this school can help the shelter. If the whole "can-do" spirit thing can be in full effect *there*, then we've *got* to be able to get it together at Clarke. Maybe if I stress how good it will look for that mayor grant money thing, Vicky will listen to me, we'll make this campaign about something . . . and I might actually redeem myself.

Donovan saunters over, picks up a flyer, and immediately rips it in half. A piece of bacon falls out of his sandwich. I grab the ripped papers from his hands.

"Hey, everybody," he calls. "Pukey's gonna blow!"

Amazingly, people seem eager to verify this, and drift over.

"Your girl is already inside," he says. "Talking about how she is going to make us pay for her college education."

Huh? A few people boo.

"What's next?" he continues. "A kindergarten slave trade?" More boos. "*V* is for *vomitocious!*" he yells. I notice Hector's grin out of the corner of my eye. "Which is exactly what you and Vicky are, Pukey." More people come over. "*V* is for *vengeance*," he continues, trying to be all Martin Luther King, "which is what We the People Who Matter will seek if you and that moose-faced hoghead get anywhere near the presidency."

I'm glad the bell ringing drowns out some of the laughter. I wait a few minutes before I start packing up, and a couple of kids come over to the table.

"Uh, hi," I mumble. I glance around to make sure Donovan's gone, and then I raise my voice. "Vicky Ross for president. Vote Vicky for . . . victory, for . . . veracity, for . . ." I look at the flyer. "Value." *Value? What does that even mean?*

My candidate and I need to talk.

A boy with binocular-thick lenses and $1 coins in his penny loafers takes a flyer.

"Thanks," I say. "I'm Vicky's campaign manager. We want to

be the voice of the people. What are your biggest concerns about life here at Clarke?"

"Not concerns, exactly. . . . We have some ideas for her campaign platform. LARPing would be really good for English, and also, we're tired of the censorship of the library computers." He rolls his eyes. "We're not all looking for porn." At that, his friend looks down at his own shoes. *Speak for yourself.*

"I'll see what I can do," I say. "Uh, what's LARPing?"

He lights up. "Thanks for asking!" He takes out a flyer. "Live-Action Role-Playing. I'm trying to spread the word. People from all over create stories and act them out, with costumes and everything. A group of kids in Vermont started a national LARP organization for teens. You can be assigned a character in an existing game, or create an original story world. People think we're just weirdos, but it's kind of a great way to get involved in stories."

"We use the same principles as official LARPers," says the other guy. "It's like we create a living video game." He finally looks up at me and I can see how much he loves this LARP stuff.

"Sounds interesting," I say. "We'll check it out."

"Tell Vicky to come to the next session at my house," he says.

His friend grins. "Yeah, he has some love scenes he wants to act out with her."

I try not to shudder since that wouldn't exactly look supportive. "I'll see what I can do," I say again. They walk away.

The second bell rings; no time for my locker. I gather up my campaign stuff and head inside. I jog down the hall, but I stop when I see Vicky up ahead. An old lady is yelling at her, finger in

Vicky's face like one of those mean army guys in a movie. Did I forget Grandparents' Day? Did Vicky? She's not saying anything. Finally, the old lady shoves a box in Vicky's arms and stomps out.

I walk up to Vicky slowly, not sure if I should pretend that I didn't see anything. She looks even more tired when she sees me.

"My mom is, um, really stressed out," she says.

Whoa. Vicky's mom is *old*. And my mom is always saying "Black don't crack," so if she looks seventy-five she must be a hundred. I remember what Vicky said about all of those brothers and sisters and being a "legacy"; after what I just saw, I'm guessing she doesn't get a whole lot of support at home.

"Where've you been, anyway?" she asks. "I . . . oh, I don't know, I kind of expect help from my campaign manager." She flashes the smile/grimace, like she's just kidding, but she's not.

"I was outside handing out flyers. What's this thing about you making people pay for your college education?"

"What? I don't know what you're talking about."

"Donovan just —"

"Oh, him," she says. "Hello? Negative campaigning? Personal attacks?" She gives me another one of her shoulder "pats." "We've got to be ready for this kind of thing from the enemy. They will stop at nothing."

"So, he was making it up?" I ask, rubbing my shoulder.

"I'm assuming he was referring to my Empowerment Fund proposal. That was your idea, remember?" She starts walking toward her locker, which is far away from mine.

"Empowerment Fund?" I fall into step beside her. "What are you talking about?"

"Raising money to start up a Clarke merit-based scholarship fund," she says. "Your idea was good, just needed a little tweaking."

"Tweaking? I said that we should raise money to help out a community organization, not for scholarships. In fact, I —"

"A school *is* a community organization. And by supporting our top students, who are the ones who have the potential to make this community great, we will be helping out a community organization."

"But, it's kind of . . . not the same thing," I say.

"You're right." She smiles. "It's better. Less chance of wasting money on people who don't . . . who can benefit from good leadership."

Time to switch tactics. "A couple of *voters* just asked me about something," I say, taking out the LARPing flyer. "They had some ideas about the English curriculum and the library."

"Maybe you should poll it later. If it's just some fringe thing, then I'm not interested," Vicky says, looking at the flyer but not taking it. "Think big-ticket issues. Fund-raisers. Honor roll parties. Award ceremonies sponsored by Junior's. Oooh — free cheesecake to the student with the highest GPA every month! See? I just came up with that one on my own. It's the feel-good stuff that matters, so get on that." The last bell rings as she grabs her books from her locker. "Gotta go," she says. "See you at lunch. And . . . what's LARPing? Sounds a little loser-ish to me. No offense, if you're into it."

"I'm not," I say. "But I was going to find out more, since they *are* part of the *voting* community." And because they cared so much. "I didn't want to judge without knowing."

"Uh-huh, that's sweet. How are you doing with postcards?" she asks.

"I'm good," I reply. "But —"

She hands me the box that her mother gave her. "Great. Here are seven hundred more." She looks at me without smiling, which is, strangely enough, a relief. "I need my campaign manager to exercise good judgment. So please, stay away from freak gatherings and boring issues that matter to two people. Your job is to get me elected. Focus on what's important."

OCTOBER 23
2:12 P.M.

"Yo. So you haven't really talked about it," says Joe C., clearing his throat a few times. "Was it intense?"

"Huh?" I say. "What's that music?" I'm kind of surprised he called. Joe C. and I used to have *Night Man* phone meetings every Saturday, but the collaboration thing has been a little raggedy lately.

"Sorry, hold up. . . ." The music gets lower, but I can still hear it. "The homeless people thing. You haven't told me anything. How was it? Did you get any ideas for *Night Man*?"

"Oh . . . yeah. It was, uh, intense." I don't know what to say, and I don't want to say much. Part of me wants to tell Joe C. that the ideas I got have nothing to do with *Night Man,* but his comments about "that place" and "those homeless people" still sting. "I interviewed this guy . . . it was pretty interesting. I'm going to go back there soon — I want to talk to him more." Then I remember something George told me. "Oh, hey, remember that show we saw about the subway tunnels? It was all true — people live underground for years and years. He said there are even informal shops and mayors and stuff. It's like *The City of Ember*."

"Yeah?" says Joe C. "Do they like it down there? Was your guy one of the real mole people? Did he eat rats?"

It's time for me to change the subject. "What's up with the music? You going on one of those celebrity dance shows?"

Joe C. laughs. "Very funny. I'm still at my dad's, working on some mixes. Gunnar gave me some equipment; he's great. I got a CD of sound effects for movies too." I hear the sound of a baby crying and what sounds like a police siren. "What do you think?"

"Sounds . . . interesting," I say.

"Yeah, I got to work on it," says Joe C. "If I get any good, Gunnar's gonna hook me up with some clubs here in Bay Ridge."

There's a pause, and for a minute I wonder if I'm really talking to Joe C., like maybe I've fallen into this alternate universe where homeless people come to life and Joe C. wears tight V-necks and dress pants.

"Hey — listen to this," says Joe C. "Andrew Johnson, who succeeded Abraham Lincoln, was born in 1808. Lyndon Johnson, who succeeded John F. Kennedy, was born in 1908."

"Spooky," I say, relieved. Same old Joe C. "Thanks for letting me know, though," I say. "I appreciate it."

"So, do you guys score points with God for the homeless stuff?"

"I don't think you're supposed to think about it like that," I say.

"I know, but everybody does. It would be pretty sweet if you could get grades that count toward the afterlife. We're awesome at getting good grades."

"I need all the points I can get to bring up my life GPA," I say.

"Yeah," he says. "So, what else? You're not giving up much info."

After a pause, I say, "Remember the kid from the Buddy program? Charlie?"

"Uh-huh, the one from Target, right?"

"Yeah. Well, he . . . lives there. At the shelter."

"Whoa," says Joe C. "I wouldn't have thought that. He, like, goes to school. And he's not all . . ."

"All what?" I ask, even though I know.

"All . . . homeless-looking," he says. "They were buying toys and stuff. Maybe his mom's on drugs. My dad says most of them are."

I pretend that I didn't have the same thoughts about them shopping. "What are you talking about, Joe C.? Do you realize how stupid you sound? Is every poor person on drugs? What's 'homeless-looking'?"

"Did you talk to him?" asks Joe C.

"Just hi. We didn't really have a chance to chitchat."

"Um, so, I should go," Joe C. says. "Gunnar said he might stop by."

I try not to sound too happy about getting off of the phone. "Yeah, I have to transcribe my notes from this thing, and then do my homework."

"Okay, see you tomorrow. E-mail me if you have ideas you want me to sketch."

"It'll probably be a while before I have new Night Man material," I say.

"That's cool — Gunnar's going to Amsterdam soon and I want to soak up as much as I can from him. So I don't know how much time I'll have. . . ."

"So we'll talk," I say. "No rush. There's a lot going on. Later."

We hang up, and I think about taking out my Night Man notebook, but I don't. After seeing the shelter and talking to George, *Night Man* feels so fake, like one of those scary fairy tales Monica used to read me where people always got chopped up with axes. I wasn't sure how happy those endings were when I was little. I'm not sure now.

4:30 P.M.

Even though it's a Saturday afternoon, Ruthie comes over later to study. We seem to have more tests than there are days in the week, and of course they will all be "a significant percentage of our final grades." I've got a feast laid out on the coffee table, but Ruthie hasn't opened the bag of organic carrot and zucchini chips that I bought especially for her. That's on her; I'm a little suspicious of something called Carrucchinis!, since I've learned a lot about the flavor of exclamation-pointed foods from Juiced!.

"Is Monica upstairs? We should ask her about some of this stuff," Ruthie says. "She helped me with my math homework once."

"When was that — kindergarten? That's about the level she's stuck at."

"I know you get the good grades and everything, and she . . . doesn't. But Monica's no fool. She's been limited to playing the unfeminine dumb jock role." Ruthie opens her notebook. "Who knows who she could really be?"

"'Unfeminine dumb jock.' Nice," I say. "I'm sure she'd thank you for that."

"You know what I mean," says Ruthie. "Women all over the world have to hide our real selves so that we don't threaten men."

"Monica is limited by her pea brain and a mean streak that's only surpassed in size by her muscles," I say. "Don't feel sorry for her, traitor."

Ruthie turns to her notes. We read and write in silence for almost an hour. Monica comes downstairs. She glares at us, mutters "geeks," and then heads out the door. I give Ruthie a meaningful look, and she shrugs.

I stretch. "When do teachers expect us to actually absorb the information they gorge us with?"

"I think Ms. A wants to change the whole school election system," says Ruthie. "I overheard her talking to a bunch of teachers about how it doesn't mean anything, and they're wasting a good opportunity to teach democracy and social change. She knows what's up. I thought you did too."

"Whatever," I say. "I'm not a politician. I'm a . . ." I stop, because I really don't know. Most of the time I feel like a blank page, and everyone else picks up a pen and fills me up before I can even get my thoughts together.

"Oh, yeah, right. You use the power of the pen to make comic books that are going to dazzle us all." Ruthie sighs. "Real revolutionary."

I hate when she says stuff like that — not just dissing comics, but like we've all got to launch some big revolution or else our lives don't mean anything.

"Or wait, I forgot — you're also . . . kind of the worst campaign manager ever." She smiles to show she's joking, but it still stings.

"Yeah, yeah, we're not the best team," I say.

"You could be," says Ruthie. "Maybe not the best, but something better."

"Give me a break. Vicky is not about to be an 'agent of change,'" I say. "And what, now you're all on the 'elect Vicky' train? Make up your freaking mind."

"I'm not talking about Vicky," Ruthie says as she stands up. "I'm getting some water. Do you want anything?" She goes into the kitchen without waiting for me to answer, then comes back with a bottle of water and a book.

"Hey, I didn't know you had this," she says. "Isn't it powerful?"

"I didn't know I had it either," I say, grabbing the book from her. "What is it?" I look: *Black Voices in Poetry: A Pan-African Anthology*. I flip through it. It feels old; the pages are yellow and a little stiff. A note falls out, and I read it. It's from Pops to me; he says that he loved this book in college, and he thought that I might too.

I'm surprised. Sometimes I consider talking to him about Night Man, but I'm afraid that he won't get it. And then it'll be tainted, like when I was little and I didn't like to eat broken cookies. I put the note back in the book.

"I found it on the table in the kitchen," she says. "It's a classic. We have the new edition with Kevin Young, Dike Okoro, and Sarah Jones — she's one of my favorites."

"It looks interesting," I say. "I think it's Pops's." As I read, Ruthie grabs the nacho chips.

"Hey —" I start, pointing to the Carrucchinis!.

"Please," she interrupts. "Look at all of the work we have. I'm too stressed out to have nutritional principles!" We laugh, and when the nacho chips are finished, we share the Carrucchinis! too.

After Ruthie leaves, I could use a break, so I decide to make a trip to Forbidden Planet comics shop in Manhattan. I love that place; it's like a world all its own, and I almost always get story ideas just being there. I don't tell Joe C. Like Night Man, I walk alone.

When I get off of the train at Union Square, there's an old guy playing Christmas songs on a steel drum. And even though it's October, it sounds right, and I stand there and listen. When he finishes that "Jeremiah Was a Bullfrog" song, we all clap and a few people drop dollar bills into his pail as they walk away. I move a little closer; he looks over and hands me the mallets. No one's paying much attention, so I pound a couple of times, and the sound is so strong and clear that it's hard to believe I had anything to do with it. He gestures for me to go on, and I just let loose, hammering and pinging and making up some crazy song while he claps along. I finish with a flourish and take a bow, even though he's clearly the only one who appreciated my musical stylings. It's all good, though. I don't even need to go to Forbidden Planet anymore. It's one of those unexpected gift moments, like looking up and finding a mirror right in front of you, and instead of food in your teeth or a booger hanging from your nose, it's really you, and you like what you see.

OCTOBER 25
8:09 P.M.

Pops has been extra busy scouring the online job boards lately; occasionally he comes out of his study looking stiff and awkward, holding a basketball that looks brand-new. He pretends that he's not looking for Monica, but it's not like he ever asks *me* if I want to shoot some hoops instead. Monica barely speaks to any of us when we do catch a glimpse of her. Apparently her supermodel friends all wear high heels, because she's gone from galumphing around in her Adidas to limping in the shoes she wore to Cousin Vinette's wedding last year. Mom's been talking about hiring an assistant to help her out with paperwork at the clinic. I want to tell her to hire Pops, but I know that he wouldn't go for that. I can tell she's more stressed than ever; this week I've woken up to find four former "special occasion only" foods on the counter: festival and fried fish, codfish cakes, coconut bread, and a bun. She even went all the way to Queens last weekend to buy real Jamaican cheese to go with the bun, not that fake stuff they sell at Good-O Market. That overly orange cheese is as wack as the college kids at the Montego Bay airport who shout "Irie, mon!" as soon as they step off the plane.

One evening after Pops and I eat a silent dinner, I'm surprised by a knock on my bedroom door. Mom comes in before I say it's okay, and I shove my plate of cake behind my pillow before she can see what it is. "Hey, Mom," I say, trying not to be obvious with the swallow. "You're home early."

She's still wearing her coat and carrying her briefcase. She's had the same one since she started working again. The stickers that Monica and I "decorated" it with so she could "think about us all day long" are still there.

"Are you doing homework?" she asks.

"Uh-huh," I say. "I've got four tests and a report this week."

"Don't overdo," she says softly, coming over to the bed. I shrug; I know she won't want me to *under*-do, so . . .

"I heard from your Aunt Daphne today," she says, sitting on the bed and rubbing my forehead the way she does when I'm sick. "How are things at school?" Aunt Daphne is Ruthie's mom, and she carries a business card that says "Full-time Wife and Mother." Talking to her usually makes my mom feel guilty, so I wonder if she's going to whip up some extra-special treats tonight. Ruthie says *her* mom feels guilty when she talks to mine, so I guess they're even.

"Fine," I say. She keeps looking at me. "Um, I got an A on my math test."

"Very good," she says. She raises her eyebrows. "And everything is . . . going well socially?"

"Sure," I say. *I'm on my way to Loser of the Year!* For a second I think about breaking down and finally telling her about my life as Pukey, how bad this year has sucked, and letting her be my mommy again; but no. I still have some dignity with my mother, at least.

"You don't see Donovan Greene much anymore, do you," she says, and it's both a question and a statement.

I shrug again. I'm not giving up anything. Monica walks by, peeks in, and makes a face.

Mom rubs my head some more, then she pulls a book out of her briefcase and hands it to me. The title: *Right Back ATCHA! Win the War of Words with the World's Wittiest Comebacks (And Vocabulary Helps)*.

It takes me a minute to figure out what "ATCHA" means. Then another to decide that I'm going to kill Ruthie. And one more to realize that I actually don't have a shred of dignity left with my mom. She must know the whole story.

"I just happened to see this while I was browsing at the bookstore," she says. "The clerk assured me that they're all clean and respectful comebacks. And educational!"

Great. Nice, clean comebacks that will improve my essays. Donovan's probably already quaking. I flip the book over. "Jimmy" writes: "I used to just cry when people teased me, but now I've learned to stand up for myself AND I raised my SAT score 200 points!" I wish Jimmy were here so I could punch him.

Mom hugs me quickly and kisses my forehead. "Don't stay up too late," she says, standing up. She still has her coat on; she picks up her briefcase and gives me another quick rub. "And don't get any crumbs in the bed." She walks out, closing the door behind her.

OCTOBER 27
3:46 P.M.

We're back at the Olive Branch. I show Dave the work I've been doing every night, transcribing the youth group's interviews.

"And Dave," I say. "There were some kids here that first day, they looked around my age . . . but I don't see them now."

Dave hands the pages back to me. "Yeah, well," he says softly. "Would you want to hang around if you lived here? Have other kids see you living here?"

I nod. I know what it's like, wanting to be invisible. But theirs must be a whole different level. I don't see Charlie around today either.

"How're you doing?" he asks. "I know it's a lot of work for one guy, all of this transcribing. I'm going to try to get someone else to help out. Gabriella . . . she kind of left you hanging, huh?"

"It's all right," I say, even though I could use the help. "It's interesting, the stories people are telling. Did you know that guy called Old Crump led a union desegregation movement in the South? And he was practically a kid. Mialonie's partner, Miss Joycelyn, had her quilts in the Museum of Modern Art." I smile. "And it figures Ruthie would get a former Black Panther."

Dave laughs as George walks toward us.

"What's up with all this chitchat?" George asks. "We got work to do." We walk over to "his" corner; there's a card table now, so we sit across from each other and I put my little bag of chips on the table, right in the middle.

"You got anything to drink?" he asks, and I shake my head. I take out my notes from our last meeting and stare at them. George stares at me.

"Um, do you want to pick up where we left off? I wanted to ask you about the subway tunnels, because —"

"No," says George quickly.

"Okay," I say slowly. "How about when you used to hang out on the Brooklyn Bridge? I was wondering —"

"Not that either."

"Uh, what is Raleigh like? I've never been down South."

"Maybe you should go down there and find out for yourself," he says.

It's like a do-over of the beginning of that first visit here — and it's going just as well as it did the first time.

"So . . ." I start, and trail off.

"Don't *you* got something to talk about?" George asks. "What's your story?"

I don't say anything until I realize that I will always lose the stare-down battle with George. There's no contest.

"Well, I've got this project, that, uh, maybe I can ask you about?" Of course my voice goes into squeak mode at the end of my question.

"Another project?" he mutters. "Is that the new thing, every-thing's a project?" He looks at me. "Every*one*'s a project?"

"No!" I practically shout. "I mean, no, I . . . It's something . . .

something I'm writing, really. A graphic novel. I mean, you know, like a comic book, but —"

"I know what a graphic novel is." Suddenly a smile breaks open his face. "That's all right! I used to write my own comic books when I was coming up."

Now it's my turn to smile. "You did? What were they about?"

"Oh, I had this rapping detective character, you know. . . ." He grabs some chips and looks down. "It was just fooling around." He takes another handful of chips. "I did it for about four years."

"Why did you stop?" I ask.

He shrugs. "Moved on, I guess. Or the creative juices just stopped flowing."

"I know what you mean," I say. "See, Night Man — that's my character — I've been working on it since kindergarten, and my friend Joe C. does the art, and it's cool and everything, but —" I stop. "Rapping detective?"

"Yeah," George laughs a little. "Whenever he solved a crime, he would get all lyrical and wrap everything up with a rhyme." He glares at me. "What's your guy? Night Man? What does he do?"

"Well, he's, uh, homeless. . . ." I glance at George, but he just stares. "He's really a superhero, but nobody knows it. They can't see the real guy behind the homeless part."

George nods. "But the homeless guy is part of the real guy too, right?"

"Yeah, exactly." I nod. "He uses his knowledge of the streets to help him. Like he built a community center in an abandoned subway tunnel for all these street kids with his reward money for saving the city from an enemy attack. All of the gifts that he gets for saving people's lives and stuff, he uses them to create this perfect underground community where everyone watches out for one another. The mayor thinks that he destroyed them when he sealed the manhole entrance to the tunnel, but Night Man knows a way in through a local storage center."

"Interesting," says George. We're quiet for a few seconds.

"But lately I've been having a hard time working on it. It's . . . different now."

"Now, meaning since you started coming to this place?"

I nod.

"That's good, then," he says. "That means you pay attention."

"And I got all involved in this school election. . . ."

"You running for office, Obama?" he asks.

"Nah, I'm just helping this girl who is. But . . . the whole thing is so fake. I mean, it could be something more, but she's just . . . I can't even explain it."

"So why are you doing it then?" George asks.

I shrug. "I guess I thought I could help," I say. "Make a difference at school and all that. But maybe I'm wasting my time, putting myself out there like that. See, there's this guy at school . . . we used to be friends."

"And what?" asks George. "He's running for president too?"

"No, but he's helping this guy who is. It's obvious that he's just trying to get to me."

"Seems like it's working," says George, pouring crumbs from the bag into the palm of his hand.

"What?"

"Him getting to you." He drops the bag on the table.

"It wrecks my nerves!" I blurt out. "Why can't he find something better to do?" I start to crumple up the chip bag.

"Why can't you?" George asks. He takes the bag and manages to pour a few more crumbs into his mouth.

"Huh?"

"I mean, seems like you got enough to work with . . . your girl running for president —"

"Vicky is *not* my girl," I interrupt.

"Your candidate, then. And your graphic novel . . . and coming here . . . Like I said, you got a lot of projects. What's important to you?" He hands back the empty chip bag.

I pause before I speak again. "This isn't a project," I say. "It's like, I've been so sick of how fake my school is — we talk all about community service and community spirit, and it's just the same old thing every year. But this place, this is . . . real. And I want to be a part of it."

He smiles again. "That's because you're paying attention. Just keep paying attention, smart boy. You'll figure it out." He points to my Night Man notebook. "Let me check that out. Homeless superhero, huh? You sure his name isn't George? Cuz well, you know . . ."

"As a matter of fact . . ." I start, and we both laugh.

OCTOBER 28
7:56 A.M.

I run up the steps at school, and today I don't trip. Progress. Pops made me a BLT for breakfast this morning, one of those don't-tell-your-mother meals. He remembered the election and asked how it was going; I said "fine." It's not often that Pops says something to me that doesn't start with "Why can't you . . ." so I didn't want to ruin things by telling him that I haven't been the best campaign manager around. He even gave me a couple of bucks "just because." Still, I've already missed the first bell, and I start running, hoping that I look athletic and not panicked and sweaty.

Charlie's standing near my locker. His fists are clenched and his eyes are slitty, just like George's when he's mad.

"Hi," he says, like he's daring me to do something.

"Hey," I say. "Good to see you the other day. Sorry we didn't get to talk."

"Yeah," he says.

"Have you been sick or something?" I ask. "I've been looking for you at school."

Charlie shrugs. "Sometimes I don't feel like coming. My stomach hurts sometimes. And my mommy doesn't feel good sometimes either."

"Well, I'm glad you're here," I say. I keep it light and casual and like it's totally normal for him to live at the Olive Branch. "I went back to the Olive Branch too, but I guess you were out."

"Maybe it was when I went to the doctor," he says. "I didn't have to get any shots."

"Great! So I'll be back there to do more interviews; maybe we can hang out then. Uh, I'm kind of late. . . ."

"Did you just take a shower?"

"No," I answer, and I keep walking fast. He has to jog to keep up.

"You're all wet," he says. "You have big patches under your arms —"

"Shouldn't you be going to class?" I interrupt.

"Yes, because today I'm sharing for show-and-tell, and I was going to tell them about you and the fun stuff we're going to do together but I have to ask you what we're gonna do because we haven't done anything yet because I know you're real busy and my mom said I have to ask you ahead of time and make a plan because big boys make plans." He takes a breath. "So I wanted to know if we're going to go to the zoo like you said. Or something."

"How about this," I say as the last bell rings. "Lunch." He's just looking at me, so I add, "To celebrate you being here today. You can sit with me and my friends."

"Really?" he says. "We can even trade lunches if you want. And I can share my juice box. Do you like juice boxes?"

"Um, you should talk to Joe C. He's really into juice," I say. "So, we got a deal? We can have lunch together a lot, if you come to school."

He nods.

I realize that the last bell rang about a hundred hours ago. I'm in trouble. "Listen, I'm really late, and so are you, so I'll see you later." I start backing away.

"Okay," he says. "I have to tell you something too. Something important."

"See you later, okay?" I turn around and start running. The door to Ms. A's class creaks as I open it, and everyone looks up from . . . a pop quiz? I look at Ms. A: She fake smiles back and points to the test paper already on my desk.

"You've lost some time, Reggie," she says. "Better get to it." Joe C. gives me a "don't worry about it" look as I head to my seat. Audrey Glassman is already done with hers, and she raises one eyebrow at me. Whatever.

I look at the quiz. It's on NATO. No wonder Joe C.'s not worried. NATO is at the top of Ruthie's New World Order Collective action list, and we've been getting a crash course in everything from the Cold War to the Riga Summit. I raise my hand and smile at Ms. A. "Will there be extra credit?" I say.

11:38 A.M.

Bonded with Pops and aced a pop quiz. It all gives me enough confidence to say hi to Mialonie and Josie as I pass their table in the cafeteria. (I'm always surprised to see Mialonie eating; I keep expecting her not to do things like eat and go to the bathroom like the rest of us.) Then I slide into my seat next to Ruthie.

"I never thought that I'd say this," I start, "but your NATO sermons came in handy."

"Don't sleep," Ruthie says. "I know which way the winds of the world blow." She takes out her journal. "I've got to write that one down. 'Winds of the World,' I love it. Could be the future title of my book."

"Don't talk anymore," I say. "Please. Just don't." I pick up my slab of pizza.

"Hey, Reggie!"

I look up; it's Charlie. I shove Ruthie a little to make room for him. "Hey, Charlie, have a seat!" He puts his brown bag down and climbs up onto the bench. He just sits there for a minute, so I give him a pat on the back and Ruthie makes a series of "awww" sounds.

"What do you have for lunch?" I say.

"Peanut butter and jelly," he says. "And grapes. They're cut in half. Halves are semicircles." He looks at my tray. "My mommy made me lunch today because I told her I didn't like school lunch. I have to finish every bite. But I meant the tacos. I love pizza, though."

I give him half of my pizza. "So, what's your secret? Let's talk now, because we don't have much time."

He looks at Ruthie, who makes a big show of taking out *The Week* magazine and holding it up in front of her face.

Charlie takes a deep breath. "Well," he starts, "um . . . there's somebody mean. . . ." He lowers his voice to a whisper. "A bully. She's really, really mean!"

Uh-oh, *she*? Already, this is not good.

"Is she bigger than you?" I ask.

"Yeah," he says, popping a grape half into his mouth. "Lots bigger."

"Well, what does she do?" I say. Joe C. arrives and sits down across from us.

"She's always poking me in the back," he says, "really hard, and she calls me Chupacabra Charlie."

"Chupa-what?"

"El Chupacabra," answers Joe C. "The goat-sucking beast. Originated in Puerto Rico. Some say it's an urban legend, but tell that to George Thurston of San Antonio, Texas. One took a chunk out of his leg on December 18, 2005."

"You remember my friend Joe C.," I say to Charlie. "Fanatical juice drinker and hoarder of useless information."

"You just needed it," Joe C. reminds me. Ruthie snorts.

Charlie keeps looking at me. "I hate her! I never did anything to her, and she's so mean to me! What should I do?"

"Um," I say. "What do you do now?"

"I try to tell her to stop, but usually . . ." He stops, and motions for me to bend down so he can whisper in my ear. ". . . I start crying." He looks like he's about to cry right now.

I think about it for a minute. "Just don't say anything," I say finally. "And walk away before anything happens." Charlie keeps looking at me like he's waiting for more. I shrug and eat one of his grapes.

I feel a tap on my shoulder. I turn around: Vicky's standing there with her lunch tray balanced on yet another folder.

"Can we talk?" she asks, looking for a spot to squeeze into at the table.

It's pretty crowded, but if we shove over a little . . . No one moves. Vicky waits a few seconds, and I don't know what to do. I raise my eyebrows and shrug a little.

"Um," I begin. "Well . . ."

She laughs, and it's not very convincing. "Yeah, I'll just catch up with you later," she says, and almost collides with Vijay and his camera as she walks away, trying to hand out "Vote Vicky!" flyers without dropping her lunch. She sits at a table by the door, alone.

"Yo, Reggie," Joe C. says. "Do you want to go on the Hip-Hop History tour with me?"

"What? What's that?" *And do you have to talk about it right this second?*

"It's this tour in Manhattan where all of these oldheads take you to the places where hip-hop began."

"Hip-hop began in Africa," I say. "West Africa."

"You know what I mean," he says. "*'Manhattan keeps on makin' it, Brooklyn keeps on takin' it, Bronx keeps creatin' it, and Queens keeps on fakin' it'* . . . Boogie Down Productions," he adds. "'The Bridge Is Over.' *Criminal Minded, 1987.*"

"Thanks, Professor," I say. "I knew that. My parents have that album. It's a classic." Joe C. better not get all Columbus on me and share all of his new 'discoveries.'

"Yeah, it's a good one. I figure a DJ's gotta be a scholar in a way," he says. "So, you want to go? It sounds like fun."

Maybe, but it also sounds like it has a high awkward quotient. "I don't think so," I say. "I don't think Black people go on those tours. We know all of that stuff already." I know I sound silly, but I'm picturing riding through the 'hoods on a bus with Joe C. and a bunch of Germans wearing Kangols. Not. Good. At. All.

Joe C. sighs. "Yeah, I figured you wouldn't go. I may ask

Gunnar to go with me." After a pause, he adds, "He's pretty cool. You really should come by."

I focus on sharing my chips with Charlie, who's finished all of his lunch. Joe C. gives me a nudge, and I look up. Blaylock has come in and pulled Justin aside; now Donovan's coming this way.

"How's it going, Pukey?" he asks. Vijay moves a little closer to us with his camera; he can smell blood. Donovan notices too, and raises his voice. "Hey, is *Talkin' Trash* doing a special episode on all-time losers?"

"Shut up," I mutter.

"Did you tell them about those stupid comic books you make?" he says. "You're probably into all that freak role-playing stuff by now too. That would be a good story: 'Pukey Geek Goes All-Out Freak.' Is that why you're supporting that witch? It's pretty sad, watching you make an even bigger fool of yourself this year. And I didn't think that was possible."

"Why are you so worried about it?" says Joe C.

"I just feel sorry for him," answers Donovan. "Everyone knows that Justin and I are going to win. We don't even have to campaign. Theirs is so bad, it's like watching a train wreck." He looks at Ruthie. "On second thought, that would be your face."

Ruthie turns away. I feel like I should say something, but I just want to run, especially because Vijay and Charlie are so interested in this conversation. All I need is a televised version of Donovan cutting me down while I'm in headlighted-deer mode.

"I'm out," I say, grabbing my stuff. "I'll see you guys at the lockers." I start walking.

"Pukey punk," calls Donovan.

Charlie follows me out of the cafeteria, not saying anything. I don't look at him, and before he can tell me that he's just experienced a Ghost of Christmas Future moment and might jump off the Brooklyn Bridge, I talk fast.

"Hey, um, Charlie, I'll see you later. I'm really busy right now, there's a lot going on. 'Bye." I practically run down the hall before he can say anything.

"Hey, Reggie!" Great. Vicky.

"Vicky, I know you want to talk about your Miss Clarke proposal, but —"

"While I *have* been working hard on the Academic Pageant plans, that's not what I want to talk to you about."

"So, what is it? I'm kind of in a hurry." To bury myself under some covers.

"That, back there, in the lunchroom. It's not a good look for me," she says.

"What are you talking about?"

"Donovan totally punked you, and honestly, you had the camera right there and not only did you fail to promote me and my brand, you looked like a fool."

"Thanks a lot, Vicky," I say. "Can we talk about something else right now? Like the service-learning idea? I think that Olive Branch, that shelter I told you about —"

"This is what I mean. I'm talking about winning the election, you're talking about street people who have nothing to do with us."

"No, see, that's what *I* mean," I say. "There are kids there, kids from Clarke even, and old people . . . and kids our age who could come to Clarke for after-school projects and fund-raisers and stuff. We need to change our message. I'm not even sure we have one."

"Look, I want to win, not get blamed for inviting a bunch of hoodrats to our school. I'm sorry, I know you want to help, but my reputation's at stake. You've got to pull yourself together, for my sake."

I open and close my mouth a few times.

"I hope we understand each other," she says.

"I don't know if I'll ever understand you, Vicky," I say.

She smiles the poor-little-puppy smile again. "How about we both think about it a little? I'm usually able to do something with your ideas. We'll figure something out." She hugs me. Gross. "Glad we had this little talk." She whips out some "Vote Vicky!" pencils and bookmarks and pushes them into my hands. "New swag. See, I *am* changing things up. Remember: Focus on me. And by me, I mean ME." She leaves.

I'm not cut out for politics. I'm leaning against my locker, trying to recover, when Ruthie and Joe C. get there. Ruthie just grabs some stuff from her locker and walks away.

"What's her problem?" I say. "Like it's my fault Donovan's a jerk."

Joe C. shrugs and closes his locker. "I gotta get up to the fifth floor."

"Later," I say. As he walks away, I stay at my locker for a few more minutes. I don't care if I'm late.

OCTOBER 31
11:03 A.M.

I leave my parents in the sanctuary and head over to the church library to meet Dave and the group, and not just because Reverend Coles said in an e-mail that he's planning to "rock da house" with his sermon. We have another group session at Olive Branch coming up on Tuesday, and Dave wants to talk about the project, so everyone shows up today.

Ruthie barely says hi to me; guess she's still got something up her butt about the things that Donovan said. I don't know why *I'm* getting blamed. I grab a spot on the old saggy black couch in the corner of the room and take out an unfinished snack bag of onion and garlic–flavored chips and a new notebook. As I lick chip crumbs from my fingers, I feel someone standing over me and look up. It's Mialonie.

I can't help it; I take in a big, deep breath, and then I'm sitting there staring at her, holding my breath like a fool.

"Hey," she says, in that low, sweet voice.

"Hah — hey," I let out my breath with a *whoosh*. My *onion and garlic* breath. *Good job, Reggie.* She sits next to me, and I really have to fight to keep from taking another deep breath.

Dave claps his hands. "Okay, real quick, I just wanted to find out how you're feeling about the Listening Ears Project." He scans the room. "How is it going?"

Silence, and then Jeff shrugs. "It's depressing. Is that what you want to hear?"

"I want to hear the truth," says Dave. "Go on, I'm listening." But he looks at his watch as he says it. Dave isn't completely focused on us, and that's not like him.

"You could have warned us more," Jeff continues.

Ruthie breaks in. "What did you expect? Homelessness is depressing. It's a shame that we let it happen to people."

"What *we*?" says Tiffany, glancing at Dave. "I mean, I feel bad, and I want to help, but it's not *my* fault."

"Whose fault is it?" asks Dave.

Some people mumble, but don't speak up. I do. "It's everyone's. And no one's. And theirs, and ours . . . I mean, it sounds corny, but the most depressing part for me was feeling like that could be my . . ." I'm not going to say Pops, so I finish ". . . someone I know."

"So," says Jeff, "it's okay if it's someone you don't know?"

I'm not going to get into it with him; this is real. "No," I say. "I'm saying I realized that there's no one that I don't know." It's only when the words come out of my mouth that I understand them.

Mialonie says slowly, "I know what Reggie means. Remember when we talked about grace, and hospitality? It's like . . . I can't walk past the guy who sleeps in front of Dunkin' Donuts anymore without looking at him. I mean, I knew he was there, but now . . . I really look."

Silence, and then a snort from Gabriella. She hasn't been around in a while; I wonder if she's going to come back to the shelter. Or help me with the transcripts.

"Give me a break," says Gabriella. "You do one good deed — and I still don't get how good it even was — and now you've got eyes into people's souls? Come on."

"Well, I got something out of it," shoots back Mialonie. "And maybe you would have too, if you'd gone more than once."

"Why do we have to get something out of everything anyway?" asks Jeff. "Everything is not some lesson." He looks at Dave. "Or Jesus parabola."

"You mean parable, bonehead," says Ruthie.

"My partner, George, told me a lot of things about New York City that I didn't know," I say. "He's real cool, actually. I'm getting a lot out of this, so it would be cool to give back."

Jeff sneers. "You'll get your medal in Heaven, then. Congratulations."

I ignore him. "I'm just saying. There are kids there and everything. And some of the adults can teach us more than anything we learn at school. I mean, we're supposed to be listening; we should do something about what we hear." I rip a page out of my notebook. "We can ask people at the shelter what they need. Put a wish list together and then find community resources to fulfill it."

"That's a good idea," says Gabriella slowly. "I'll help." I look down because I don't want her to see my skepticism. "Seriously," she says. "I will. Just . . . I might need you to remind me that it really *is* helping, Reggie."

"Well, that place needs to be painted for one thing," says Jeff. "Guess Home Depot had a sale on Depression Gray when they painted the first time."

Ruthie smiles, but not at me. "We can be 'The Hope Depot'!"

Everybody groans, but I'm kind of liking this whole idea. I don't need Vicky to get involved at Olive Branch. The youth group is already there.

Dave looks at his watch, then shifts a little. "Guys, this is one of the better discussions we've had, but I need to be somewhere this afternoon, so let's get going."

"That's it?" I say. "Don't *you* have anything to say?"

Dave is already packing up his stuff and moving toward the door. "I have an announcement, but it's no big deal, another time. We'll talk later, I promise."

For once I don't feel like I can bank on Dave's promise, and it doesn't feel good.

NOVEMBER 2
2:O8 P.M.

"Why are you doing this?" George asks. This is my fourth time here, so I'm getting familiar with what George calls his "chill" days. I call them Grumpy Old Man Days, but not to his face. His eyes are closed, and we've been sitting in silence for fifteen minutes.

"Hey, I'm the interviewer," I say, trying to be jokey and bold at the same time. "I need to ask the questions here." When I was doing the transcripts, I realized that George and I talk more about me than anything else. I came up with some great new questions so it wouldn't be all about me, but he hasn't answered any of them yet.

"What, I'm not allowed to ask questions?" George opens his eyes. They're bloodshot.

"Um, no ... Of course you can ask ... I'm just, um, you know, trying to finish the interview."

"Uh-huh." He closes his eyes again.

Pretty soon I realize that I'd better answer him about why I'm doing this. "I don't know, I go to church every week with my parents," I say. "And this is a youth group thing."

"What kind of answer is that?" asks George. "I asked why

you're doing this, and you tell me about church and projects and your parents." He sits up and leans forward. "Why. Are. You. Doing. This?" George enunciates every word in a way that Mr. Stanzione, who runs the debate team, would go crazy for. "Stop playing around. You know exactly what I mean."

The problem is that *I* don't know exactly what I mean. I take a deep breath.

"I like youth group, okay? I told you, this is . . . real, and, um, you're interesting, and you're teaching me a lot." I take out a bag of chips and open it. I start to tip the bag to my mouth, but I stop and offer it to George first. "I hope people buy the book with all the interviews so we can raise some money for the shelter. And I was telling the youth group that maybe we could help out here more. Satisfied?" I look at George, who takes the bag and tips it to *his* mouth.

"Church is all right sometimes," he says. "I used to win the Sunday school prize every week for memorizing verses, and not just that old 'Jesus wept' trick. I was good at that. But we didn't have no youth group or nothing after that. When you got too old for Sunday school you had to sit through all that preaching, and I couldn't get down with that for too long."

"Dave lets us have real discussions and we try to figure things out. How to talk the talk and walk the walk."

"You got the Christianese down," George says, making me feel silly. I wonder when he's going to give up the chips. "I thought the whole point was that we can't figure Him out because He's God and we're not. So, smart boy, what you got figured out?"

"Mostly that I can't figure God out," I say, and he laughs.

"When I was little, I thought God was like a superhero," I say, keeping my eyes down. He doesn't respond, so I look up. "I wanted to be a superhero too. Not like I wanted to be God, I mean. Just . . . you know. I wanted to have some kind of power that zapped everything perfect."

George takes another swig from the chip bag. I can tell it's already down to crumbs.

"How's Night Man? You haven't mentioned it for a minute."

"Pretty dead," I answer.

"Don't give up on the superhero thing," says George after a while. "It'll make you feel strong."

We both look over at Dave, who's talking to Wilma and using his hands a lot.

"I wish I was as sure as that guy is," George says, finishing the crumbs and crumpling the bag. "Your boy Dave looks like he could have been one of the twelve apostles. I'm the guy on the outside looking in." He looks at the crumpled bag in his hand. "Just looking in." He's quiet a moment. "Jesus was cool, but sometimes I think He could help a brother out a little more, you know?"

My thoughts exactly.

He stretches. "I keep some Scripture with me all of the time anyway. When it gets down to it, I like having something to hold on to. It kind of goes with your comic book." He takes a tiny folded piece of paper out of his cracked leather wallet and passes it to me. "Read it."

I start reading, and he taps my hand. "Out loud, smart boy."

I look around to see if anyone's watching, then I clear my throat and start.

". . . in all these things we are more than conquerors through Him who loved us. For I am convinced that neither death nor life, neither angels nor demons, neither the present nor the future, nor any powers, neither height nor depth, nor anything else in all creation, will be able to separate us from the love of God that is in Christ Jesus our Lord."

"What do you think?" he asks when I stop.

"It's . . . it sounds powerful," I say.

"Yeah," he says, taking back the paper and folding it very carefully. "It was one of my memory verses when I was a kid. Makes me feel strong when I read it now." He slips it back into his wallet. "Sometimes I don't have the strength to read it, though. I just can't pull the little piece of paper out of my pocket." He sighs.

I try to lighten things up. "You just reminded me of one of Dave's favorite sayings: 'If you want to walk on water, you've got to get out of the boat!'"

"Or get pushed out," says George. He doesn't laugh. I'm hungry. "Man, I wish I could have voted in the elections today. Gotta get some batteries so I can listen to the returns later. Speaking of that, how's *your* election going?"

The pause goes on long enough for me to know that I have to answer. "Not great. I'm just not sure there's anything I can do to get Vicky to take the issues seriously, and not just herself. It's not even about issues anymore. It's about people, and she doesn't get that."

"You know who Rosa Parks was, right?" asks George. I resist the urge to roll my eyes and just nod. "Of course you do," he says.

"But you probably heard the old tired lady story. 'She'd been working so hard, she was just too tired to stand up.' Nuh-uh, don't get it twisted. Rosa was an activist. She was part of the Civil Rights Movement long before she got on that bus. She knowingly took that risk, to say, 'No, I'm not getting up.' Everything that she'd been through, that she was, she used it that day. And after."

George was leaning forward while he spoke, but now he slumps down in the chair, and I see the scars running up and down his dangling arms.

"That superhero thing is right there, Reggie," he almost whispers. "Just do your thing, and be cool."

I don't know if he's talking about Night Man, or God, or the election, or what. I wish I had more than chips for George. Because right now he looks like he has nightmares just behind his eyes.

I wait awhile, but he seems like he's done, so I say good-bye, and head to the steel doors.

NOVEMBER 4
3:30 P.M.

As Joe C. and I leave the school building, the posters announcing Holiday Jam committee meetings remind me how much I looked forward to winter break when the school year started. It was a relief to tell George that *Night Man* isn't working, but I don't know how Joe C. will react.

We pass the Crazy Sock Man, who's in the middle of the street, wearing shorts and screaming about White people and black cats.

"That guy should be in a home or something," says Joe C. "He's dangerous."

"He's not hurting anyone," I say quickly.

"Just my feelings," he says. We both try, and fail, to laugh.

"I'm surprised you're coming with me," he adds as we walk to the 2 train. He wants to do a little browsing for *Night Man* inspiration at Bergen Street Comics before we go to his house to study. "We don't really talk about *Night Man* anymore."

"Lots going on," I say. A kid runs by who reminds me of Charlie. I haven't seen him at school in a while; even though I have no idea what to say to him, I keep looking for him in the halls.

"You and Vicky don't have meetings or anything?" Joe C. asks. "Not that I think you should."

"I know," I say. "At lunch I told her that maybe we should propose a canned food drive for the shelter, something totally easy, and all she wanted to talk about was her proposal for a merit-based lunch voucher system."

"What's that about?" Joe C. asks.

"She wants people who get the best grades to get discounts in the cafeteria. She thinks that the more we support the top students, the more everyone will benefit. Ruthie called it a twisted Talented Tenth trickle-down theory."

"Whatever that means," Joe C. answers. "And they should be paying *us* to eat that food."

"I've gotten some interesting e-mails from people about cafeteria food. Vegetarian options, kosher options . . . 'not-nasty options' . . ."

"My mom wants the school to go totally organic." Joe C.'s mom is a lawyer.

"I'd like to avoid people making any connections between me and nasty food with a high you-know-what factor anyway." I try to laugh but it comes out like I'm choking.

"Yeah, I guess you would," Joe C. says. "Look, it's not the best nickname, but it could be worse. What if you were Acid Face Johnson?"

Good point. Everyone used to call this girl "Pizza Face," but after Ruthie did a current events on women in some country getting acid thrown in their faces, it became "Acid Face." Last week, Hector asked Acid Face if he could use her as a model for his presentation on the moon's surface.

Joe C. looks at me. "You can tell me. You do realize that you made a mistake, right? With Vicky?"

"I don't know what to do," I say, taking out my campaign notepad to look over some of the suggestions that I've heard. "There are kids who are actually coming to talk to me about the election, and there's a lot we can do. I just wish I didn't feel like I was the one running against my own candidate . . . and Donovan. I mean, Justin."

"Yeah," says Joe C. "Sucks to be you."

Is he being sarcastic? I let it go.

"You do have a lot going on," he continues. "The homeless thing, Vicky . . . When are you going to have time for Night Man? The things you really want to do?"

I take this as a rhetorical question; at least, I take it as one I don't want to answer right now. A police car weaves through the traffic, siren screaming. Miss Yvette, who's lived on my block "since before these yuppies were old enough to spell 'gentrification,'" she always says, calls out a hello as she drops soda cans into a shopping cart. (Those nickels she gets from recycling send her to Atlantic City every weekend.) A couple of old guys playing chess in the park challenge us to a game.

There's a couple slobbing each other down in front of a nail salon. They're almost horizontal and I'm expecting a baby to pop out of the girl any minute. What if that were Mialonie and me, and . . .

I look away from them, fast. "I heard Justin did it in fifth grade."

"Did what?"

I just look at Joe C. until he gets it.

"No way."

"Yeah," I say, stuffing my hands in my pockets. "That's what I heard."

"You believe that?" asks Joe C.

"All the girls at school are in love with him."

"I guess . . ."

I look at Joe C. "What about you?"

"What about me?"

"Have you, you know . . ."

"Oh. Well, no. Anyway, you would know."

"I thought maybe with that girl from computer camp . . ."

"What, are you crazy? Anyway, she wasn't that cute. And Maria, remember?"

"So, you would have?" I say it real low, even though no one is close to us.

"I don't know. . . . What about you?"

"I guess . . . I don't know. Yeah, probably. It depends." I'm almost whispering now.

"My mom tries to talk to me about that stuff. It's so embarrassing."

"Yeah, Pops gave me a book," I say.

"Any pictures?"

"Naw, it's one of those Christian books. . . . You know, 'Save it for marriage.' "

"Oh." We're both quiet for a while. Then he laughs. "Maybe your parents will set it up so you and Ruthie can lose your virginity to each other. They'll have to fight off Vicky first, though."

I chase him for two blocks before he apologizes, and I still make him pay for the fries we pick up at the Chinese takeout place.

When we get to the subway station, we just make it onto the train, and I know right away that it's the wrong one. A bunch of older guys are laughing and playing around; with all of the labels on their jackets and shoes, they don't even need real names. It's quiet, and I can feel them staring, and it's one of those times when Joe C. seems Whiter than ever. Joe C. squeezes onto the bench next to a guy who's opened his legs even more to make the space smaller. I stand in front of him, grab the rail, and pretend to read the vocational school ads posted over the windows.

Joe C. pulls out a Gargantua comic book.

"I found it," he says, way too loud. "Remember we were looking for the one where Gargantua and Velvet Steel work together?"

I glance down and away real fast, hoping he gets that I don't want to look at the book right now. It's a long time until the next stop, and low profile is the way to go.

He opens up the book to a pullout spread. "Look at these lines. I think I can do something just as good as this," he says. One of the guys across from us lets out a snort. I shake my head a little. Joe C. goes on, and it's like he's shouting. "We should write them a letter too. Because if Gargantua and Velvet Steel work together in this issue, then what happened in Number 613 is impossible."

The snorty guy says something I can't hear, and some of the others start laughing. Joe C. looks right at them (*nooo!*) and shrugs, then turns back to me. "Here." He waves the book at me. I don't do anything right away.

"Your friend is trying to give you something," says Snorty. "Why are you being rude?" His friends laugh some more.

I know what they're thinking. My clothes and my hair are a little too corny. My friend is a little too White.

Joe C. looks at me, and at them, and then at the floor. "Anyway," he mumbles after a long minute, "it's just stupid."

Snorty looks at Joe C. "I used to read those books. Do they still have the Space Brawler?"

"Yeah," says Joe C. "Only he lost his powers and he's on this pilgrimage to find out why." Snorty reaches for the book; Joe C. hands it over. He flips through it for a minute.

"So you draw and stuff? You want to make your own comic books?" he asks Joe C. It's like I'm not there.

"I'm okay," says Joe C. He nods toward me. "We've been working on some stuff." I try to catch Snorty's eye, but he's not having it. He just focuses on Joe C.

Joe C. pulls out his art journal and shows it to Snorty, who's impressed.

"You're pretty good," he says, showing his friends. "Keep it up. My uncle is an illustrator; he's done a lot of picture books. It's good work."

We pull into our stop. Joe C. gathers his things; Snorty and a couple of the other guys give him a pound. I feel like I have too many limbs and trip as I head to the door. As I head out, I hear one of the guys mutter "stupid Whiteboy" under his breath. I'm so glad Joe C. didn't hear that, but when I look up I realize that the guy is looking me full in the face.

NOVEMBER 5
8:42 A.M.

I've got organic gummy bears in my pocket, and I'm waiting for Ruthie to get to homeroom so that I can grovel. She walks in, sits at her desk, and opens a book without looking my way. She's still all frosty because of that run-in with Donovan in the cafeteria the other day, and I admit it: I miss her. I haven't gotten one IM or e-mail from her in days.

"I'm sorry," I say, in my most pitiful voice. "Are we friends?" I add a pout; I'm laying it on thick like chocolate frosting.

She looks up from *Their Eyes Were Watching God*. "What's wrong with your face?" she asks, not smiling.

"This is me being sorry," I say. I poke my lip out more, and raise my eyebrows. "Really, really sorry."

"For what?" She goes back to her book.

"You're not going to make this easy, are you?" I say. I can't tell her that I can't even stand up for myself with Donovan, much less anyone else.

"You're not going to make this right, are you?" she shoots back.

"Make what right?" I ask. I'm not sure what we're talking

about anymore. We're interrupted by Hector, who strolls over and leans on Ruthie's desk.

"Excuse you," she says. I smirk, and Hector reaches over and snatches my pen out of my hand. He turns back to Ruthie.

"So, um," he starts, "I . . . w-w-what I'm thinking is . . ."

When did he start stuttering? Dare I hope it's permanent?

Hector takes a deep breath. "I want to find out more about . . . the Fort Benning thing you were talking about last week, and, uh, the garment industry too." He sits up a little straighter. "I want to help."

My mouth drops open, and so does Ruthie's. Then she gives Hector the smile I thought she reserved for her Malcolm X poster. "Well, I . . . that's great! What do you want to know?"

Hector smiles back. "Everything, I guess. I want to be a part of the solution, you know?"

I can barely stifle my groan. I wait for Ruthie to remind him that he is firmly implanted on the problem end of that equation.

"Let's talk, then," says my temporarily insane friend. "Do you want to meet after school? My piano lesson was cancelled."

"You play the piano? That's cool," says Hector as Ms. A marches into the room. "Yeah, after school is good. I'll meet you at your locker."

Hector slides into his seat behind me, throwing in a punch to my back. Ruthie, the traitor, doesn't even say anything.

Ms. A drops some stuff on her desk and starts writing on the board.

"Hey," I whisper to Ruthie. "As I was saying before we were so rudely interrupted, will you accept my apology if I treat you to a slice after school?"

Ruthie shrugs and whispers back, "Don't worry about it, it's all good. Maybe another day on the pizza." She looks at me and smiles. "Seems like I'm booked today."

NOVEMBER 6
5:32 P.M.

"Monica, it's been a while since we've done any drills," says Pops, scooping up a mound of mashed potatoes as big as a snowball. After daily pop quizzes, state test prep, and three early mornings of begging people to take "Vote Vicky!" postcards, I'm grateful for the weekend, even if it means sharing space with my gremlin of a sister. Mom had soca playing in the kitchen all day while she was cooking, and I even saw her and Pops dancing for a minute. I take a bite of her oxtail and stew peas. We had an early snowfall yesterday, but this food tastes like it's summer and I'm a little kid again, and I don't know yet that there is evil in the world.

Then Evil speaks. "Mom, the chicken is too spicy." Monica has been talking in this weird whiny voice lately. "It's going to wreak havoc on my pores."

"'Wreak havoc'? Did Dick and Jane teach you some new vocabulary words today?" I snicker, and Mom gives me a light backhand to the head.

Monica puts more callaloo on her plate, watching me the whole time. I look away first. I've been pushing it lately. Last week, I threatened to tell Mom about the night she went clubbing when she was supposed to be studying with her friend Asha. I asked her how many baby seals she got; I thought that was a good one, but she didn't get it.

"Don't eat it, then," says Mom, real calm because she knows that it is impossible to keep from eating her fried chicken. She says she took this Saturday off to get some rest, but I think it was for Pops. He's smiled more today than he has in two months, and I can tell she's been working hard to keep him up.

Monica grunts and sucks the meat off of a bone.

"Am I invisible?" Pops asks. "Inaudible? I thought that I just asked Miss Monica a question." He takes more mashed potatoes, and they fall off of his spoon as he points to Monica.

"It didn't sound like a question," she says in a phony "who, me?" voice.

Mom slides her eyes over Monica's way, and her *Don't push it* is almost audible.

Monica smiles. "Just playing, Pops. . . . Actually, I've been wanting to talk to you about that. About basketball, I mean."

"Good," says Pops. "I know you think you've got game, but it takes hard work and perseverance to separate you from the pack. Let me tell you, when St. Joseph's needed someone to step up and be a leader on the football team, they didn't have to look far. . . ."

I sneak a look at Monica, who's already looking at me. We share an eye roll, then look away before it gets too friendly.

Pops stops talking and clears his throat. "Anyway, that was all a long time ago." He coughs a little. "So what did you want to say, Monica?" he asks.

"Oh, yeah . . . um, well, I don't want to play ball anymore. I'm not going to try out for the varsity team next year. I've changed my mind."

Three heads snap up so fast they almost come off. Monica drew a face on her first basketball and would push it around in a toy stroller. I've seen the pictures; Pops keeps them in his wallet. And March Madness? It's straitjacket time around here; she tapes every game so she can replay each one in slow motion, and she and Pops scream at the screen. This must be a joke. I wait for the punch line.

"I'm trying out for cheerleading," says Monica.

Now, *that's* a punch line!

"Be serious, Monica," says Mom, standing up and collecting plates.

"I *am* serious," Monica says.

Mom sits back down. "Monica, what is going on with you? I have been letting you go around with those silly girls, wearing too much makeup and acting the fool. And don't think I don't know about that trashy *Cosmopolitan* magazine in your room. But this is ridiculous."

"I can't believe you were snooping around in my room! That's such an invasion of privacy!" yells Monica. I make a mental note to check my room for contraband. "What does *Cosmo* have to do with anything anyway? Why are you even bringing that up? Anyway, cheerleaders are athletes. They work hard —"

"— boosting the egos of boys with below-average grades," cuts in Mom.

"You guys don't understand anything. That's not what it's about now. Cheerleading is a competitive sport."

"Monica . . . you used to be a serious child, you had an interest in science, and we've always encouraged your athletics," says Pops, who's been sitting there looking like he got sucker punched.

"Look at your brother: He's involved in school politics. That's respectable." He looks at me and nods. "And he's involved with that homeless shelter."

"Uh . . . yeah, but you know, it's just a little youth group thing." Pretty nice to have Pops's approval heading over my way, but it makes Monica glare like she is going to stomp me to death.

"That's good, Reggie. Just be careful," says Mom. "You," she turns to Monica. "Cheerleading. Why would you want to spend your time doing something so mindless?"

"I can't explain it because you wouldn't understand."

"I don't have time for this," Mom says, standing up. She starts dumping the food into plastic containers; I wouldn't have minded a little more. Monica picks her plate up, drops it hard into the sink, and then stomps upstairs. Mom starts to say something, then just mutters under her breath. Pops is still sitting there, looking dazed.

Why did Monica have to go and ruin things? My summer day's gone, and the chill in the air makes me want to go to my room and crawl under the covers.

"May I be excused?" I ask, and leave before I get an answer.

What burly ball-playing beast is an aspiring booty-shaking pom-pom waver? That's a quiz I would have failed for sure. Cheerleading?!?! My lumberjack gladiator of a sister? There's got to be another angle. I lie in bed and wonder if the cheerleaders at Future Leaders are actually a gang of master criminals who plan and execute ATM robberies. Monica as thug I can believe. But Monica all short skirts and sexy smiles? Not even close. I used to wonder what Mom and Pops would say if I told them about Night Man, but I'm guessing it would look like I've been writing a textbook compared to Monica's latest news.

I can hear Mom and Pops murmuring in their bedroom. I've got to give it to my sister. No one will ever ignore Monica. They may shudder, run screaming, or even wonder how the God who created Mialonie could also create something so monstrous . . . but she makes an impression.

NOVEMBER 8
3:47 P.M.

Back at Olive Branch, I'm determined to get some interviewing done. George is all "less me, more you" every time I come here, but I'm supposed to be leading this project, and it's not a good look if I'm not doing the assignment properly. I push the heavy doors open and almost take out Charlie's mom.

"Sorry!" I say, as she jumps back.

"No problem," she says, and smiles.

I've been trying to cut back on the awkward silences lately, so I clear my throat. "Um, we're doing a wish list for the shelter," I start. "I posted it over there. You can write down anything that you think Olive Branch needs and we're going to see what we can do."

"That's nice," she says. "Reggie, I want to thank you. Charlie was afraid that you'd laugh at him because he lived here."

"Laugh?" I say. "But it's not funny at all." *Oops.* "I don't mean . . . I just . . ." I trail off.

"Don't worry about it," she says, sighing. "It's not funny. But we're getting out of here soon. I'm on a list for a place in the Bronx."

"Oh. That's good."

"I just wanted to let you know how much you've helped him. He talks about you all the time. You're like a superhero to him. He says he wants to be a writer. All he used to ever say was that he wanted to be someone else." She hugs me and walks away quickly before I can say anything back.

I walk over to George, my notebook and pen already out, and wait for him to notice me. He's kneeling down on the floor, surrounded by kids and cardboard boxes, paper, glue, and a bunch of stuff that looks like it could either be art supplies or garbage. Charlie brings over a box full of empty milk cartons and dumps them out. He came over to my house a couple of days ago with a whole bag of train stuff and we set it up in my room. I even cleaned up a little. He left all of it there "so it would be nice and safe."

"Uh," I move closer to George, and try to sound serious. "So, I guess we should get started with the interviewing. . . ."

George glances up at me. "Can't you see I'm busy?" A couple of the kids look at me and raise their eyebrows. Charlie moves a little closer to me, like he's got my back.

I clear my throat. "Um, yeah. Sorry. I guess it won't take too long, I just wanted to follow up on some of the things we talked about. . . . And we have a deadline. . . ." I trail off, because he stands up.

"Check this guy out," he says to the kids. A couple of them giggle. Charlie doesn't. "He's got a deadline for his project. Guess he doesn't see that we've got a project of our own going here, huh?"

"We're building a CITY!" says Charlie. "A whole city!"

"I'm in charge of commerce, that means business," says a girl. "You're standing on the place where the big train station is going to be." I move a little to the left. She shakes her head. "Now you're at the bus station!" She and more kids start laughing, and not for the first time am I glad you can't see the blush through the Black.

"Come over here," says George, motioning me away from the group. I follow him, doing a few exaggerated steps to show that I don't want to King Kong the city anymore. This time when the kids laugh, it's okay.

"Don't you go to some big-time school?" asks George.

"Uh, yeah," I say. "What does Clarke have to do with —"

"I don't know what they're teaching you there," George says, "but you need to learn a few things." I look around the room at the other kids from youth group sitting with their interviewees and recorders. I don't see Dave. When I look back at George, he's all slitty-eyed again, so I just nod.

His voice softens. "I'm not trying to be down on you or anything. But I'm doing something here with these kids that's important too. And needs to be done right now."

Playing? I think. I try not to let *Whatever* show on my face. I guess it doesn't work, because George continues.

"It may look like just playing, but these young cats are engaged, man, they're dreaming and being productive." He points over to the group, all gluing and cutting and working. "A kid got stabbed last night," he says out of nowhere.

"What!?!"

"By another kid." His voice is dead. "Neither one of them more than eight years old."

"Don't they have rules or something? What about the metal detectors?" George just looks at me. I shift a little. "Is the kid okay?"

"We don't know yet. But what are you talking about, 'okay'? None of these kids is okay. That's what I'm trying to do here, make it a little more okay." He pats my shoulder. "Do you get it now?"

I don't know if I do, or if I know what I'm even supposed to get, but I nod again. George gives me a friendly but hard punch on the shoulder.

"All right, Reg-dog, let's get to work."

"Uh, okay," I say, not sure what to do. He looks at me, then at the interview equipment in my hand. "Oh — um. Let me put this stuff down. I'll be right over." I put everything into my backpack and stick it behind Wilma's desk, then I hustle back to the group.

"Mr. George," Charlie says, "can Reggie help me make a really tall tower?"

George hugs him. "Of course, little man." He nods me over to Charlie and the two of us get to work. George starts grabbing stuff, and he's smiling, and the kids are watching him and working hard. Something about the whole scene is like Santa's workshop or something; I can look at this little group and almost forget the gray walls, the industrial-strength smell, and the old woman talking to herself in the corner.

After we finish our tower, Charlie and I sit down next to the commerce girl, who's bossing a bunch of other kids around. "How can we help?" I ask.

She doesn't miss a beat, handing me a couple of shoeboxes.

"Start cutting a door and some windows. That can be McDonald's."

George's head snaps up. "I know I didn't hear nothing about no McDonald's in this town. What did we talk about?"

"Happy, healthy people in a happy, healthy town," a couple of the younger kids yell. Commerce Girl is light enough for her blush to show.

"Oh, yeah," she says. "Well, it can be a fruit and vegetable market then."

"You got it," I say. And I get to work.

NOVEMBER 10
2:48 P.M.

I asked Ruthie if she wanted to walk home together today, and she acted like I should have made an appointment or something. So I wait quietly at her locker while she talks to Cristina Rodriguez, who keeps giving me dirty looks.

"We should get our Little Buddies together for a playdate," says Ruthie when we finally head outside. "They'd be so cute."

"You're such a girl," I say.

"Oh, I forgot to tell you — Ida's home, and she says hi." Ruthie's big sister Ida is a freshman at Cornell and she is beautiful. So beautiful that to call her hot would be an insult. So gorgeous that you forget she has a name like Ida. The crazy thing is that she used to look just like Ruthie.

We walk down Lafayette Avenue without talking for a while. I am not going to ask about her "date" with Hector. We pass Gruenwald's Market, and I laugh. "Remember when we read the diary of Anne Frank in third grade and you stormed into Gruenwald's to demand accountability for the Holocaust?"

Ruthie grimaces. "Don't remind me. I still buy stuff there just because I feel guilty."

We're passing the playground, and kids are screaming and

running around like they just got released from Rikers instead of school.

"Hey," I say. "Thanks for encouraging me to do the Buddy thing. That was . . . deep when I found out Charlie lived at Olive Branch."

Ruthie nods. "He's a nice kid. Reminds me of a little you."

"His mom came up to me to thank me, and I don't even know what for," I say. "It's not like I'm doing much of anything."

"I don't know," she says. "There's something going on at the shelter. Like there was already a spark, but it's gotten bigger. My Listening Ears partner told me that the youth group is bringing a new energy to the place. And I mean, maybe you don't see it, but Charlie lights up like a Christmas tree every time he sees you."

"I wish we could do more stuff together," I say. "But homework is killing me. How are we supposed to give them wisdom if we don't have time to absorb it ourselves?"

"I took my Buddy Jamila to rallies at the UN and the Botanic Gardens," says Ruthie, all sunny and smug. "Tomorrow we're going to the Carousel in Central Park."

"You don't need me to tell you to shut up, do you?" I ask. As she opens her mouth, I cover it. "Rhetorical, Ruthie. Rhetorical."

"Don't hate, congratulate," she says, all proud like she's saying something cool, and not something that was in when Pops was in "primary school." Then she gasps. "Oh my God, look!"

It must be something big to make St. Ruthie forget to say "gosh." I see my Little Buddy Charlie curled up on the sidewalk next to the playground gate. Donovan's standing over him and a bunch of other kids are there, laughing. For once, I don't think; I just run over and pull Charlie up. "What the — what's going on? Are you okay? What happened?"

Charlie's doing the usual — gasping, snot, hiccups. I scan the group for clues about what happened. Hector wanders over and shouts "Fight!"

A little boy raises his hand. "Um, he was talking about his shoes."

I'm guessing the first "he" was Donovan. I look at Charlie's feet and he's wearing . . . Dora the Explorer sneakers.

Oh.

Charlie looks the way I feel after a Donovan encounter. And he's a little kid! He's five years old and already he's broken.

I turn to Donovan. "Why don't you pick on a personage of your own size? Oh wait — I guess you're doing that."

Score! That gets a big laugh from the crowd, which has gotten bigger since Hector yelled "fight." Surprise knocks most of the mean from Donovan's face. *Yeah*, I think. *I'm saying something today. And yeah, I got help from a book my mom gave me, but you don't know that.*

I continue: "You mad that he's got your girlfriend's picture on his shoes?" That one's a little weaker, but the crowd's with me so they laugh anyway. Donovan snorts.

"Whatever, Pukey. Of course you're gonna defend *her* — oh, I mean him. He's like your Mini-Me; it must be like looking in a mirror."

"At least I don't crack mirrors," I say. Getting weaker; I need to end this.

"Why are you hiding out with the babies anyway, Pukey?" Donovan sneers. "I never see you handling your election business.

Scared of the spotlight, maybe? Afraid you're gonna have to get up on that stage again?" He turns to the crowd. "Puke alert avoided! Don't worry about bringing your protective gear to the election assembly!" He smirks. "You are the most ghost campaign manager ever. You don't have her back at all."

He's got me there. Charlie's stopped crying; he's actually standing next to me with his fists balled up like he's about to do something. In my head, I hear George say, *Don't give up on the superhero thing, smart boy.*

I turn back to Donovan. "You should talk. You're trying to be big and bad with a kindergartener. And you wouldn't even exist without Justin. You feed off him, parasite. It's like you need him to be a human being, and you're a pretty commiserable excuse for that. By the way, where's your boy now? Maybe he's having second thoughts about you."

More than a few *oooh*s and I hear one "Is 'commiserable' a word?"

"Whatever," he says, and that's when I know I've won. He turns away first, and walks off alone.

"You okay?" I ask Charlie. He nods. I pick up his backpack, which I realize is brand-new and just like mine. "Come on," I whisper. "Don't look anybody in the eye." We walk away from the crowd. I know Ruthie will understand that I'm not dissing her by leaving. "Don't look back," I mutter. "I'll walk you home."

He's staring at me like I'm Night Man. And I look at him, at those ridiculous shoes, and just like Night Man, I know what I have to do.

"So . . . I couldn't find my size," I say, since my oblivious friends haven't glanced at my feet.

"What?" says Ruthie, pulling out her iPod earplugs. "I'm trying to catch up on my BBC News broadcasts before school starts."

"Listening to no-longer-current events," Joe C. says. "Always productive."

I sigh and point to my shoes. They look. And say nothing. I'm feeling a little less confident than I did at home this morning. It helped that Monica was already gone when I left the house.

"Uh . . . did you puke your brains out again or something?" says Joe C. finally.

"Ha ha," I say, but the second "ha" catches in my throat a little. Maybe turquoise high-tops with orange stripes are a little over the top. It was the cheapest color, but they seem like they're glowing now, especially with the picture of Dora the Explorer on the toe.

Ruthie gets it and grins. She wraps herself around me, laughing. "You are the best. I should have thought of that." She looks at my sneakers again. "How did you find those?"

"I made them," I say, realizing that it's been a while since she's hugged me. "I took Charlie to Cold Stone Creamery after school. Those sneakers he had came out of a donation van the other day. And he was going on and on about how much he loved Dora and Boots and should he like somebody else instead, and he cried some more. I felt so bad."

"So you decided to reveal your crush on Dora too?" Joe C. shakes his head. "I knew Mialonie had competition, I just thought it was three-dimensional."

"Donovan was looking for another way to get to me, so he started on Charlie."

"I don't know if it was about you," shoots back Joe C. "The boy was wearing Dora shoes. And now you are too."

"I want to know how you made them," says Ruthie.

"Stickers, mostly. And stencils . . . they have a bunch of stuff at Target." I shrug and try to look casual. I don't think it works because they both start giggling. I look down at my sneakers and laugh too. They are almost completely covered with images of Dora and that stupid monkey friend of hers. Charlie went on and on about the monkey yesterday.

"I know I look ridiculous," I say. "But I don't care." At Joe C.'s skeptical look, I nod. "Okay, I care. But I care more about that look I saw on Charlie's face. I'm tired of Donovan's persecution party. I'm tired of the way every little thing we do has to get picked apart and judged and categorized. I mean, he's only a little kid. Does it have to start that early?"

Ruthie nods. "Standing up for the downtrodden. I'm so proud of you, I'll forgive you for shopping at a chain store that doesn't respect the basic human rights of its labor force."

The first bell rings and Charlie comes running up. "Reggie! Reggie, look! I told my mom what happened and look what she got me!"

He's wearing Spider-Man sneakers.

11:46 A.M.

Charlie wants to go home to the Olive Branch and switch back to the Dora sneakers, but I tell him it's okay. Donovan's not at school, and that helps. Ruthie says that the story got around and people are on my side. Maybe. I get a lot of looks, but I can't read them. After a while, I just look back. As the morning goes on, I walk through the halls without hoping for invisibility and I toss Hector a bunch of pens before he even asks.

By lunch, I sit down to eat my tuna salad sandwich without worrying about who's watching. Just as I pull my Night Man notebook out so I can fake it in case Joe C. asks if I've done anything new, Vicky slams her stuff down next to me.

"Are you kidding me?" she says. "Really? Please tell me this is some misguided joke."

I don't pretend I don't know what she's talking about; I wish I could pretend I don't know who she is. "Some stuff went down yesterday with my Little Buddy Charlie and Donovan at the playground," I begin. "And —"

"Yeah, yeah, I heard," she says. "Donovan punked you again and your Little Buddy's a girl. Whatever. You have a campaign to represent."

"Vicky, you are such a —" I start, as Sparrow runs up and almost sticks her microphone in my mouth. Vijay follows, but for once his camera isn't on.

"Pukey — the public needs to know — what's with the shoes?" she asks, all breathless like she's reporting on a hurricane or something.

"My name is Reggie," I say. "Is this a slow news-day or something?"

"Get some close-ups of his feet," she orders Vijay, before turning back to me. He ignores her. "Where exactly does an eighth-grade boy get those shoes? And is there some sort of significance to your apparent Dora the Explorer obsession?" Without waiting for an answer, she turns to Vicky. "Vicky! Is there a particular message that you're trying to send with your campaign manager's shoes?"

"This has nothing," Vicky starts, "absolutely *nothing* to do with my campaign." She throws me a glare and leaves. Sparrow runs after her. She doesn't notice that Vijay isn't following. He gives me a nod and walks away.

My friends haven't arrived yet, and my tuna salad sandwich has raisins, celery, red onions, and carrots, so I dig in.

"That looks good," says a female voice behind me.

I gulp, and some of my tuna salad falls onto the table. I turn. It's Mialonie. I can't help it; I move my feet a little more under the table in case she hasn't given me a pass.

"Um, yeah, it is. My mom made it." Why do I have to go and mention my mom? It's like I am determined to kill any suave potential with extreme geekery. "Do you want some?" I hold up a triangle. More tuna salad falls on the table.

"No thanks," she says. *And sits down next to me.* "I've been meaning to tell you, I liked what you said that day. About civic responsibility." She checks the table before she puts her stack of books down.

I look in the general direction of her face. "Oh, uh . . . really?" I smile a little, and aim closer to her eyes. "I didn't say much."

Mialonie smiles back. "But I can tell . . . there's more."

There's a long pause. Can she hear me swallowing? I notice that the top book in her stack is called *Be Extra: How To Be Yourself Plus (For Tweens and Teens)!* What more does she think she needs?

I point to the book. "Plus what?" I ask.

"Plus everything," she answers, and she must have swallowed the sun at some point today because she is dazzling like you wouldn't believe. "It's about going beyond, not being satisfied with your own status quo."

"Oh." I nod like I know what she's talking about.

"We should talk. It would be so good for you."

You would be so good for me.

"You've changed so much since . . . school started," she says. "This book tells you how to talk, dress, even eat in a more productive way so that you can maximize your potential." She pauses and smiles. "And you do have potential."

Just having this conversation makes me feel like I'm getting to wear the superhero cape for a while. I smile back even though I can't think of anything to say.

"What's *that*?" She points to my Night Man notebook.

Oh. So much for being more powerful than a locomotive. I've got my own social kryptonite on display.

"Nothing," I say, turning the notebook over. "Just some ideas . . . fooling around."

"'Night Man' — is that a superhero? Is he classic, like Lobo or Luke Cage? Or more Black Thunder or Agent 355?"

I forget to think and look her full in the face. "How do you —" I stop, because I realize how stupid my question is going to sound. But still . . . Mialonie is into comics?

"Are you Marvel or DC?" she says, shrugging. "I'm DC all the way. I guess I'm just old-school like that."

"Um. I like both," I say. "I mean, DC can be kind of corny, but they had John Stewart. Marvel had Lucas Bishop, so . . ."

She raises one eyebrow in a way that I didn't think could happen in real life. "Oh, are you too cool to pledge allegiance to one or the other?"

I shrug, because we both know *that's* not the case. I'm tired of feeling off balance, so I say, "And of course, there was Spawn." *This is a game I can play.*

"Yeah, McFarlane's good," she says, casually dropping the name of the Image Comics creator. "He makes you think." She points to my Night Man notebook. "So tell me about Night Man." Her nails are sparkly.

"I made him up when I was just a kid," I say, trying to emphasize what a long time ago that was. "He's, uh, homeless, and that's all people see, this street bum . . . but he's holding it down in this whole underground city. But like I said, I was just a kid when I started this. Now that we've been going to the shelter — it's different."

"Yeah, I can imagine. . . . Can I read it sometime?" she asks. "Maybe we can collaborate."

"You for real?" My voice goes up at the end of the question, but still, it's not quite a squeak.

She gets up. "That's all I ever am," she says. She sits a few seats away and starts whispering to Josie. They both smile, and so do I. Even if I haven't worked on *Night Man* in a long time, he's working for me in surprising ways.

3:15 P.M.

I think these shoes give me power. For the rest of the day, I'm floating. In chemistry, I don't hear Mrs. Rostawanik call on me three times to recite my epic poem based on the periodic table (progressive, integrated curriculum = weird assignments). No "Pukeys" all day. After last period, Charlie brings a couple of little kids over to my locker to meet me, and he makes the words "Big Buddy" sound like "President of the Universe." I feel too good to go home; Joe C. is going beatboxing or something with Gunnar, and Ruthie is going to the Brooklyn Museum with Cristina Rodriguez, so I decide to swing by Olive Branch unannounced. Wilma says that we're always welcome. I can finish interviewing George, and today I've got my own story to tell.

When I get there, I notice that the cardboard box town is growing, and Commerce Girl giggles when I ask if she's the mayor. I catch George's eye and we head over to our corner.

I figure my sweaty foot funk will go unnoticed here, so I take off one of the Dora shoes and hand it to George.

"Check it out," I say to him. "Would you believe that Dora the Explorer took down my nemesis?"

George holds my shoe, turning it over and staring like he's memorizing it.

"Nice work," he says. "Didn't realize you were that much of a fan. I know a guy who can set you up with the whole series on DVD for five dollars, if you want. Including unreleased episodes."

"No thanks," I say quickly. I point to Charlie, who's playing tag with a group of girls. "I just did it for him. This guy I know was making fun of him at school, just ripping him apart because he had on Dora shoes. It made me sick."

George hands back my shoe. "Put your shoe on, boy. You realize how funky your feet are?"

"So for once I didn't just stand there," I continue as I slide my foot back into the shoe. "I said something this time." I laugh. "And he didn't like that at all."

"I guess things are getting better," murmurs George, looking down at his own black old-man shoes. "I remember the days when we were killing each other for shoes." He looks up at me, and I wonder how he can see out of eyes so bloodshot.

"So, you said something. Good. Elaborate . . . what'd you say?"

I pause. "I don't know. You know . . . I just kind of told him off." Maybe I need to write the whole thing down, because the details are getting fuzzy already.

"Okay," he says. "So you made a statement. And you're making one now, with the shoes."

"I didn't even think about what I was doing," I say. "I just . . . did something."

"So now that you've had a chance to think," George says, "what's next?"

Can't I just have my moment? I shrug.

Something flashes across his face, but then he smiles. "I'm proud of you." I grin. "Are you proud of yourself?"

"Well . . . yeah!" I say. "I'm glad I could be there for Charlie. That's mostly what matters."

"Mostly?" he asks.

"I mean . . . I was just having his back . . . I wasn't thinking about making any statement," I say. "That's not really me."

"What's really you, Reggie?" George asks, and then he points to my shoes. "That?"

I shrug again. I wish we could have stayed on the "I'm proud of you" track. George closes his eyes and we sit for a while, until I wonder if he's asleep.

"I saw that wish list thing you put up," he says. "I was working with the kids the other day, and I had some ideas for an after-school program. Maybe you and your smart friends could come do some tutoring, get these kids involved in some sports. . . . I got a few notes together," he says, rummaging around in the gym bag on the floor. "And you've got some elders here who could teach all y'all some real stuff."

"I know! I was thinking the same thing," I say. "Ruthie told me that her partner told her about something called Friday Freedom School that old — I mean, where people used to teach about activist movements and community leaders. The youth group is going to start painting this whole place in a few weeks. Jeff saw us doing that little cardboard city thing, and he had an-idea for a mural based on it. And maybe my school could open up the gym on the weekends and stuff so kids from here could come and use it."

"I'm proud of you," he says again suddenly. "Let's go celebrate." He reaches into his back pocket and pulls out his wallet and I can see the duct tape holding it together. "A big bag of those chips you like," he says. "My treat."

"Better than a five-course meal," I say, smiling.

NOVEMBER 12
11:12 A.M.

So I'm handing out more meaningless Vicky propaganda in the cafeteria doorway, and I am not in the mood for this at all. I'm sorry everybody hates her, but it's become painfully clear that they have good reason. I spent a lot of time at the Olive Branch over the weekend, and what's going on there is so real that her campaign just seems even more fake. At this point, I'm just doing this because I said I would, but one more crack and I'm out.

"I can't believe you still have this many left! What are you doing?" Vicky grabs a bunch of flyers out of my hand. She shoves them at kids, and a few teachers, as they walk in. Some people crumple them up right away; she doesn't miss a beat and gives them another. I move a few inches away from her as she practically throws them at Veronica and her Cruzers-in-waiting. Sean Glanville takes a bunch, and now we're out.

Vicky turns to me. "That's how you get things done. How can I get this through to you? If you're going to work for me, you're going to have to actually work. Don't try to ride on my accomplishments."

She is not human. I'm thinking that I don't even have to be gracious about getting out of this when the first red spitball hits her in the middle of the forehead. She turns, and another hits her ear. Donovan is standing on a table, laughing and throwing spitballs our way, hard and fast.

All of a sudden there is a hailstorm of red spitballs, and everyone in the cafeteria has the aim of a major league pitching legend. Vicky is getting hit in the face, in the chest, all over. I get myself way out of range, and watch as she flinches at the first barrage. Then she just stands there, kind of laughing and holding her arms up, like she's inviting the spitballs to a party. People are picking them up and taking multiple throws. Donovan yells "Here's my vote!" each time he launches one. It's mean, and it's vicious. . . .

And it's not directed at me.

I gotta give it to Vicky, I'd have been out of here after the first one.

I gotta give it to everyone else, Vicky is a pain in the —

A few spitballs land near me. Some little kids run over and snatch them up and throw.

I wonder if a teacher is going to stop this; then I wonder if there are teachers throwing spitballs. It's possible. It's Vicky.

I should do something. I am her campaign manager, after all. What would Night Man do? I imagine myself standing in front of her, spitballs bouncing off of my puffed-out, super-muscled chest.

Donovan looks at me; his grin widens and his eyes narrow.

I take a few steps backward, toward the door.

I don't even like Vicky. She doesn't respect me, and she's not going to change. This whole thing is a waste of time.

She gives a few bows and finally turns to the door; everyone is laughing and cheering and you could almost pretend that it's all in fun, we're all in this together, just good-natured horseplay.

I take a few more steps back, until I'm almost out of the cafeteria.

Vicky turns and looks directly at me. She's still smiling, and her nose is high enough in the air that I can see straight into her flaring nostrils. I can also see that there are tears in her eyes. She brushes past me as she walks out, and the cheers get louder.

I've been there. Right where she is.

But now, I'm over here. On the other side.

It doesn't feel like I thought it would.

NOVEMBER 15
7:00 A.M.

Dave answers the phone on the first ring, all high energy even though it's seven in the morning. He wasn't in church yesterday, which was weird.

"Sorry to call so early," I say. "I just wanted to tell you that I've been talking to George about doing more stuff at the shelter, like painting and workshops and stuff, and I wanted to sit down with you sometime and go over my ideas."

"I knew you had it in you!" says Dave. "Sure, we can talk. My schedule's a little tight right now, and we've got to make sure we wrap up Listening Ears. We've got less than a week to turn everything in."

"I'm not slacking on that," I say. "I've got everybody's interviews transcribed."

"You're not pulling too many all-nighters, are you?" Dave asks.

"I'm used to it," I say. "But, listen, I wanted to ask you —"

"I'm sorry, Reggie, I've got to get out of here, I have to catch a train. But I'm proud of you, my man! What did I tell you? I knew you could do this."

"Okay, but I have to talk to you," I say. "I'm ready to work, but I need your help."

"We'll talk soon, I promise," he says. "Adios."

I hang up the phone slowly. I didn't even get to tell him that Wilma sent me an e-mail yesterday saying that George had offered to supervise any tutors that I bring in; she says that some of the older kids want to talk to me too. Vicky asked me for a meeting this morning, and I'm thinking maybe we can talk to Blaylock about just starting that after-school program before the campaign is over. I'll emphasize how good it will make her look to voters, and then she'll get on board. I know she's all kinds of wrong, but after Friday, I know I'm not that right either.

7:26 A.M.

Vicky is rummaging in her locker; I figured she'd get here early. I take a deep breath and wonder if I should open with an apology. But maybe it's better not to bring it up, pretend that the whole spitball thing was no big deal.

The inside of her locker door is covered with "Vote Vicky!" posters in different colors; no school pictures of friends, none of those silly photo-booth pictures that girls always take when we go on school trips to the amusement park. Not even a note or a chain letter that's been passed around under a teacher's nose. Vicky's best, and I now realize only, friend is clearly Vicky.

"Hi, Vicky," I say, for once tapping her on the shoulder first. "That idea I had about opening Clarke facilities for the shelter kids? I've been thinking, and —"

"Your job," she says slowly, without looking up from her locker, "was to work on my campaign for president here at Clarke.

Not to be a lame community activist or charity-case collector." She's holding a shopping bag full of rubber balls with "Vote Vicky!" on them. I can't help but think that after the spitballs, that's pretty . . . ballsy.

"And *your* job," I snap, because she has such a knack for squashing any feelings of sympathy, "or at least the one you want, is to focus on the needs of the community you'll serve. Clarke has students at the shelter. Clarke is blocks away from the shelter. Are you really going to pretend that what's going on there doesn't matter?"

"Are you really going to keep pretending that you're my campaign manager?" she says, looking up. "You were supposed to focus on *me*. Nobody forced you into this, you know," she continues, and while I might argue with that, I keep my mouth shut because I can see her hands shaking a little. "You have made one mistake after another and have just created more work for me. All I do is clean up your messes. I mean, those stupid sneakers — was that supposed to be funny? I don't need that, and I don't need you."

"Does this mean I'm —" I start.

"Fired!" she says, just as I say, "— free?"

"I don't care what you want to call it, we're done, okay?" she says, more softly. "I thought we could be — work together, but obviously that's not going to happen."

Was she about to say *friends*? Or something even worse? I want to feel sorry for Vicky, but that's what got me into this mess in the first place.

"That's it, then," I say. "Um, good luck with your campaign."

"Thanks," she mumbles, and starts to walk away. I head down

the hall in the opposite direction, and she calls, "Reggie!" I turn and look.

"Vote Vicky!" she yells, and tosses me a Vicky ball. She aims low (no surprise there), and my Very Special Binder comes in handy to block it. I guess Coach was right about how useful they can be.

NOVEMBER 16
3:21 P.M.

I asked Joe C. to meet me at the park today after school. There's a "Black people" side to the park, where family reunions set up their grills right under the No Barbecuing signs, and a "White people" side, where bikini-clad skinny girls ("mawga gals," my mom's always saying) stretch out on the doggy grass as soon as March rolls around. The wind is a little strong; I zip up my jacket and pull my hat down lower. Still, I almost feel like laying out myself, I'm so relieved about being done with Vicky. Plus I'm exhausted from carrying my own overstuffed backpack, along with another holding a surprise for Joe C. I haven't seen him much, between the shelter and school, but he sent me this really funny drawing of me in my Dora shoes, with a cape blowing out behind me. He's always had my back, even when he doesn't get what I'm doing, and last night I came up with a way to let him know that I've got his too.

He walks up to where I am in the middle, near the Vanderbilt Monument. He takes a Juiced! out of his backpack as we settle onto a park bench. "I left my sketchbook in my locker," he says. "Sorry."

"No problem," I say. "I don't want to work anyway."

"Yeah," he says. "You're the guy who's too busy to work."

Okay, this isn't going to be easy. "I'm the guy who's free at last," I say. "As of yesterday, I'm officially free from the Vote Crazy campaign." I'll start with that.

"Woot!" shouts Joe C., high-fiving me. "I can't believe you didn't say anything!"

"The important thing is no more Vicky Ross," I answer.

"I heard she got pelted with her own flyers on Friday. You didn't tell me about that either. . . ." he says. "I always miss the good stuff. First, the Donovan smackdown, and now this." He gulps down his Juiced! "Everybody's still talking about the Donovan thing. You did good, with the Dora shoes and everything."

"I wish you could have seen the look on Donovan's face," I say. "Vijay should have gotten *that* on camera. Talk about *Talkin' Trash!*"

I don't have the shoes on, but they're in my backpack. I didn't have them Monday, and I wonder if I would have done something different when those spitballs started flying if I'd had the shoes on. I know it's silly, but they're kind of like my talisman. I've been on a quest for the new me, and I think these shoes got me a few steps closer.

A bunch of kids from school come into the park. Some high school guys are there, and Justin. And Donovan. He's holding a basketball. My first instinct is to hide, and I hope it doesn't show. Donovan's not looking this way, though; he's dribbling the ball between his legs and concentrating like he's trying out for the NBA.

"Speak of the devil . . ." Joe C. says.

". . . and the devil appears," I finish. "He didn't see us; he's too busy trying to be a baller."

"You want to go?"

Yes, I think. "No," I say. "Let's hang out for a little while longer." If I can hold it down for five minutes, I'll win. What I'll win, I don't know, but it's important enough to risk public playground humiliation.

Joe C. shrugs, and we watch the basketball game start. Donovan's good. He's always been good at basketball; he used to beg Monica to play with him all of the time. It's weird watching him like this. I'm expecting a lot of trash-talking and clowning, but he's serious and smooth. He plays fair, and doesn't complain when he gets fouled hard. And he does, a lot. He gives up a lot of shots to Justin, who plays lazy and shoots confidently. Justin doesn't miss a shot, and neither does Donovan when he takes them. Supposedly Donovan's dad was almost in the NBA. That's what Donovan used to say all the time, but he could have been lying. He also told us that his dad was a spy and a sniper. His dad left when he was two, so he was never around for us to see if the stories checked out.

"So are you going to the shelter again soon?" asks Joe C. after a while. "How's that wish list thing going?"

"It's all good. I'm going to be there a lot," I say. "You can't go there and then forget about it. It's exactly what," I swallow, "what the Clarke Pledge is talking about." Joe C. is one of the only people that I can even mention the Pledge to now.

"You've really gotten into this thing," he says slowly. "You're all serious about it."

"Yeah, I am."

"Does it make you feel better?" he asks. "Holier or something?"

"I don't know about all that. It's just . . . I have a good time, I'm more myself there. The Listening Ears Project is almost done, but a lot of us from the youth group are planning to stick around. We're going to clean up the place, paint it and everything. George, my partner, he wants to have a whole after-school program. And it's not all about projects. I can do my thing there, talk to George, hang out with Charlie, not worry about . . . stupid stuff."

We sit for a minute.

"I thought this was some Ruthie thing," says Joe C., "but it's all you, isn't it?" He pauses. "I want to check it out. I want to help. But . . ." He stops.

"But what?" I ask, looking up.

"It freaks me out a little."

"Try anyway," I say after a pause. "I still do."

Some pigeons move toward us, and they look so mean I'm expecting them to take out their knives and snatch Joe C.'s MP3 player.

"Listen," I say, taking a deep breath. Joe C. looks at me.

"Night Man . . ." I stop again. "I think it's done."

Neither one of us speaks for a while.

"I know," he says. "It was fun, though." He shrugs. "I could never come up with something like that. Thanks for letting me work on it."

I watch the pigeons fight over a bagel. "It was kind of an X-Men rip-off anyway. But yeah, it was fun. And, uh, I couldn't have done it without you. Thanks."

He nods and adds, "So . . ." Another pause. I wait.

"Nothing," he says, looking away. "It's cool."

"Huh?" I ask. "What are you talking about?"

"Nothing," he says again. Then he looks at me. "I'm just saying. Man up and tell me if you don't want to hang out with me anymore."

"Whoa, Castiglione," I say. "What are you talking about?" But we both know, and it's complicated, and I don't know what to say. I hope I don't have to go on that hip-hop tour to prove my friendship.

Joe C. looks at me for a moment, then shrugs. "Sorry. Just seems like things are changing."

"Got a lot on my mind," I say. "But it's not about you." And then I do know what to say. "It gets messy sometimes. But we will always be boys. Just don't say 'man up' anymore."

"Always," he says. "I got your back."

Looks like it's getting heated on the basketball court. Some guys are arguing, and Justin and one of the older guys are trying to break it up. At the other end of the court, Donovan's got the ball, and he's not even watching the argument, he's just shooting baskets. He looks like he's in a bubble, just shooting and shooting and not paying attention to anything else. His mouth is a little open, almost like he's praying. He looks like someone I might be friends with.

"I think there's going to be a fight," says Joe C.

"Yeah," I say. Pretty soon, without the game going on, Donovan will sniff me out. I look at Joe C.'s Juiced!. "This might be a record. I can't believe you haven't told me about some three-legged midget with no toes."

"Ha ha," Joe C. shrugs. "I'll tell Ruthie you said 'midget.'" He cracks it open and then looks at the bottle cap. "Anthony Duda officially changed his first name to Zipardi in 2002."

"That's it?" I ask. "What's the punch line?"

"Zipardi," Joe C. says. "Get it? Zipardi Duda?"

It takes me a minute. "Oh!" I say. "That's not disgusting, that's just stupid. And weird."

"Admit it," he says. "You would miss it if I stopped."

"Um, no," I reply. "Really, don't keep it up on my account. I just tolerate it because you're like a brother to me."

He smiles.

"And before we actually turn into girls by talking like this, I've got a surprise for you." I unzip the second backpack and show him the old records that I had to pry out of Pops's hands. There are names like Sugarhill Gang, Kool Herc, and Eric B. & Rakim on them — I promised Pops I'd get a full scholarship to Cornell in order to get him to give these up. "These are for you," I say. "From Pops's collection of vintage hip-hop — or 'old-school JAMZ,' as he likes to say." I draw out the Z and Joe C. laughs. "There's some dancehall in there too. Since DJ-ing is your thing . . . I got your back too."

"Thanks!" he says, like I just gave him a car. "Wow!"

"My pleasure," I say. He takes the second backpack, and I pick up mine. "Do you think the Goon guy is around now?"

"Gunnar," Joe C. says. "Probably. He wakes up around lunchtime and he doesn't go into the club until later. Why?"

"Let's go over to your dad's," I say. "We can start working on the sound track for *Night Man: The Movie*."

Joe C. grins again as we stand up. And I don't even glance at Donovan as we leave.

7:28 P.M.

The Goon guy *was* pretty cool, and I liked fooling around with all of that DJ equipment. I'm a little late for dinner, but it's pizza, so Mom's cool. Still, the dinner table atmosphere is downright cold. Pipitone gave us a pizza with anchovies by mistake, and even though we're sitting there with a nasty sea-worm pie on the table, Mom and Pops don't want to bother to send it back.

It doesn't help that the Wicked Witch Who Didn't Get into Clarke sings "The worms crawl in, the worms crawl out" under her breath when we open the box. She also starts talking about how "those cheerleaders are stuck-up" and Mom tells her to shut up. Mom actually uses those words. I expect a pig to fly in through the living room window, or Satan to walk through the door wearing a fur coat and shaking off the snow. Nobody says anything else. Then Mom and Pops don't even eat with us — they go into their bedroom and talk in those annoying low voices that are impossible to hear, even with a glass against the door.

I grab a slice and start picking off the anchovies. Monica stares at the pizza for a long time, then gets a bag of baby carrots from the fridge and starts crunching. She whips out a copy of *American Cheerleader* and ignores me. I feel bad for her about the "shut up" from Mom, so I decide to give conversation a try.

"You've been eating rabbit food forever. Is there a new diet in the Land of Evil? Is that how you ogres keep up your strength?"

"Whatever, Biscuitbrain. If you really need to know, I *am* on a new diet. I'm trying out for the school play. It's *A Raisin in the Sun*. I'm going for Ruth."

We saw that on Broadway a few years ago; real dramatic. Wait, isn't Ruth the pretty wife? I start laughing. Then I'm laugh/choking. Then it's a full-on choke thing and I'm rolling on the floor, gasping for air. Monica gets up and leaves, brings back a glass of water, then drinks it right over me.

"What is so funny, geek?"

"You . . . in a school play? Playing a woman? Dr. Evil in a dress!" I start laughing again and she pours some water on me.

"You don't know anything about it," she says. "Mrs. McMahon encouraged me to try out; she thinks I have talent." She finishes pouring the water on me and looks like she might get more.

I decide to get up before it gets worse. Monica sits down and goes back to her magazine. I watch her for a minute. Cheerleading? School plays? What is up with her?

"Are the Black Barbies — I mean, Tatia and Renee trying out?" I ask.

"I don't know," Monica mumbles. "They made cheerleading, so maybe not."

"Wait, how come you didn't try out? After all that drama you started . . ."

"I did," she says, not looking at me.

Oh.

"I heard Diane Anderson might drop out; rumor has it she's pregnant. They're going to have tryouts for her spot."

"Are you gonna try again? Mom will kill you," I warn.

"She wouldn't even notice," says Monica. "She'll be too busy trying to keep Pops together if he doesn't get a new job soon."

She's probably right. The murmur-y discussions they used to have only late at night aren't always so murmur-y or so late anymore.

"I don't care anyway," says Monica. "I'm so over cheerleading."

What's the magazine for, then? I can almost relate to my sister at this moment. Will rejection make her a better person?

Monica looks up at me. "Can you move? I don't want to get loser dust on me."

I guess that answers my question. "Why are you reading that magazine? One of Joe C.'s dogs would make a better cheerleader than you. A cuter one, anyway."

"I'm going to come to your school and tell everyone what a punk you are," she says. "I'll bring pictures."

"Why don't you get off my back," I say. "This time I'm gonna tell."

"'This time I'm gonna tell,'" she repeats. "You would. You don't have the guts to do anything else."

I go upstairs and take the Dora shoes out for school tomorrow. School's been okay for the last week — at least, no one's been calling me Pukey lately. It looks like the LARPing kid with his bow ties and penny loafers is next in the line of fire. Mialonie talked to me, and Charlie thinks I wear a cape for real. I got what I wanted, I guess. But it's not the total zero-to-hero transformation I thought it would be. Do I need to put the shoes back on? Will I have to wear them every day for the rest of my life?

NOVEMBER 20
10:30 A.M.

Joe C. makes good on his promise to come with me to Olive Branch, even though I can tell he's freaking out as soon as we step through the doors. I don't see George or Charlie, but Gabriella is watching TV with some of the hard-core basketball fans, and she stops what seems like a sort of friendly debate to wave at me.

After I introduce Joe C. to Wilma and a few of the residents, and Mr. James challenges him to a game of dominoes right away, a girl walks over carrying a box of books. She looks like she could be my age. I meet her halfway so that I can help with the box.

"Thanks," she says. "There's another box outside," she says, looking at Joe C. He goes to get it.

"I'm Carmen," she says. "You're Reggie, right?"

"Yes," I say, surprised that she knows my name. "I didn't realize other schools were volunteering. Did you come with a group?"

"Come with what group?" she asks. "I've been here. I *live* here."

"Oh! Great! I mean . . . um, what are the books for?" *Nice going, Reggie.*

But she doesn't seem to mind. "I've been trying to get a lending library going for the last few months, and people are finally coming on board. Old Crump built some bookshelves from scrap wood, and we got a few more donated. And Dare Books just gave me a bunch of brand-new textbooks for free. I'm going to set up over there," she says, pointing to a corner next to Wilma's office. As Joe C. returns with the box, she looks at me again. "I heard you've been making things happen. Maybe you can get some other people to help me collect donations. Spread the word." She hands me a piece of paper. "Here's a list of places that I still need to hit up."

"Uh, sure," I say. "But I don't want to be all up in your project. I mean, I'd feel kind of funny, like I was taking credit for your work."

She rolls her eyes. "Okay, you can stand around and feel funny, or you can help me get this done."

"Good point," I say. I take the list.

"Thanks a lot," she says. "I'd been kind of discouraged about this whole thing, but there's been some new positive energy around here lately. I'm ready to make things happen." We make plans to talk again in a couple of days, and she heads to Wilma's office.

"She was cool," says Joe C. "And cute. If it weren't for Maria . . ."

Yeah, yeah. "So, you see what I was saying?" I ask. "Not what you were expecting."

"Yeah," he nods. "Even after we came in, I kept thinking about what a dump this is. But when I take a second look . . ." He points to the kids' town. "Cool. Is that the town you were telling me about?"

"Yeah," I say. "And this guy Jeff is painting a mural to go with it, and if you knew Jeff, you'd never expect him to do anything like that. Hey! You should talk to him; I bet he could use your drawing skills. I'll give you his e-mail address."

"No wonder you've been so busy," he says. "Sounds like you've been getting a lot done here."

"We all have," I say. "It's the community thing that makes it work. I wanted Vicky to get behind that for the election."

"Well, one of the candidates was listening," says Joe C., looking at the door. I follow his eyes; Justin Walker is coming in and walking toward us.

"Hey," he says. "Mialonie told me you had something going on here. I came to check it out."

"Uh, yeah, thanks," I say. "Um, are you alone?"

"Uh-huh," he says. "I want to do something to help. Who should I talk to? Her?" He points to Wilma, and I nod. "Thanks. See you," he says. Justin walks over to Wilma and Carmen, and within seconds they're all smiling together like old friends.

As Joe C. and I are leaving, I notice that Justin has gone over to the basketball-watching crew and he's telling some story that makes everyone laugh. Gabriella comes over. "Wow, Reggie," she says. "Before now, I wouldn't have thought a guy could pull off something like this."

"Thanks," I say as I take Carmen's list out of my back pocket. "Here. See that girl over there?" Gabriella nods. "She needs some help with a project, and I think you'd be perfect."

She takes the list and smiles. "I'm glad I came back," she says. "Thanks for making it happen."

"The Man Who Makes It Happen," says Joe C. when we're on the sidewalk. "Sounds like the start of another graphic novel." When I roll my eyes, he adds, "And it sounds like my boy Reggie."

NOVEMBER 22
6:30 A.M.

When the doorbell rings, I wonder if the Jehovah's Witnesses are on some early-morning overdrive kick. I open the door; it's Ruthie. She looks surprised, and that annoys me. Who does she expect to see?

"Hey," I say. Her hat and scarf almost cover her whole head, except for her eyes, which are bright and shiny. They look like they're what's really keeping her warm.

"Oh — hi!" she says. "I'm supposed to meet Monica to go over some lines." She walks in without an invitation. "I'm freezing!" She hugs me hard.

Whoa! I could use a binder right now. Coach Conners wasn't kidding when he said *unexpected*.

"What?" I say, turning away to hide my body's betrayal. I hope it doesn't show on my face. "Why Monica and what lines?"

Ruthie sighs. "You heard she's trying out for *Raisin in the Sun*? She called me and asked if I would help her practice."

There's an amusement park ride called the Pirate Ship, and it swings back and forth in the air until you're certain that you're going to fall out no matter how strapped in you are. First Joe C. is breaking beats, and now Ruthie is . . . I don't know *what* Ruthie is. Consorting with the enemy.

"Oh yeah. Dr. Evil in a dress . . . I can't believe she asked you to help her."

"Well, she knows how much I like it, and she knows that I," she stops and gives me a look, "have a flair for the dramatic."

"No kidding," I say, and it's almost like old times. "You?" We stand there grinning at each other for a minute, and then Monica appears at the top of the stairs.

"Get up here, Ruthie!" she roars. "I don't have much time." When Ruthie just looks at her, she adds, "Please." I'm impressed.

Ruthie smiles and starts up the stairs. She turns and looks at me. "Uh, see you at school," she says.

"Oh, okay, see you."

I linger at the kitchen table, letting my Cheerios get soggy, while I hear them mumbling and moving around upstairs. When I think I can't wait any longer, I hear Ruthie's shoes coming down the stairs, so I run out to the hallway to look like I'm just going out the door.

"Oh, hey," I say. "I was just leaving. Do you want to walk together?"

"Sure," she says, and we head out.

"So how's the Monster's acting?" I ask. "I still can't believe she's trying out for a play."

"I think she's good," says Ruthie. "We had a good talk about the story, and she relates to the themes." I don't even try to mask my skeptical look, and Ruthie nods. "I'm serious. The dream deferred . . . feeling held back by outside forces — Monica gets that."

"Yeah, whatever. Monica *is* outside forces holding people

back." I laugh. "And I bet John Wilkins has something to do with this. She has a crush on him, which is the funniest thing I've heard in years."

Ruthie rolls her eyes. "You are such a bonehead sometimes." Then she gives me a sidelong glance. "But in the interest of full disclosure, he is trying out for the male lead."

I let out a whoop. "Ha! I knew it! Fat chance, fathead!" I yell back in the direction of my house. Ruthie sighs and we walk on in silence. I sneak looks at her all the way to school.

8:55 A.M.

The morning is quiet, and I look away fast every time I see Vicky, looking tired, handing out flyers. I'm starving by the end of second period, and decide to grab some of my lunch out of my backpack on the way to third.

"Have you seen this?" screeches Ruthie as soon as I get to my locker. She gives me a red flyer with a big purple *V* on the bottom. I scan; the centerpiece of Vicky's new solo campaign seems to be pushing for a special "community achievement fund for more appropriate recognition of student accomplishments." Basically she wants to raise a whole lot of money for a formal banquet at the end of the year, where we celebrate our collective greatness with steak and lobster tails.

"What, are we senior citizens or something now? And we already *have* an awards assembly in June," I say. "I slept through it last year." Joe C. walks up and I hand him the flyer.

"Apparently, it's not enough to pat ourselves on the back," huffs Ruthie. "We need to have a *group mastur —*"

I clap a hand over her mouth, even though I know she hates that. "Please don't go there. I get the point." I think I'd rather have the sex talk with Mom, Pops, *and* Reverend Coles than hear Ruthie say that word.

She pulls my hand off, all fired up. "There are so many real issues we could be focusing on! I gave her *Bling: Glistening Instruments of Death*, my annotated report on the exploitive realities of the diamond industry."

"In that case, I would have gone with the banquet plan myself," says Joe C. "For real. And do people even say *bling* anymore?"

I notice his belt buckle. "Is that a nameplate? Who's 'THE GODSON'?"

"It's my DJ name," he says. "I won a junior mixtape competition last night."

"Godson? I don't get it," says Ruthie.

"You know, *The Godfather*," mumbles Joe C. "*Junior* competition . . . God*son*. . . ." At least he has the sense to look a little sheepish. But he looks proud too.

"Congratulations," I say.

"Thanks," he says in a way that makes me glad I congratulated him. "I used some of those records you gave me in the bonus 'Way Back in the Day' round." He smiles.

The second bell rings as I feel a tug on my shirt. "Charlie!" I say, turning around. "What's up, little man?"

He's wearing his Dora shoes and he's got a big smile on his

face. Then he looks at my Adidas and his mouth starts to quiver. I reach into my locker and pull out my own Doras.

"I didn't want to mess mine up," I say. "I was just about to change."

10:46 A.M.

A few people glance at my Dora shoes, but no one says anything. Ruthie's not in English, so I wonder if there's some kind of international border crisis. Joe C. and I are walking down the hall to our lockers, and as we pass the girls' bathroom, Ruthie bursts out and slams right into me.

"Ow," I say, bending down to pick up my books.

She opens her mouth to say something and then just bursts into tears. Ruthie doesn't cry. "Ruthie?" I whisper. "What's wrong?" I put my arm around her and wonder who did this and how I'm going to get them back.

"Does it smell that bad in there?" says Joe C. "I figured you girls had some flowery scent piped in." I give him a look, and Ruthie makes a face and wipes her eyes.

She turns to me. "Joelle Johnson fell asleep in study hall and somebody used a Sharpie to play connect-the-dots on her face," she says, sniffling. "I can't believe how cruel people can be. We spent all of last period in the bathroom trying to scrub it off."

Joelle Johnson? Oh yeah, Acid Face.

Oh. Ouch to the infinite power.

"Why do we have to be so mean?" Ruthie wails. "Human nature sucks. I'm so sick of it."

"She must be a heavy sleeper," says Joe C.

"Excuse me, but she has to babysit her five brothers every night until her parents get home. She doesn't even start her homework until after midnight." Ruthie leans against the wall. "But does anyone care about that? No one cares about anything in this place. . . . 'Community' — it's such a joke."

I know this, and everyone does, but it always made me feel better to know that Ruthie stayed stubbornly clueless. I don't want that to change. I look at her; she's rummaging through her big bag made out of a pair of jeans. She pulls out a tissue and blows her nose. I reach out again, but she brushes my hand away.

"Oh, leave me alone," she mutters. "Like you don't call her that awful name, both of you. You're just as bad as whoever did this."

I recoil; does she really think that? And then I wonder: Is she right?

"Maybe she can borrow Suheir's scarf thing," says Joe C.

"A hijab is worn for religious reasons, you ignorant —" She takes a deep breath. "I'm going back in to help." She disappears into the bathroom, and Joe C. and I stand there for a minute. Kids brush past us, and I wonder which one of them was the culprit. I want to pin it on Donovan, but I know that there are so many people it could be. . . . Ruthie has a point.

"A Sharpie . . . that is pretty cold," says Joe C.

" 'Does it smell that bad?' " I say, mimicking Joe C. "Nice."

"Hey, it got her to stop crying," he replies. We walk on to our lockers.

Joe C. clears his throat. "If you tell her this I will have to kill you." He glances at me. "Just once . . . she was talking about something, maybe the G8 Summit, I don't really remember, but I was looking at her and it was like she got all . . . glowing, or something." He looks down. "I'm sure that sounds dumb to you."

"No," I say, after a minute. "It doesn't."

"Anyway, it was just a spur-of-the-moment thing . . . before I met my soul mate."

"Oh, yeah, of course. Maria," I say with a sigh. "Mysterious Maria."

"I'm going to get her to come hang out with us next week," he says. "Really."

I shrug. We close our lockers and start walking.

"Ruthie wouldn't go out with me anyway, because I'm White," he says.

There's not much I can say to that because he's probably right. I look at Joe C. My Uncle Terrence is always saying "Never underestimate the White man." I see what he means.

11:41 A.M.

When I get to the lunch table, Ruthie's already there. "I'm sorry, I shouldn't have yelled at you," she says. "It wasn't your fault."

"I should have been more sensitive," I say.

She gives me a smile that makes me feel like my last puzzle piece was put in place. She starts to bow her head to whisper grace, then looks up. "Do you want to pray together?" she asks softly.

"Um, right now?" I edge away from her a little. When we were in Sunday school, Ruthie used to belt out "This Little Light of

Mine" every time we sang it. She didn't care how bad she sounded, or who was there; she would really let go. At first, it scared me, but then I'd stand next to her because I liked the song and I wanted to sing it out too. The Sunday school teacher used to tell us to sing "loud and proud," and I know it's cheesier than a pizza, but I used to roll like that, full blast, and the more I did it, the more I felt like there was a little ball of fire in my belly, getting bigger and bigger with each verse. We'd be there, all off-key and screechy, but singing anyway. Then we got older and Ruthie kept belting it, but I started noticing that people were noticing us. I sang a little softer. Then I just stood somewhere else, next to Jeff and the other people who never sang, just mouthed the words.

"Uh . . . maybe later," I say.

When she's done, I clear my throat. "Here's what I was thinking," I start.

"Don't hurt yourself," says Hector, leaning over me. His tray is piled high with fish sticks, tater tots, and chocolate milks. He grunts as he squeezes himself into the spot on the other side of Ruthie.

I can't stand Hector. And he's all pushed up in here when he could have just sat at the next table. Joe C. comes over, looks at Hector, then at me, then shrugs and sits down.

"Can I borrow a dollar?" Hector asks him. "I forgot to get some butter crunch cookies."

"Didn't get enough in your daily kindergarten shakedown?" I ask.

"He doesn't do that anymore!" says Ruthie, shoving me. Then she looks at Hector. "Right?"

"Baby!" he says. "Come on!"

"*Baby?*" Ruthie says, a warning in her voice.

"Uh, sorry," he mutters. "Slip of the tongue."

Heh. Joe C. gives Hector a dollar, and he lumbers off to get his cookies.

"Did you know donkeys kill more people every year than plane crashes?" says Joe C., gulping down a Juiced!

"I thought you gave that up," I say, sighing.

"It's an addiction," he says. "One day at a time . . ."

"Joelle!" calls out Ruthie, waving. "Over here!" I look up and see Acid Fa — *Joelle* standing in the cafeteria doorway. Even from far away, you can still see the traces of Sharpie on her face. She doesn't move for a minute, and there are stifled snickers and whispers. Ruthie waves her over again, and she walks fast toward our table, her face down and her books up. I know that walk.

I'm not sure what to say, so I just say "hi," and try not to look at her face. But then I wonder if she'll notice me trying not to look, so then I look, but not for too long. Her eyes are really red. Her face is really messed up. I realize that that was all I knew about her until Ruthie told us about her brothers today. I say "hi" again because I don't know what else to say, and fiddle with my lunch.

A little girl runs up to me, crying. "You're mean!" she yells. A few people at the table look our way. Who is this kid? Charlie comes over, and I don't recognize his swagger.

"Nah nah nah," he says to the crying girl. "That's what you get."

"What's going on?" I ask, as more people look at us. Ruthie pats Crying Girl on the shoulder.

"This is the girl who's always mean to me, Reggie! And today I got her back, just like you!"

"What are you talking about?" I ask.

"He talked about my MOMMEEEE!!" the girl wails.

"Yeah," says Charlie proudly. "And it was good, just like the ones you said to that mean guy."

Uh-oh. "What exactly did you say, Charlie?" I ask.

He giggles. "I said . . . I said, 'Your mommy's so old, she was at the Virgin Mary's baby shower!'" He cracks himself up, falling on the floor. Ruthie gasps and glares at me. Joe C. chokes on his Juiced!. Crying Girl cries harder.

I almost keep a smile from my face. *Hey, that's a pretty good one.*

"Charlie, I never said anything like that," I say, trying to look serious.

"Yeah, but I heard some guys saying stuff to each other at the playground and it sounded just like the things you said, so I knew it had to be good. And I was right, 'cause it worked!" He cackles. "Whatcha got to say now, huh?" he says to the girl. "Your mommy's so —"

"Charlie! Um, it's not good to talk about people's mommies like that," I say.

He thinks for a minute. "Okay." He turns back to her. "You're so ugly —"

I've created a monster. In my own image.

"Charlie!" I raise my voice a little, and he looks at me. "Listen to me —"

"Hey!" It's Vicky. Great.

"What can I do for you, Vicky?" I ask. "I'm kind of in the middle of something."

She shoves a small spiral notepad and a pencil in my hands. They are both purple with big red Vs on them. She's changed things up. Yay.

"Just a token of my appreciation for your vote. Thanks for your support!" She lowers her voice. "You owe me, since you practically killed my campaign." Her eyes hold mine for a moment. "I may even give you another chance. You can start by handing these out." She almost jabs me with a bunch of pencils.

I don't have to take this. I swallow my *Right-Back-Atcha!-*styled retort. *Or give it.*

Vicky hands Joe C. a notepad and pencil, and he starts doodling. Charlie grabs two sets. Crying Girl cries harder. Hector returns with his cookies and a chocolate milk for Ruthie, who smiles at him like he just gave her a copy of a peace treaty. I am in the eye of the Tornado of Crazy.

"I can't vote for you, Vicky," I say as I edge a little closer to Ruthie. *This little light of mine.*

"Whatever," she responds, not looking at me. "Remember: Vote V!"

"I mean," I speak a little louder, "I won't vote for you." Her head whirls around. I stand up. And gulp. "I can't vote for you because —" Everyone at the table is looking at me now. I'm already putting on a show, might as well make it good. I get up on the table and hope my zipper's up. "Because *I'm* running for president now!"

I throw up a fist. Charlie cheers. Loud.

And that's it. The rest, as Hamlet said, is silence.

"What are you talking about?" says Vicky.

"Uh, yeah, Reggie," Joe C. adds. "What are you talking about?"

"And why are you on the table, fool?" says Hector.

Good question. Joe C.'s mouth is hanging open. Ruthie looks surprised, and happy. I see Mialonie in the doorway, looking like a model; Josie whispers something in her ear. This is like being on stage, and I want to puke. I think about picking something or someone to focus on so I don't lose my nerve, but I just close my eyes instead.

"I'm announcing my candidacy for president of Clarke Junior School," I say, opening my eyes. "I am running for . . . for . . . civic responsibility . . . community service . . . um . . ."

"For Blaylock brownnosing!" someone shouts, and that elicits woots and cheers.

"No," I say. "For people right here in our community. Kids just like us." *Come on, come on. Think, Reggie. Come up with something good.*

"There's a place called Olive Branch right here in the neighborhood that needs our help," I start, and I sneak a peek at Ruthie, who's smiling. "It's a homeless shelter, but it's more than that. I've been part of a documentation project there, learning from people who are true community resources, treasures even. I've gotten a lot out of it, and I want to give back. People are already helping to clean it up, and paint it, and they need more. Tutors, sports clinics — even just hanging out with some of the residents would be welcome. I propose that we show the world that Clarke students are about something," I glance at Vicky, "other than ourselves." She rolls her eyes.

A few people are laughing, but only a few. The paraprofessionals are coming over, looking like they're about to haul me out of there, so it's time to wrap it up. Out of the corner of my eye I see Vijay with his camera on me.

"Let's do something positive," I say. "Stay tuned for more tomorrow, when me and my, uh ... campaign managers over here," I wave in Ruthie and Joe C.'s direction, "will present my platform." I jump down from the table just as the paras get to me. One of them jerks her head in the direction of the door. As I gather my stuff, Ruthie grins at me.

"Well, well, well," she says. "I always knew you had it in you."

"Campaign managers?" says Joe C. "Will you please put your regular shoes back on? I swear those have some weird power over you — you have gone crazy!"

Charlie's standing there, looking a little lost. I give him a quick pat on the back.

"We'll talk," I say. I point to No-Longer-Crying Girl. "And you have to apologize. That wasn't nice." He frowns. As I am hauled away, a few people start cheering. I throw up another fist on my way out.

12:03 P.M.

Blaylock's office is a mess, and so is he. His tie, which even I know is too wide, is flipped over one shoulder, and one of his shirt buttons is missing. Once I notice that, I can't stop looking at the gap.

"What is this about, uh . . ." He looks down at a manila folder. ". . . Reginald?"

We've both been here for nine years and there are only two classes per grade; he doesn't know my name?

"What was the meaning of the disturbance you caused in the cafeteria today?"

"Mr. — Dr. Blaylock, sir, I apologize." He rubs his temples like he's got a headache. But he's been all hyped up about this election thing, and I'm just doing what he talks about all of the time. What's the problem? I didn't even have a sound track like Justin's announcement. "I, uh, am running for president, sir."

"Oh?" he says. He's not looking pleased. "I don't recall your candidacy announcement, or your candidate registration forms." He makes a point of flipping through the manila folder as he speaks.

"Yeah, um, well, that's what I was doing today. Announcing."

"I see. You do understand everything that needs to be done in the coming weeks? You have no campaign presence, you haven't participated in the debates —"

"Debates, sir?"

He looks at his papers again. "Oh. Yes, we seem to have forgotten about those this year."

"Did we have them last year, sir?"

"Ahem, that is not the issue here. Next week is the Step Up And Lead candidates' rally, and because of Clarke's illustrious history (and I dare say also because of my modest efforts at innovation during my tenure), the mayor will be in attendance. It's an opportunity to showcase Clarke's legacy as one of the nation's top schools, and is meant for our brightest stars. I have it on good authority that Clarke is a lock for that grant money, as long as no one screws this up. It is not something to be taken lightly, so decide now if you have the . . . stomach for it."

Yeah, even though he didn't remember my name, he does remember the first day of school, and the part he played in my . . . accident. I just look at him and nod. He really doesn't seem happy about this at all. I don't get it. What about all of that "step up and be a leader" talk? I try again. "Uh, sir? I was thinking that I would take your words to heart, and, um, become a force for positive action in our community."

He looks at me like he doesn't know what I'm talking about. "I would not have expected you, er, Reginald, to run for president. As a matter of fact, I was just speaking to Justin Walker about his plans for the rest of the year."

"Excuse me, sir, but doesn't he have to win first?" Talk about heir apparent. Except it's obvious Blaylock was never the Justin when he was a kid.

"Well, erm, of course, but . . ." Blaylock smiles a little. "Students like that do the school proud."

I just sit there. How am I supposed to respond to this?

"It would be unusual for me to let you enter the race at this late date," he says. "Highly irregular."

"Uh, I understand, sir. . . ." I keep my eyes down. "But is there a rule against it?"

He looks at me for a long moment. Then he sighs and shuffles some papers around on his desk. It's getting a little weird, this just sitting here, and then I realize — he has no idea what to do.

"No," he says slowly. "There's no such rule. I suppose that if you do want to enter the race, you may." He leans forward and hands me some papers. "Fill these out and return them immediately. And watch your step, Reginald. I will not have a repeat of last year's debacle. This process is a dignified one."

I almost laugh, but I turn it into a cough.

"And I expect you to respect that. Understood?"

"Um, yes, sir," I say. "May I be excused?"

He clears his throat. "Yes. And remember what I said."

Yeah, right. But I'm feeling good as I leave the office.

Let me reintroduce myself, sir. I'm Reggie McKnight, and I'm in this thing.

2:39 P.M.

By the end of the day, I don't mind the whispers, which I'm used to anyway. A couple of people come up and ask me about Olive Branch, and I tell them to meet me there after school. Every once in a while, someone looks at me like they hadn't known how crazy I was, and I want to say, "That makes two of us!"

I get a bathroom pass near the end of last period and head to my locker early, hoping to slip out before the rush. I need to clear my head, and I want to talk to George. When I get to my locker, Charlie's there. "What are you doing?" I ask. "Does your teacher know you're over here?"

"I got a bathroom pass," he says.

"You're gonna get busted," I say, pulling on my lock. "You're gonna get *me* busted."

Charlie mutters something.

"I can't hear you," I snap. "What did you say?"

He looks up. "I said," he starts, kicking the locker next to mine, "I don't know why I have to apologize to Anndalisa. She's always mean to me!"

"Two wrongs don't make a right," I say automatically.

"But . . . when that boy was saying mean things to you, you said mean things back, and it was COOL!" he says. "And everybody was laughing at him, not you." He takes a deep breath. "Anndalisa always says mean things to me, and everybody laughs. But today they laughed at her."

"But Charlie," I say, "how do you feel when people laugh at you?" Good. Classic turnaround stuff. Ruthie would be proud.

"Bad!" he says, like I'm not as smart as he thought I was.

"So do you want to make someone else feel that bad?" Hey, I'm pretty good at this.

"Yeah!" he crows. "Especially Anndalisa!"

Oh. Well.

"Okay," I say. "Uh, here's the thing . . ." I look at my watch; the bell's about to ring. "See, that guy who was making fun of your shoes, we have a history. We used to be boys, but then he turned on me for no reason except that he's a jerk and he's always trying to humiliate me — I mean *really* humiliate me, and I try and try to ignore him but he's always in my face, and then I didn't like him picking on you, so I had to speak up. And yeah, okay, it felt good for a little while, but it doesn't mean you should do it because it's not really right." I take a breath. "Understand?"

"No," he says.

Join the club. "Um, have you ever heard someone say 'Do as I say, not as I do'?" I'm hitting new lows. Referencing hypocritical adult sayings. Nice.

Charlie shakes his head.

"Scratch that," I say, as the bell rings. "Listen. It's just that . . . when you do that, say mean things like that, it's like you give the other person power — superpowers — over you, like they're controlling how you behave."

"What would Night Man do?" asks Charlie. "Nobody could have superpowers over him, right?"

"Night Man would agree with me," I say. I take a deep breath. "Okay, I'll be honest. It felt good to say those mean things to Donovan." Charlie giggles. "But . . . it felt better when I wore the Dora sneakers to show that I was *your friend* instead of saying mean things to show that I was *his enemy*." Aha! "That felt *much* better," I finish. "Because it was the right thing, the Night Man thing to do."

He just looks at me, and I don't know if he gets it. People are rushing by; a few glance over at us and our matching shoes.

"And Night Man always apologizes when he makes a mistake," I improvise. "Because even Night Man makes mistakes."

"Even though he's a superhero?" asks Charlie.

"Yeah," I say. "Being brave enough to make mistakes is, um, part of what makes him a superhero." There's a click in my brain when I say that.

I start packing my backpack. Someone bumps into me, hard. I turn around and Donovan is passing by, giving me a look that Joe C. would illustrate with laser flames shooting out of his eyes.

Charlie's eyes widen. "Are *you* gonna apologize to *him*?"

Smart kid. He's got me. I bend down and take a long time untying then retying my laces. I try to think of something

Blaylock-ish to avoid answering the question. I search for a movie or quote or even a Bible verse to get me out of this one. Then I take a deep breath and look Charlie in the eye.

"Yes," I say.

I walk Charlie to his classroom, and head back to my locker to put the Dora shoes inside before I leave. Some people are waiting for me there, and I end up answering a bunch of questions about Olive Branch. Veronica Cruz thinks that posters of her would be a great fund-raiser, but other people have actual good ideas. This gets me all pumped up, so I change my mind and decide to take the shoes to the shelter with me. Wait until George hears what happened today! He's not going to believe it.

4:09 P.M.

When I push open the heavy doors, my black-and-gray Adidas look right at home inside the community room at Olive Branch. But I see the rollers and cans of paint sitting in a corner and know it won't be long before this place is looking more like *Hope Depot* than a people dump. I scan the room for George, and I don't see him right away, but I do see Commerce Girl sitting on a chair not reading a magazine in her lap. I go over.

"Hey," I say. "Remember me?"

She shrugs.

"Where's the town?" I ask, squatting next to her and looking around. "Do you guys keep it in a closet or something?"

She looks at me like I'm crazy. "We don't have closets," she says. After a pause, she adds, "We don't have a town anymore. That game's over."

"What do you mean? Where's George? Don't let him hear you talking like that."

She looks me full in the face and it feels like a smack. "Why don't you shut up?" she snarls. "He's not even here anymore."

"What —?" I look around some more like George is going to pop out from behind one of those big black garbage bins. "Did he go out or something?"

She sucks her teeth and gets up. "He left this morning. He took all of his stuff with him, so he's not coming back. And he gave his table to Marcus. He promised we were going to build a playhouse." She walks away, dragging her feet a little so her shoes make a hissing sound on the tiles. I look down at my sneakers, and when I look up, I see Charlie and his mom. She's nudging him, but he's not moving. It's obvious from the scowl on his face that his mood has changed since I saw him a little while ago, so I go over.

"Hey Buddy," I say.

"Hi," he says, not looking at me. His mom smiles at me and goes to talk to Wilma.

"So, um, I heard, George stepped out for a minute," I say.

"George left," Charlie says. "I came back to tell him about what happened today, when you got on the table and everything, and he's gone."

"What are you talking about? He'll be back."

"No he won't," Charlie mutters. "He took all of his stuff! And some big boys knocked down our town. And you'll probably leave too. Everybody leaves."

"Hey," I say. "Remember all we've been through together? I'm not going anywhere. We're a team."

"Yeah, sure. People always run away. And I will too, one day. I hate living here."

Okay, I don't blame him really, but I know I'm supposed to say something Big Buddy-ish. "You can't run away, Charlie. Just, um, keep your head up."

He looks me full in the face. "I *am* gonna run away. And you always leave too, to go to your house. *You* run away."

"But —" I start.

"Leave me alone!" Charlie runs to join Commerce Girl and I stand there for a minute. Wilma is marching over to a group of old ladies fighting over an overstuffed laundry bag, and I follow her.

"Hi, Wilma," I start, and then watch in awe as she swoops in and snatches the bag away from the old ladies in one smooth motion without breaking her pace.

"Yes?" she says. "Can I help you, Reggie?"

"I was looking for George. . . ."

"George isn't here," she says.

"Yeah, that's what I was wondering. I mean, do you know when he'll be back?"

Now *she* looks at me like I'm crazy. "I don't keep tabs on a grown man. I guess he'll be back when he's back." She drops the bag into a pile of similarly overstuffed bags. "Or he won't." She motions to a young woman who looks enthusiastic and out-of-place. "Charmian! I need you to start sorting these clothing donations before we have a riot up in here." Cheerful Charmian bounces over and starts opening the bags. Wilma marches away and I have to jog to keep up.

"But he didn't just leave, right?" I ask. "I mean, he was doing projects with the kids, and he told me that he was going to start a sports program here. And a tutoring program."

Wilma stops marching and looks at me like I'm still crazy, but also pathetic. "Look, hon, George is one of our more active residents. That means he does a lot to help out when he's here, and it also means that he comes and goes. I can't do much about it except pray that he's staying out of trouble and that he doesn't bring any back with him."

I think of those bloodshot eyes, and that smooth, oily voice talking about getting high, and I'm scared. "So you think he's not coming back?" I say, and I'm surprised by the panicky squeak in my voice. I clear my throat. "That little girl just said he took all of his stuff, and gave away his table. He loved that table. Maybe you should call the police or something. George is my . . ." I pause. "He's my friend."

Wilma looks at me like she's known a thousand guys like me, and she feels sorry for all of us.

I shrug. "We talked about a bunch of things. . . ." I sound so lame. I sound like someone who thought that sneakers covered in Dora the Explorer stickers had superpowers. I sound like someone who was too much of a punk to keep those shoes on.

Wilma looks over my head; I turn and see a couple of kids doing some obviously fake but ferocious-looking martial arts moves. I'd told George that maybe Joe C. could teach karate here. The kids must feel Wilma's eyes on them; they stop and wander away. She starts sorting through a box of dirty clothes. A couple of T-shirts are torn and there's a red dress with a huge blue stain in front.

"Uh, do you want me to put those in the trash?" I ask. Maybe if I do some work she'll take this George situation a little more seriously.

"Trash?" she murmurs, not looking at me. "These are donations that just came in today."

"But . . ." I point. "They're kind of . . . *old*." Did people really send this crap for Olive Branchers to wear? Would I have sent "the homeless" some old, broken-down gear before I started coming here?

Wilma shrugs, but I notice that she takes a few of the really jacked-up shirts and the stained dress and puts them to the side. I just keep standing there while she sorts. The bad pile gets bigger. She turns, looking a little surprised to see me.

"Oh, I forgot — here's that list you started." She walks to her desk and returns with some pages that she hands to me. "It got longer. Old Crump is all fired up and he wants to do some kind of apprenticeship program; can you see about getting tools donated? Oh — and I never knew this, but Nancy over there was an actress. She thinks an acting class for the kids would be fun."

I fold the pages up and shove them into my backpack. The wish list. All of those big plans. How am I going to pull that off without George? Why did I think I could pull *anything* off? I'm not ready for this.

Wilma reaches out and rubs my head a little, but it's like she does it for emphasis. "Hon," she murmurs, "you gotta understand that these people are struggling. Even the ones like George —

especially the ones like George, who help out a lot and got a lot going for them. They got a lot against them too." She pats me on the shoulder. "Sometimes, it's mostly themselves. But it's real. There's not too much we can do." She pats me again and calls out, "Charmian, after you finish with those, I need you to come and help me set up for dinner."

I've been dismissed.

Wilma is a fraud. She looks and sounds like she's all about getting things done, but when it comes to a real person, she's just giving up. I'm not going to give up. I'm going to do something. I look at Charlie, and even though he can't hear me, I whisper, "I'm not running away. I'm coming back, and I'm bringing George with me."

4:46 P.M.

Dave is pulling books from the church library shelves. He jumps a little when I knock.

"Reggie! Come on in, I wasn't expecting anyone."

"Is the library closed?" I ask, looking around.

"No. But you know how it is — I wasn't expecting anyone." We both chuckle — nobody ever comes here besides Dave. I drop down on a couch and cough when the dust rises.

"We gotta do something," I say. "George is gone."

"Huh?" asks Dave. "Who's George?"

"George. The guy who was my Listening Ears partner. I just went by the shelter and he's gone."

"Oh," Dave says, rubbing his head and yawning. Another sign

of the apocalypse — Dave doesn't get tired. "Did you talk to Wilma?"

"Yeah," I say. "She was all, 'He's a grown man, just pray, blah blah blah.' That's why I'm here. You've got to do something."

Dave raises his eyebrows. "Like what?"

I shrug. "I don't know. . . . Find him, make sure he's okay. Take him to rehab or something. I don't know." Why is he asking me?

Dave sits down in a chair next to the couch. More dust flies. "Reggie, it's not such an easy thing to track down a chronically homeless man on the streets of New York. And Wilma's right — he's a grown man. We can't be responsible for him."

"What about all that 'He ain't heavy, he's my brother' stuff you always say?" I ask. "Doing for the 'least of these'?" I can't believe Dave hasn't already rushed out to start looking.

He sighs and looks down at the patchy carpet. "Reggie, I've got a lot going on here. I'm glad that you're concerned, though. Why don't you go look for him?"

"Me?" I ask. "Come on, Dave. I can't —" I stop.

"Can't what?" asks Dave, sounding more like the Dave I know, ready to pounce on me with a couple of verses. "You sound like you think something needs to be done." He stands and starts pulling books down again.

"Yeah, I do," I say. "That's why I'm here. I thought you'd agree."

"So, if you think that looking for George is the thing to do, then why don't you go ahead? You don't need me for that."

"Thanks for the support," I say. "Thanks a lot."

Dave stops messing with the books and looks at me. "Reggie," he says, "I'm glad you want to help. I applaud your passion. But you don't need my seal of approval. You don't need me to help you do what *you* think needs to be done."

"I don't know what needs to be done!" He opens his mouth, but I go on. "I know you're gonna say 'All I need is God,' and yeah, I get that . . . but I have no idea what I'm doing here." And suddenly I'm not talking just about George but about life. "I'm the guy just trying to get through the day without" — I can't talk to him about the Pukey stuff — "falling on my face."

"What's wrong with falling on your face?" asks Dave. Then he looks me right in the eye. "Again?"

We have one of those I-know-that-you-know-that-I-know moments, and if it was anyone but Dave, it would be excruciating. But I'm kind of relieved. I should tell him about the lunchroom today, but it's George who's the main character right now.

"Where do you think he is?" I ask, looking at the mangy rug. "Maybe he got a job — he's almost an engineer, you know — maybe he found a place and everything . . ."

"Maybe," says Dave.

"He was really into that project he was doing with the kids; he wouldn't just leave them hanging." I'm talking fast now. "He was talking about a whole after-school program. I was going to help out, and get some of my friends to do it too."

"You could still do the after-school program," says Dave. "That would be a good project for Clarke. I'm on the Board of Advisors there, you know."

"You are? I didn't know we had a Board of Advisors," I say. "What do you guys do?"

"Well, I'm going to be a chaperone at that Holiday Jam you have coming up. . . . Got your date lined up?"

"I'm working on it," I mutter. "Go on."

"There are two hundred and thirty-seven of us advisors, including the governor. Not a whole lot gets done."

"That's the thing about Clarke," I say. "I know it's corny, but all of that stuff we're supposed to be about, civic responsibility and community service? I wish it were for real." Standing on the cafeteria table and announcing my candidacy feels like a dream now.

"Reggie," says Dave, sounding impatient again, "you do a lot of wishing and dreaming and hoping. That's all well and good, but you've got to get past that. You know, 'faith without works is dead.' James 2:20."

"I want to have faith. But I'm not like you."

Dave gets up again. "I've got two words for you: mustard seed." When I just look at him, he adds, "I know you'll get it. Hit the Book."

Yeah, yeah. He stacks books in boxes while I sit there for a few minutes. I look around; the room's looking pretty sparse.

"What's with the cleanup?" I ask. "Is the bishop coming to review the youth group again?"

Dave doesn't say anything for a minute. He doesn't look at me either.

"Hello?" I say.

"Remember when I said that I had an announcement?" Dave starts. "I was planning to tell the whole group at our last meeting, but . . ." He sighs. "I'm leaving."

"Huh?"

"I'm moving. I've taken a teaching job in Jersey. It's full-time. I won't be able to do the youth group anymore."

"What are you talking about?" I stand up. "You're just messing with me, right?" I force a laugh. "The Jersey reference was a little over the top." Dave always tells us that he's been in Brooklyn so long, he went to Dodgers games.

"South Orange," he says without smiling. "You're looking at Columbia High School's newest English teacher. I'll start in January." Then he does look at me and smiles a little. "I'm going to miss you guys. But I'm looking forward to this. I've always wanted to teach English."

I can't believe this. I don't believe this. "You're abandoning us?"

"I'm not 'abandoning' anyone," Dave starts, but it's sinking in and I'm getting mad.

"What, deserting, then? Is that better? Let's get to the 'meat of the sammich,' Dave. Isn't that the way you like to roll?"

"I like to be honest, and I like to be real," he says, and there's no apology in his voice. "I've enjoyed working with you guys, and I've been inspired. But I'm ready to challenge myself in a new way. I've always wanted to teach — that's what I studied in grad school. And I need to make more money."

"What happened to 'seek ye first His kingdom and his righteousness'?" I ask, and my tone is so nasty that I don't recognize my voice. "Or don't you practice what you preach?"

"I try not to preach," says Dave with a sigh. "Maybe I'm not always successful. But I'm a human being, Reggie, not your guardian angel. And I believe I can serve wherever I am."

I don't know what to say. So I just leave. At least this way, I'm doing it first.

5:39 P.M.

The BBC News is playing on the kitchen radio when I get home. I don't want to get any more depressed, so I try to run upstairs without seeing Pops. The creaky step betrays me.

"Reggie?" he calls. "I've been waiting for you. Come in here."

I drag myself into the kitchen. He's standing over the stove. "Can you run to the store and get some sugar? I need it for the meat sauce."

"Can't we just do without it?" I ask. "I just got home, and it's been a long day."

"Excuse me, Mr. Eighth-grade High-Powered Executive," he says. "I didn't realize that you had it so tough."

"You never do," I say without thinking. Oops.

Pops stirs his meat sauce, and then points to the five-dollar bill on the counter. I sigh, grab it, and head back out.

I skip the fancy new organic market because I'm not in the mood to be followed around by the woman who thinks I'm going to steal her jars of imported whatever. I go to Ralph's Bodega and grab a box of sugar and a bag of plantain chips for myself, along with the *Brooklyn Courier* and *Our Time Press*, the free papers that keep my parents grumbling over the State of Black America. When I get back, I drop the sugar on the counter and start to head to my room. I figure he's going to send me there anyway.

"There's a salad to make," says Pops without looking at me. There's a smart answer on the tip of my tongue, but I swallow it and get the lettuce out of the fridge and start washing it. Pops and I work in silence for a while.

"So tell me about your long day," he says. I look at him, and he nods. "Go on. I'm interested."

I don't really want to talk to Pops about it, but I know I'm skating on thin ice.

"Well, um, you know that project we've been doing with Dave? The homeless shelter thing?"

"Listening Ears, right?" he says, nodding. I'm surprised he remembers the name.

"So, the guy who was my partner —"

"George," says Pops.

"Yeah, George. He's gone. Like, really gone. I went there today to tell him — something that happened and he was gone. Nobody knows where he is."

"Couldn't that be a good thing?" asks Pops. "Maybe he's gotten on his feet. You said he was a pretty together guy."

I did? I don't even remember talking to Pops about George.

"I happened to hear you and Dave talking at church the other day. I wasn't eavesdropping," he adds quickly. "I was there already."

Pops on the defensive! That's a first. "Yeah, maybe," I say slowly. "But . . . I don't know. . . ." I don't want to tell Pops why I'm scared. I don't want him to judge George. Or call me a fool for believing in him in the first place.

"But what?" he asks. "You're worried that he's not okay?"

I nod slowly. I can feel him looking at me, so I raise my head. "Is he involved with drugs?" he asks.

I just shrug, which I know he hates. He lowers the flame under the meat sauce and sits at the table.

"What does this" — he shrugs — "mean?"

I know I'm pushing it, so I look up. "Yeah. He used to be on drugs. But he's clean now, and anyway it wasn't his fault, he was under a lot of pressure. . . . He had a tough life," I finish. My voice sounds thin and squeaky and I hate it.

"Many of us have tough lives and are able to refrain from drug use," Judge Pops begins, but then he adds, "And many aren't. And we cannot judge either way. Addiction is a complicated thing."

I'm shocked, and I don't even bother to hide it.

"You thought that I would say something else?" He smiles. "*You* judge *me*, Reggie. I thought you'd know better than that."

"You always think I should be better than something. Why can't you just let me be me? Just leave me alone and get a job!" My words shatter in the air.

His voice gets hard and his accent gets stronger. "And who exactly are you to talk to me like that?"

I open my mouth but nothing comes out. What finally does is a whisper. "I don't know. . . . Nobody, I guess." I'm ready to send myself to my room. "Can I go now?"

Pops nods. I start to leave, and then he says:

"Reginald Garvey McKnight. Sit down."

He used my whole name. I sit down at the table. I am a jerk. It's so quiet, I think that I can hear the minutes go by on the microwave clock. Pops sags a little in his chair.

"Pops." He doesn't look at me. "Pops, I'm sorry. I'm really sorry. I didn't mean it."

He nods, and it looks like that's all I'm going to get. I wish he'd sit up straighter. I don't know what else to do, so I just keep talking.

"I got all involved with this thing George was doing, working with little kids . . . and now he just leaves." I take a breath. "And then I go to Dave for help, and he tells me he's leaving too."

"Dave's leaving?" Pops looks up.

"Yeah. He's gonna be a teacher. In *Jersey.*" I spit the word "Jersey" out and Pops smiles a little. "And I know you've been looking for a job, I don't know why I said that. . . ."

"You're feeling abandoned," Pops says, sitting up. I shrug again, and he lets it go. "It's been a stressful time around here," he says slowly. "Lord knows it's been hard for all of us. I never expected to be out of work for this long, and I will tell you the truth —" He pauses and looks right in my eyes. "I'm ashamed."

I broke Pops. I hate myself. "Pops," I start, and I don't care that my voice is shaky, but he puts his hand up.

"I know you're at an age when you're going through some things that we should probably talk about."

Please don't say sex. Please don't say sex.

"Like sex," he says, and for a minute I think that I really am melting into the floor, but he's looking over his glasses at me with a question in his eyes.

"Huh?" I shift in my chair. "Come on, Pops. Of course not."

"Just checking," he says. He picks up the lettuce and starts shredding it. "I don't tell you enough how proud I am of you."

He looks at me. "Or should I say that I don't tell you at all." He goes back to shredding. "You are a responsible young man — doing that Big Buddy project, working with the youth group, studying hard. . . . I tell you, you are way ahead of me when I was your age."

"What?" I make a face. "You were that Head Guy thing. You had the respect of your peers."

Now he makes a face. "I cared too much about being popular. I didn't even like football. And I was so busy trying to be everyone's buddy that I wasn't a friend to myself."

That sounds like something Ruthie would say. Or maybe she's actually said it.

"And when the chips were down, I didn't have a real friend to speak of." He sighs. "It was a hard lesson to learn, but I will always be glad that I did, especially after what happened at the job."

"Uh, what *did* happen, Pops?" I ask.

He sighs again. "Nothing I can prove in a court of law, as I was told. I witnessed discrimination over and over. . . . Young, qualified brothers who got passed over because they weren't members of this unofficial 'club.' I was 'in,' you know, because being Jamaican made me 'different.' But when I couldn't let it go any longer without asking questions, my membership card was revoked."

"Wait, how can you get fired like that? That's not fair."

"Life is not fair, Reggie. Layoffs had to happen, and since certain people weren't 'comfortable' with me anymore, I was first on the chopping block. I don't regret what I did, though. It's not been easy, but I would stand up and speak out again."

"Did anything change? Did any of those guys get promotions or anything?"

"I don't know," he answers.

Pops clams up. We sit together for a while as he shreds the lettuce.

"So, you want to go out and look for your friend together?" he asks.

I'm glad I don't have a heart condition, because I'd be stone-cold dead with all of the surprises hitting me today. "Uh — you serious?"

Pops shrugs.

I think about it. "I guess it doesn't make sense, does it? I wouldn't even know where to start." I shred a few pieces of lettuce myself. "But I don't want to do nothing, you know? And those kids — if you had seen how excited they were, happy, even in the middle of that dingy place. And today, the bossy one was all defeated. . . . George was helping them forget where they were, and I was helping. I was even forgetting who *I* was."

"Maybe you were being who you really are," says Pops, standing up. "You know, I left a book in here for you the other day. Did you see it? Black poets. Powerful stuff. It really affected me when I was your age, and I see you with this notebook all of the time, so I just thought . . ." He looks at me. "Did you get it?"

I want to lie, but I don't. "Yeah, I did. But, um, I didn't read it yet. Ruthie told me that it's really good, though."

"Smart girl," is all he says, but I know he's disappointed.

"Pops," I start, remembering something George said once. "Who's Samuel Sharpe?"

"Daddy Sharpe!" he says, grinning. "Maybe they *are* teaching you something at that school." He shuts off the stove and starts to clean up all of the shredded lettuce, and I think that father-son time is over, but he laughs. "Looks like we need another head of lettuce," he says. "You want to go? We can stop by the shelter, see if George came back. I'll tell you about Samuel Sharpe. An educated man, a deacon, and a leader of a slave rebellion — one of Jamaica's bravest."

"Sure," I say, starting to get up.

"Wait, let me go get my shoes," he says. "And you can tell me a little more of what's been going on. How's school? And what's happening with that new image you were going for?"

I have to laugh. "Let me go get MY shoes," I say. "And I'll tell you."

George hasn't returned to Olive Branch. No one's seen him either, or they're not saying. Pops and I walk around the neighborhood for a while, grabbing some Yummy Taco on the way as a snack; we don't see George, and I'm glad about that. Because if we see him on the street, I'm thinking it wouldn't be good.

By the time we get home, I'm exhausted. In one day, I've announced my presidential candidacy, lost two people who were a big part of the reason for the announcement, and — biggest shocker of all — had a real conversation with my dad. We eat a fast dinner and I go to bed without taking off my clothes or my shoes or worrying about this whole election thing. I just sleep.

NOVEMBER 23
7:16 A.M.

When I wake up, it's late and I want to squeeze my eyes shut and clamp my hands over my ears, but then I see a Post-it stuck to my Dora sneakers. I stumble out of bed to check it out. It's from Mom — a heart-shaped smiley face. It's corny, but I smile and it gets me going. When I go downstairs to say thank you, Mom's already gone. Pops is out, and I guess Monica left without bothering to wake me up. I run back upstairs and get Mom's Post-it. I fold it carefully and put it in my pocket, and I grab the Dora shoes and put them in a bag. Then I run all the way to school.

Sparrow Barrow is blocking my locker and has a microphone in front of Ruthie's face. This can't be good. I speed up and get close enough to hear Ruthie speak.

". . . Just think of him as 'Dark McKnight'!" she's saying. "You know, like the Superman comic books."

We are not friends.

"She means Batman," says Joe C., who's trying to stay off camera. It doesn't matter; Vijay's obviously got the camera locked on Ruthie. He smirks. Then they all notice me.

"Hey, Puke — um . . ." says Sparrow.

"It's Reggie. Reginald Garvey McKnight, and don't you forget it," says Ruthie so loud I'm sure people in Jersey can hear. I glare at her and try to catch my breath.

"Sorry, Reggie. We're taping for *Candidates Get Real*, the election reality show, giving the people a chance to see who the candidates really are behind the scenes. We've been taping for a while, and we'll air a couple of specials next week."

"Why didn't I know about this before?" I ask. "I was a candidate's campaign manager."

"We've got hours of Justin on camera. We only started covering Vicky yesterday, after your dramatic lunchroom betrayal designed to brutally undercut her hard-fought journey."

"Sounds like I'm already being misrepresented by the media," I say.

"Exactly! This is a chance to show us who you truly are! That's the beauty of reality television!" Sparrow chirps. Ruthie sighs and rolls her eyes.

"Justin and Vicky are already on board," says Vijay. "It would be, like, kind of bad if you don't participate."

"Justin's poll numbers are setting a record," says Sparrow. "And Vicky is dying a slow painful death, and it's great to have it all on camera. So, what's up? Are you gonna do it?"

I look at Joe C., who shrugs. "We just found out about this," he says.

I turn to Sparrow. "Uh, I don't even know if I'm really running, actually," I say. "The whole thing might be kind of a mistake. . . ."

"You don't have to do the show if you don't want to, but . . ." Sparrow trails off so it sounds like a chirpy threat.

"But if you don't, you'll look like a punk," says Vijay.

"Punky McKnight," says Sparrow, giggling.

I can't let them do this to me. "Okay, I'll do the show," I say too loudly. "Start rolling, or 'action,' or whatever you guys say."

"We're already taping," says Sparrow.

Ruthie grabs me. "This is stupid, Reggie, let's —"

"Shut up, Ruthie," I say.

Sparrow turns to me. "So, Pu — Reggie, why do you think you should be president?"

I clear my throat and try to stand up straight. "Well, I —"

Faintly familiar music blasts behind me. Real heavy bass and a thumping beat. My locker pops open. I turn around and it's the Justin Party Train again. Running out of ideas, Donovan? They can't possibly fall for this reheated crap.

"JW's house!" yells Donovan. "Join us at Justin's place after school for a rally — free food, good music, and prizes! Become a part of Justin's crew and learn more about Justin's plan for a new, feel-good Clarke! Say *no* to outdated letter grades and useless testing! Say *yes* to Justin!"

The chorus of "Woo hoos!" is so loud that I feel like I've been punched. Justin cuts off the music and Donovan starts handing out PayDay candy bars. But he just pushes past me and my friends, which makes Joe C. drop an open Juiced! bottle on Ruthie's foot. Ruthie squeals in pain. The Juiced! makes a little puddle on the floor.

Blaylock comes out of his office. "Justin, can I speak to you for a moment?" For a second, I think that FOR ONCE Justin is going to get in trouble, but Blaylock actually hugs Justin as he ushers him into his office. Donovan tries to slip in behind them, but Blaylock brushes him off.

Donovan looks over at me and nods. "What's up, Pukey? Good luck trying to hang with the big dogs." He tries to stroll off, but his shoulders are so slumped that they remind me to stand up straight.

"Let's wait here," Sparrow says to Vijay. "We can talk to Justin after he comes out. What a campaigner! Um, later . . . Reggie," she says, glancing at me. "We got enough of you for now, we'll get more tomorrow."

"I didn't even say anything," I mutter, but they're crossing over to the other side of the hall and don't hear me. I slam my locker shut, but it pops open again and everything falls out.

"They're just going to make you look stupid and Justin look cool," says Ruthie. "The whole reality-show thing is a waste of time. We should focus on the issues that kids care about."

"They couldn't make me look any worse than *you* did," I say, grabbing my papers and books. I throw a bunch of stuff into my backpack without looking and close my locker carefully.

"First of all," says Ruthie, "you're the one who was all up in the middle of the cafeteria yelling about being an agent of positive change. Second of all, we got here early to meet you and you didn't show up. Third of all, if this is the kind of candidate you're going to be, then I don't want to be your campaign manager anyway!" She hits my locker and it pops open and everything falls out again.

Joe C. holds up his hand like a ref. "Hey, hey . . . Let's all have a drink and calm down." He opens up a bottle of Juiced! and reads the cap. "Did you guys know that no word in the English language rhymes with month?"

Ruthie and I both stare at him. Then we all start laughing.

"Now I'm going to spend the rest of my life trying to prove that one wrong," gasps Ruthie. "Like the one where you said it's impossible to lick your elbow." She tries to lick her elbow. "See?"

"Not only do you remember them," I say, "you're doing them. Don't let him get you, Ruthie! Must. Resist. The Juiced!!"

"She's just living the dream," says Joe C. We laugh again. "You've gotta admit, that beat Justin uses is pretty sweet. From a purely professional point of view," he adds quickly.

"I think his whole thing is style without substance," says Ruthie. She looks at her watch. "Okay, it's really late. Class starts in two minutes, and I have to stop at the library. Tell Ms. A I'll be there soon." She looks at me. "Maybe the Dark McKnight thing was a little too much, okay? Friends?"

"Yeah," I say. "Friends." My smile is almost real. "I'm sorry I was late; I overslept. And I'm sorry I told you to shut up. I do want to have a meeting, though, somewhere kind of private. Any ideas?"

"I've got a rapport with Cutler; we talk union sometimes. I'll see if we can get into his office for a few minutes," says Ruthie.

"And one more thing," I say. "I never, ever called myself an 'agent of positive change.'" Ruthie hugs me and runs down the hall, her jacket flapping around her waist.

"She runs like a girl," says Joe C. He helps me restuff my

locker, and we start walking down the empty hall together. "We are so late for Ms. A."

"Forget Ms. A, what about me? What was I thinking, taking on Justin?"

"Calm down, we'll come up with something. You've got me and Ruthie behind you — what more do you need?"

I'm not sure if he's being funny or serious.

"Let's talk later," he says. "Don't count yourself out."

When we get to Ms. A's room, she doesn't seem too angry that we're late. In fact, class hasn't started yet. Vicky's eyes are red and watery; she's sniffling, but no one offers her a tissue. People are whispering and everyone turns to look at me, and my attempt to slide unobtrusively into my seat is made even more unsuccessful by the fact that I trip over Sean Glanville's backpack. Hector doesn't ask for a pen; he actually offers me one.

"Okay, everyone," says Ms. A. "Let's settle down. I know there's a lot of election talk going around today, which is a good thing for once. But we've got work to do."

She makes a little speech about how she's looking forward to a spirited, sincere campaign, may the best person win, and I swear she looks at me and winks.

10:55 A.M.

"Thanks, Mr. Cutler!" calls out Ruthie, holding open the supply closet door. Cutler holds up a lumpy muffin and grins. I don't think I've ever seen a school custodian smile before. "I gave him one of my homemade apple-broccoli muffins in exchange for ten minutes in here," she explains, ushering Joe C. and me inside. "Perfect spot for a quick top-secret strategy session."

"Ouch!" says Joe C., as he hits his head on a shelf and a lightbulb crashes to the floor. "Did you tell him it was apple-broccoli? He's probably going to lock us in."

"I said it was a delicious home-baked good, which is the truth," retorts Ruthie.

"Okay, guys, whatever . . . Look, we don't have much time," I say. "We need to figure things out."

"Speaking of which," says Joe C., looking at me, "when did I miss the whole I'm-gonna-jump-up-in-the-middle-of-the-cafeteria-and-run-for-president conversation?"

"I know it was kind of crazy," I start. "Everything happened all at once. . . . I was thinking about Acid — I mean Joelle, and Charlie, and George, and trying to help those kids, and then . . . uh, I guess I did this. I wanted things to be different. And I got tired of just wanting it."

"Exactly!" jumps in Ruthie. "It's what I've always said. Well, Gandhi too."

"I don't know about Gandhi," I say. "I just saw how even though George was homeless and struggling, he inspired those kids. And here I am, inspiring Charlie to talk about somebody's mom. And I . . . wasn't much help to Vicky."

Joe C. chuckles. "Virgin Mary's baby shower. That was a pretty good one," he says. "And I'm Catholic so I probably shouldn't laugh."

Ruthie unrolls a long sheet of paper. "I've got some talking points for you," she says, "things that will call attention to some of the real issues we have here at Clarke, such as the deplorable bias in our history books, and de facto segregation at lunchtime."

"Remember when I thought it couldn't get worse than this morning?" I say to Joe C. "I was wrong."

"Ha ha," says Ruthie. She shakes her head, but she's smiling a little. "And we've got to work on your big speech." She writes something down. "Not just the rally next week, but the one at the assembly on Election Day, in front of the whole school — that's gotta be BIG."

I stop smiling.

I forgot about the speech.

"Figures they'd have a punk like you do this."

I know without looking that the voice is Donovan's. The fake bass and genuine sneer in it are unmistakable.

I try to focus on the Pledge — the Clarke Pledge of Proactive Community Living, which we've had to say all together on every first day ever since kindergarten. The teachers pick one student to lead the Pledge at the assembly every year, and this year is my turn. My chance to be someone spectacular. That Guy. I pretend it's not so different saying the Pledge on stage in front of everyone. I haven't been up here since kindergarten, when my Frederick Douglass wig fell off in the middle of the "Every Month Is Black History Month" assembly.

Donovan makes the puking sound he does every time he sees me, but this time it reminds me of Mom's first day of school Breakfast of Champions, and not in a good way. She believes in starting the day off with a meal large enough to feed the entire Caribbean. She made me eat a boatload of oatmeal with cranberries and walnuts, a cheese omelet, then fried dumplings with two mounds of Jamaica's national dish, codfish and ackee, for "back home fortitude."

"You know you're going to mess this up."

I still don't look at him. Always a mistake to catch his eye. Just face forward and don't think about the fact that my stomach is somersaulting like a circus clown.

At least I'm not wearing a wig this time. And I don't cry in front of people anymore. (Please, God, no. Anything but tears.)

He starts laughing. "I guess you're the right choice, if they picked someone to represent WEAK. You are weak, Reginaaald. How's your voice? You know you like to squeal like a girl when you're nervous."

I clear my throat, and can taste the omelet remains in my mouth. I swallow.

Blaylock is wrapping up his big intro, and I can hear that the crowd on the other side of the curtain is restless. Everyone waits for the first day Pledge. Not because we care about it, but because the person who leads it always does something spectacular. Last year, Julie Glover used the flag as a baton and did a whole routine while she recited. The year before, Sam Chen break-danced.

It's the first day of school. Eighth grade. New me, the warrior. Night Man creator. Superhero simulator.

My plan for the Pledge? Wait, what was it again? Oh, right. I'm going to be "reporting" on Night Man's latest good deeds at Clarke — cleaning up the school yard, starting a recycling program, bringing back recess for all grades.... And then I'll quote Night Man saying the Pledge. I worked with Joe C. on some special art just for this that I'm going to show on the big screen. (Ruthie *wanted me to dress up as Night Man, but no way I could have pulled that off.) This way, I can use Night Man to finally show everyone the real me. This way, I can be That Guy. And no one will guess that I'm terrified up here.*

I swallow again, and this time, I can taste the codfish.

Blaylock says my name, but the crowd is already screaming and cheering, and it's almost loud enough to drown out the roaring in my ears.

Just before Donovan pulls the curtain, he hisses, "Good luck, Frederick Douglass. You've been making a fool of yourself since, what, kindergarten? This will bring back memories."

The curtains open and I am up on this stage, and everyone is looking at me. The cheers get louder. I take a deep breath, and I think the oatmeal is stuck in my lungs.

There are a lot of "shhh!"s and giggles, and finally, silence.

You can do this. Just make it fast and get your butt off this stage.

You can do this. People do it every year. DJ Johnson said the Pledge backward.

Don't think about wigs.

Or crying in front of the entire school.

Don't think about breakfast.

Especially not the eggs.

Or the fish.

Or fish eggs.

I open my mouth, and —

I puked up my guts on the first day of school.

I cannot get back on that stage.

Donovan sneering.
My stomach rolling. And rolling.
Overflowing. Spilling out onto the stage. All over the stage.
Splatter on Blaylock's shoes.
The silence. Then the "ewwww!"s. Then the laughter.
Cutler limping out on stage with his mop and bucket.
And the nemesis, the instigator, Donovan. Laughing the loudest of all.

I'm feeling a little dizzy. I want to sit down. Oh, wait — I am sitting down. What have I done?

I was the guy who wanted to get up in front of the whole school and show them Reggie McKnight, Night Man creator. I ended up the guy who spent the first day of eighth grade in a T-shirt with a pink and silver unicorn across the front (courtesy of the nurse's "Oops! Cabinet," since renamed "Regurgitation Station").

I cannot get back on that stage.

"Come on, Reg," says Joe C., nudging me. "Remember the cafeteria?" He looks down at my feet. "Maybe you should put on the shoes."

"Those shoes are how I got myself into this mess," I say. "What was I thinking? I'm going to make a total fool of myself. I forgot about the stupid speech! Haven't we seen that show before? No need for reruns."

"It's all going to be fine," says Ruthie. "You may think the odds are against you, but it's like a David and Goliath sort of thing." She rubs my back a little, and that feels pretty good, but I shake her off.

"Ruthie, this is my life, not some inspirational Bible story or some charity project for you to organize. It's hopeless. Justin's talking about getting rid of grades and tests. That's what stressed-out superachievers want to hear. Even *I* would vote for that. I'm not making a fool of myself, *again*, for nothing."

"The trouble with the David and Goliath analogy," muses Joe C., "is that people really *like* Justin. He's cool for real. It won't be the good little guy battling the big evil giant."

"Thanks for the comforting words," I snap. He shrugs. "It *is* like facing an evil giant, though, because I know Donovan's behind this whole thing. He just can't stand to see anything good happen for me —"

"Get over Donovan," says Ruthie. "Get over Justin. *You* can make a difference. You can do the things that kids really care about. You can make it *not* a popularity contest!"

"Thanks a lot," I say.

"You know what I mean. You talk about being Somebody. I mean, I think you already are, but this way you can show the world who Reginald Garvey McKnight really is!" Ruthie gets all worked up. It's kind of nice that she's so loyal. "And besides," she continues, tapping her mile-long list, "there are so many things we could do as president!"

"We?" I say.

Ruthie goes on. "What are the biggest problems at this school? What do we really need? You've got to show what you're about. Standing up for the meek, liberating the oppressed!"

"You want me to show what *you're* about," I reply.

"Touché," whispers Joe C., smiling.

"The thing is," I say slowly, "I don't know if I can take any more humiliation."

"Did you mean what you said before, about helping out the kids and standing up for the right thing?" Ruthie asks, folding her arms.

"You know I did," I say. "I just need people to take me seriously."

"Then take yourself seriously," she says.

"Don't go out like a sucker, because you're not," Joe C. adds. "And we're only in eighth grade. We've probably got years of humiliation ahead of us."

"That shouldn't help," I say, "but it does."

"And what are the odds —" starts Ruthie, and stops.

"— that the same thing will, uh, happen again?" finishes Joe C. "I mean, that was once in a lifetime, right?"

Ruthie and I are silent. We sit there for a few seconds, and I think of Charlie all slumped over, of eating chips with George, and bragging about standing up to Donovan. I think of the Dora shoes in my backpack, and of the days when I thought that, if I wished hard enough, I could be Night Man myself. I remember the kids who asked me about Olive Branch and take my notes from the wish list out of my pocket. "Okay. There are a lot of little kids like Charlie at Olive Branch. I don't want to let them down. There's Carmen and her library, and Old Crump with his tools . . . I know my ideas could be good for Clarke. I don't want to let George down. I'm *not* going to let any of them down. Let's do this!"

"That's what I'm talking about!" says Ruthie.

The doorknob starts rattling, hard. Joe C. and I look at Ruthie.

"Cutler must have tasted the muffin," says Joe C.

11:17 A.M.

When we get to the cafeteria, the usual cacophony stops, and a hush blankets the room. I think I really do need superpowers to withstand this kind of scrutiny. *How would Night Man handle this?* I think. Then I hear George's voice. *Be cool. Just pay attention, and be cool.*

The three of us walk to our table together. Donovan looks over and smirks. I notice a line of girls near Justin; he's handing out little pocket mirrors. As each girl comes up, he holds the mirror up to her and says, "Look who's voting for Justin." It gets a giggle every time.

"I'd like to congratulate you," says a voice. It's the LARPing kid. He's wearing a striped polo shirt and dress pants, and he has Sacagawea coins in his penny loafers.

"Who are you?" asks Joe C.

"George Henderson, at your service. Sixth grade."

I didn't realize that his name was George. Is this a sign from God?

"Hey, George," I say. "LARPing, right?" He nods. "I'm sorry I never got to a meeting. I tried to talk to Vicky about it, but . . ."

He nods again. "You don't have to say anything. Actually, I wanted to congratulate you on your candidacy."

"Our first supporter!" squeals Ruthie. "Would you like to join us?"

He slides into the seat next to me. "I'd like to sign on to your campaign. I've got an original perspective, and I am well versed in the art of the teen movie turnaround and happy ending."

"Huh?" says Joe C.

"It's about image," continues George Henderson. "It doesn't matter what you say, or what you mean, it's all about perception."

"I guess," I say, a little dazed. "But that sounds kind of . . . phony."

"It's the drama, the story," continues George. "Creating a compelling narrative. I know about those things."

I have an idea. "Hey, George, you know the Olive Branch shelter that I talked about?" He nods. "Would you be interested in teaching people about LARPing there? Maybe get a club or something going?" "Drama club" was on the wish list, and this seems pretty close.

He grins. "Sounds interesting — I've got a costume collection like you wouldn't believe." He gives me a business card. A business card! "Text me. We'll talk image." He slides out and walks away.

"That was weird," says Joe C. "And I think I believe the costume collection."

"He had a point, sort of," I say. "Image counts." I look over at Justin's never-ending line of ladies. "I do need people to see that I'm more than just Pukey. And more than 'not Pukey.'"

"Let's finish eating; the bell's gonna ring soon," says Joe C.

We eat and pretend not to watch the crowd at Justin's table. Vicky Ross walks by and glares at me. Vijay's getting the whole scene on tape.

"I wonder how the *Talkin' Trash* segment is going to turn out," I say. "They didn't tape me that much."

"That's a good thing," says Ruthie.

"Yeah," says Joe C. "They didn't tape that much. How bad can it be?"

NOVEMBER 24
8:09 A.M.

Very, very bad, actually. Even though we're just counting the minutes until Thanksgiving weekend starts, when *Talkin' Trash* starts up the next day, people actually watch. There are clips of Justin tossing a football and kicking a soccer ball around with some kindergarteners. (A bunch of girls go *"awwww."* Even Ruthie, the traitor.) There's Justin saying how he wants to make the school a better place for all students — it all sounds like Blaylock was his speechwriter — and then the *We Love Justin Show* ends with the whole Pied DJ scene, and Donovan making a big *V* for *victory* as they all dance out the door.

They flash a still image of Vicky, and that's it. She gets all huffy, but everyone shushes her so that we can watch the rest. The rest is me. Sparrow's intro is, "We all know him as 'Pukey.'" Then there's a sound effect of (what else?) someone throwing up. She goes on to say, "Our team is working really hard on getting more details of his campaign out to you ASAP, so more on that later." (Lots of giggles.) "And I'm really sure things'll really heat up as the campaign really gets underway."

How many times can she say "really"? I want to slide under my desk but I keep watching my very own train wreck. There's a clip of me and Ruthie arguing with Joe C. behind us reading a bottle cap. Then there's a long shot of the puddle that Joe C.'s broken Juiced! bottle made under my feet. Sean loud-whispers, "Did he wet his pants?"

"No Pukers for President!" is the first thing I hear after the bell rings to end homeroom. I don't even have to look to know it's Donovan. At least almost everyone else looks away as they laugh at me. Ruthie has her sympathetic face on and I can't stand it, so I just give her and Joe C. a quick wave and head out the door.

"No Pukers for President!" has already caught on by the time I get to my locker. Donovan says it over and over, and a few other kids like Sean Glanville join in. I keep my head down and my books up and pretend I don't hear anything.

George Henderson waves as I walk past his locker.

"Anytime you want to talk . . ." he says.

I nod. I don't want to talk to anyone now. I want to go underground. Maybe that's where George is, and maybe he has the right idea.

4:32 P.M.

After school, I stop by the Olive Branch for a little while, and playing trains with Charlie puts me in a better mood. Jeff is almost done with the mural design, and, no lie, it's going to be a masterpiece. I help peel potatoes for tomorrow's Thanksgiving meal, and Gabriella collects all of the peels for the composting thing she's doing.

When I get home, at first I think I'm the only one there, but when I walk by Monica's door, I hear these funny sounds like a dying animal. I pause; I can ignore the scary sounds and retreat to my room and lock the door, which is what I really, really want to do. Or, I can risk life and limb and investigate.

Hmmmm.

I knock on the door.

"Go away!" roars Monica, which should be enough, but I crack open the door. "Come in if you want to die."

"Look," I start, "I'm not trying to be all up in your business, but I heard noises, and —" I look at her. She's lying facedown on her bed. There's no dying animal in sight. So were the sounds . . . crying?

"Um, are you okay?" I ask, stepping into the room. I can't remember the last time I was in here.

"Get out," she mutters without looking up, and now I know she's been crying. Because she cries some more.

I don't know what to do, so I pick up the box of tissues on her desk and hand it to her. Then I sit on the edge of the bed. She stops and glares at me, so I slide to the floor. I just sit and look around while she winds down to sniffling. For reasons I don't have to go into, I don't spend much time in her bedroom. It's kind of neat, which surprises me. She used to have all of her science stuff around — a microscope, this plastic model of the human body where you could take out all the organs and stuff (and hide them in your little brother's cereal), and her at-home science lab. That's still sitting on her desk, though it looks pretty dusty. I can see a basketball on her closet floor, and I'm surprised to see that she still has her NBA All-Star poster up too. Her computer is on; it's at a website called "DOES HE WANT YOU . . . TO GO AWAY?"

Finally, she sits up. "So you can gloat," she says, looking in the mirror. Her makeup is streaked and all over her face in black and red smudges.

"What are you talking about?" I ask. But then I think I know. "You didn't get the part, did you?"

"Yeah, so ha ha, it's so funny that I was stupid enough to try out," she snarls. "You might as well laugh now, because I'll get the last laugh someday."

I sigh. "Monica, listen — I'm sorry about what I said, and I'm sorry about the tryouts. I didn't realize how much you wanted to be in the play."

"I'm in the play," she says and then she starts sniffling again.

"Oh!" I'm confused. "Well, that's good, right?" Unless . . . "You didn't get cast as the Walter Lee guy, did you?"

She looks up, and I'm glad there are no bricks nearby because I can see her arm twitch like she wants to throw something. "No, you brain-dead social slug, I didn't." Then she sniffs again. "But actually, maybe it's worse."

"Huh?"

"I got the part of Mama, okay? I'm the mother."

Monica's the star? My sister Monica?

"But . . . I mean, Monica, that's the lead! I mean, Mama is like the rug holding the room together! That's a big deal! Ruthie is going to be so happy for you!"

"You're so stupid. I don't want to be Mama. I don't want to be the big fat old lady in a housedress and a wig!"

I can see her point. And I start to get what Ruthie was talking about. "But . . . I mean, I guess it's not glamorous, but —"

"Of course it's not glamorous!" she says, rubbing her smeary face with paper towels. "Why would anyone ever think of me as glamorous? I'm just . . . oh, forget it. Why am I talking to you?" She falls back on the bed in a pretty dramatic way. I guess she *is* good.

"Because I'm here," I say after a minute. "And I'll listen. I promise. How about a truce? No name-calling, no fighting . . . what do you have to lose?"

Silence. I sit, trying not to look like I'm afraid she might jump up and tackle me. After a few minutes she slides down on the floor next to me.

"Whatever. I might as well talk to my stupid —" I look at her. "My baby brother. I don't have any friends anyway."

"What do you mean?"

"Tatia got the part of Ruth. I heard her and Renee laughing about the fact that I tried out for it in the first place."

"Why do you hang out with them if they're like that?"

She rolls her eyes and looks at me. "You wouldn't understand. You've got your little BFF-pinky-swear crew that sticks by you no matter what."

"Well, you've got . . . um," I trail off. She makes a face.

"Exactly. Thanks for the pep talk, I feel so much better now. Next you'll tell me Jesus loves me just the way I am, but He loves me too much to let me stay that way." She snorts.

"Or that you're too blessed to be stressed," I say without thinking, remembering another of Reverend Coles's favorite sayings.

"Or in my hour of need I've got His power indeed," Monica adds, and this time the snort almost turns into a chuckle.

"If you're looking for a Boss, just look to the Cross."

"If you've got pain and strife, try living the Spirit-filled life," she adds.

"Or, there ain't no flava like that of the Save-yah!" I say, laughing, but then she glares at me; I'm still the Enemy.

I sigh. "Monica, I'm sorry about the play. I know you're disappointed, but you really are the star. That means you must have been good." I think a little. "And what about Asha? She's cool, 'even if she's a Trini.' You guys seemed like pretty good friends before you started hanging out with the video girls."

Monica shrugs. "Nothing against Asha. I just wanted . . . I cannot believe I'm telling you this, and if you say one word to anybody I will tear your limbs off and stuff them down the toilet — I just wanted people to see me in a different way this year. I'm tired of being just the baller, the big girl . . ."

"The bully?" I volunteer. "The brute?" She does punch me in the arm this time, but not as hard as usual.

"Very funny. Joke all you want. It is a big joke, me trying to be something else. Those cheerleaders laughed at me, and I bet all of those drama-club people are cracking up right now." She gets up and literally shakes it off. "Whatever." She looks at her wall calendar and mutters, "I heard there's gonna be a step team next year. I'm gonna try out for that."

She puts some white stuff on her face and wipes the last of the makeup off. When she turns around, she looks really young, and I remember the time that I lost Mr. Tiddley Pom, my stuffed octopus, and she went out in the rain to find him. Of course, she was the one who'd buried him in the park in the first place, but I remember how sorry she was and how she hugged me after she brought him back.

"That's what I admire about you, Monica," I blurt out. "You're amazing."

"What are you talking about, SuperGee — I mean, uh, yeah. Huh?"

"You're not afraid to try things, to take action. You're all fearless."

"Don't be an idiot," she says, quickly adding, "And *idiot* doesn't count there." I let it go.

"I'm serious," I say. Then I tell one of those lies that I figure God has to forgive, if He's anything like I think He is. "You totally inspired me to do something a couple days ago that I would never have had the guts to do if it weren't for you."

She turns around and looks at me. "Get out. What are you talking about?"

"Well, I got up on a table in the middle of the cafeteria and announced that I was running for president. That I wanted to do something big for a change."

"Humph," she says, shrugging a little. "Big deal. I thought you were going to say you did something like . . . like . . . I don't know, something major."

"Come on, Monica, this is me. It *is* major! I've been trying to be invisible at school ever since . . . the beginning of the year. But, um, when I saw how you were going all out and trying new things, it got me thinking that . . . that instead of trying to be invisible, I should start taking some risks." And even though I'm totally lying, it kind of clicks, and it becomes true.

"Yeah, well, a lot of good it did me," she mutters, turning back to her mirror. "My so-called friends are cheerleaders and I'm not, I get to play a fat old lady in front of the whole school . . . My image has gone from bad to worse."

"Come on, Monica," I say. "Did you really want to be a cheerleader?" Then I take my biggest risk yet. "Or did you just want to get next to John Wilkins?" I brace myself; this could get ugly.

She doesn't say anything for a minute. Then she shrugs. "The cheerleading thing, whatever. It's just that those girls get looked at a certain way. I mean, I'm not down to hang on the fence and watch the guys play ball all afternoon the way they do, but . . ." She trails off, then she sighs. "I can't talk about this. Not with you." I wait for a minute, but she's clammed up.

"Okay," I say. "Just listen. You got the lead role in the school play. And you and John seem to get along all right."

She whirls around and jabs a comb at me. "You're the fool talking about John Wilkins. I never said anything about him."

I let *fool* go, and continue. "And will you just play ball with Pops again? He's pathetic, dragging around the house with that ball under his arm. I think working out with you helped him feel better about this whole job thing."

She comes over and sits on the floor next to me. "It's been a long time for him, with no job," she says in a low voice. "Are you scared?"

"Yeah," I say. "Are you?"

"I wish they would talk to us about it, and stop having not-so-secret conversations. We're not babies."

"Sometimes I wish we were," I say. "Or at least little kids, so we could be clueless about all the bad stuff."

"You're still clueless," she says, but it's so halfhearted it's almost a compliment.

"Whatever," I say. "Just don't cry anymore. I thought you'd killed something in here." She grabs a pillow and pretends to smother me. Then it's a little awkward, and neither of us says anything. I'm a little out of breath anyway.

"Why are you in my room?" she says suddenly. "Get out of here!" But she's giggling, and then I'm laughing; I leave with a smile on my face, and a conversation with my sister put it there.

NOVEMBER 27
10:17 A.M.

When I get to the Olive Branch, Jeff and Gabriella are already there. I don't say a word when I see the "Hope Depot" banner behind Wilma's desk. The old Jeff might have said something stupid about being an Olive Branch "resident" with all of the time we spend at this place, but I think all of us are just grateful for the way that the actual residents make us feel at home. I look at Wilma, and she knows without saying anything that I'm wondering about George, and she shakes her head.

"Check this out, Reggie," calls Carmen. "We've gotten a lot of new books; we need to get organized like a real library. Can you round up some volunteers?" She and Gabriella are all geeked out about the cataloging system they developed. I compliment them on it; Jeff comes over.

"Yeah, we want to get started on the painting too," he says. "We need the whole youth group on board, but that might not even be enough. I want to start making a work schedule, so let me know how many we'll have. We'll start on these walls first, and then hit up the mural."

"Sure, yeah . . . I'll get on it," I say. And I know just where to find some volunteers. The candidate kid is back.

1:34 P.M.

At home, after lunch, I work on trying to put Reggie McKnight, Presidential Candidate, together. I've turned in Blaylock's confusing candidate forms and need to go over Ruthie's list of ideas and my notes from my Vicky campaign days. Just thinking about that big rally makes me tired, so I lie down with Pops's poetry book for a while. I'm going to hang Gwendolyn Brooks's "Speech to the Young: Speech to the Progress-Toward" up on my wall.

> Say to them,
> say to the down-keepers,
> the sun-slappers,
> the self-soilers,
> the harmony-hushers,
> "even if you are not ready for day,
> it cannot always be night."

I shut the book and go back to my desk and campaign folder. It's time to work.

NOVEMBER 30
8:47 A.M.

"Hey, um, got a pen?" Hector sounds almost embarrassed, and I realize that even though Donovan's been relentless with the "No Pukers for President" thing, it's not catching on like it would have a couple of weeks ago. Even Hector hasn't joined in, though I still have to keep up a steady supply of ballpoints. I hand one over.

"Thanks," he says. "Pull my finger."

A *Talkin' Trash* "Justin Is King" episode airs, where he seems like a prophet, a pro athlete, and a scholar all rolled into one girl-friendly, man's-man package. Sparrow Barrow even calls him "Mr. President" a few times. Blaylock makes his first-ever appearance on the show, mostly to stress how the fate of the world rests on the Step Up And Lead rally with the mayor tomorrow. And Justin has connections (of course), so the whole deal is being covered by some local news show as a "feel-good" story about youth getting involved in their communities. Blaylock says "televised" so many times, it's like he's in a competition of people to see who can say the word *televised* the most. He makes a point of thanking Justin for his "service to the school," and is "sure Justin's efforts will be recognized by his classmates."

Maybe thanks to that, when we finally get to lunch, no one seems to notice my campaign table. Justin and his crew are leaning against his, eating McDonald's. People go up to them, and there's a lot of laughing and talking going on. Vicky's not even sitting; she's harassing people while they're in line for lunch and then following them to their tables. Vijay's getting it all on film, and every once in a while he turns his camera on me, the Lone Stranger. I sit at my chair behind the table, trying not to stare at everyone, trying to look positive but not desperate. Ruthie and Joe C. keep looking over at me; I kind of miss their company, but I told them that I'm better off doing this alone. I didn't add that I thought Ruthie's straw hat and Joe C.'s six-pack of Juiced! wouldn't help matters.

Veronica Cruz wanders over, and I take a deep breath. "Hi, Veronica. I'm running for president, and I wanted to talk to you about ways that I think Clarke can make its mission a reality —"

Veronica interrupts me. "Have you done my latest poll? Top five reasons why I would make the best First Lady for Justin?"

"Uh, what?"

She flicks her hair and laughs. Veronica will stop in the middle of a crowded hallway to flap her hair around; she also brushes it during exams. "Whatever. I don't know if I have any more forms for you to fill out anyway. Go to *Ronnie-is-hot.com* and do it there. So . . . what were you saying?"

"Never mind," I say. She's already walking away, flicking her hair all over the place. Mialonie is ten times hotter.

Ruthie comes over. "She thinks she's the only girl in the world with hair on her head."

"You're hovering," I say, but I smile as I say it. She pats me on the shoulder and wanders away.

"Can you tie my shoe?" A little kid comes up to the table and puts his foot up in my face. I look at him; it's the "Pukey-Pukey-Pukey" kid from a few weeks ago. Guess he's graduated to shoelaces. I sigh and tie and he runs away without saying thank you.

Two guys come over. I sit up straight and try to look cool.

"Do you plan to do anything about the information systems at this place?" one of them asks. "We're about five years behind the times."

Computer Club. "Uh," I start, "I'd probably consult guys like you, and I guess get an idea of what you think we need."

"PC or Mac?" the other guy says.

"I've got a Mac at home," I say.

I think they like that; they look at each other and shrug. "Here's my e-mail address," says the "PC or Mac" guy. "Let me know when you put together your technology subcommittee, and we'll talk." They high-five each other for some reason and leave.

Not bad, I think. Though I wish I'd gotten something about Olive Branch in. Ruthie comes over again. "Hey, I saw that," she says. "That's the way to go. Attract the disenfranchised, the overlooked —"

"Okay, Miss Liberty," I say. A few girls from a sixth grade table walk up. They look like they're still in fifth grade.

"So what are you all about?" says the one who looks like she wants to beat me up. "All I know is you're the guy who threw up."

"Gross," mutters the one who looks like she smells a dead animal.

I need to come up with something fast. "I'm, uh, here for . . .

the disenfranchised, the overlooked, the downtrodden," I say. I pretend not to hear Ruthie's snort.

"So, like, what does that mean?" the first girl asks. "What are you gonna do for me?"

"Well, I'm thinking more along the lines of what we can do for our community," I say. "There's a homeless shelter called Olive Branch that really needs our help —"

"Yawn," says the first girl. "Everyone needs our help — they need to start helping themselves. I'm not voting for someone who's gonna make me feel guilty and give me extra work. What about a step team? Getting rid of the corny dress code? Let me rewind: What are you gonna do for *me*?"

"What would you like me to do?" I ask.

That makes her friends giggle. She sucks her teeth. "You don't even know what you're talking about," she says.

Ruthie jumps in. "Hi, I'm Reggie's campaign manager. What he means is that this is your opportunity to express yourselves. We want to hear your ideas! This is a campaign of the people, by the people, and for the people. It's not a popularity contest."

"That's for sure," says one of the gigglers. They drift away.

I look over at Justin's table, where he's asking girls to give him thirty-second dance lessons in preparation for the Holiday Jam. I heard he's proposing something to do with more fund-raisers, but I'm not sure, and from the looks of the festive scene at his table, no one cares. They just want to be around him. And that's what's going to get him votes.

Blaylock walks into the cafeteria and smiles over at Justin. He raises his eyebrows when he turns my way.

"We've got to get it together," I say to Ruthie. "The big rally thing with the mayor is tomorrow, and I've got nothing. Meeting at Joe C.'s at four." I start walking over to George Henderson's table. "And I'm bringing a guest."

4:10 P.M.

"We have got to prove that Reggie has the credentials to make this more than an office in name only," says Ruthie as Joe C. lets us into his living room. About eight dogs come running up to greet us.

"C'mon, everybody knows that people vote for who they like. Besides, who has credentials in eighth grade?" says Joe C.

"Don't be a victim of the system, Castiglione," counters Ruthie. "It's about sincerity, the courage to have convictions. Reggie, when you speak from the heart about the ways that you want to make a difference, you will capture the voters' respect."

"Yeah, well, Justin's gonna capture their hearts," says Joe C. "Did you see those heart buttons that Lisa Vincent made? Featuring Justin's big ole head? He's got the girl vote on lockdown."

"So superficial," says Ruthie.

"Like you don't think Justin looks good. I saw you batting your eyes at him yesterday," says Joe C.

I raise my eyebrows and look at Ruthie, who blushes. "That's ridiculous. I was just showing Justin the latest statistics on the effects of inefficient waste disposal."

Joe C. rolls his eyes. I don't like the way this conversation is going. Ruthie says "JUSTIN" like his name is all in capital letters.

"Ruthie," I say, "I don't need one of my campaign managers drooling over the competition." We follow Joe C. to the kitchen so that we can pick up some extra snacks while he feeds the dogs and gets out a couple bottles of Juiced!.

George Henderson has been watching and listening to all of this like we're a reality show. He smiles. "I think you're in good shape," he says. "You're developing a following already, from what we saw at the shelter. And I heard Mialonie Davis talking you up. Getting girls like that on your team is the way we want to go."

"Girls like what?" asks Ruthie.

George Henderson clears his throat and Joe C. laughs.

"This really is going to turn into a teen movie," Ruthie says, looking at me. "We all know what's going to happen. You'll get a makeover and then you'll get popular, learn to dance, discover your hidden jerk, and desert your real friends. Then something catastrophic will happen and you'll be humiliated and unpopular again and listen to a lot of sappy ballads and have to come crawling back to your old friends, who'll be stupid enough to forgive you."

"Give me a break, Ruthie," I say. "I may like the occasional slow jam, but a sappy ballad? Never!" We all laugh.

"That reminds me," says George Henderson. "My cousin Bobo Dollar is an up-and-coming hip-hop artist. I might be able to get him to give Reggie a shout-out on his podcast." He pulls out a piece of paper. "We should also talk about tomorrow's television appearance. We've got to establish a brand. I think 'regular guy' is fine, but a variation of that might switch things up a little.

You could wear more baseball caps, different jeans, get really hood with it . . . or go the hip-hop impresario route, with some nice pinstriped suits . . . and different shoes —"

Ruthie grabs the paper from him and reads. "Wardrobe budget?" she asks. "Celebrity endorsements?" She turns to me. "Let's be serious."

"I think G-Henny is right," says Joe C. "You've got to establish a name brand."

"G-Henny?" the rest of us repeat. Joe C. has the sense to blush.

"Just kidding," he mutters.

"As I was saying, people need to get to know the real you," says Ruthie. "Not just —"

"— Pukey McKnight," Joe C. finishes. I give him a look. He shrugs.

Ruthie jumps into a speech about getting to know the people I'm trying to reach, finding out what they want, what they need. She sounds like she's been saving it up.

"That's real integrified, Ruthie," says Joe C., making me wonder if he's been talking to my Uncle Terrence. "The thing is, WE know Reggie's all right, but other people don't. And to get them to pay attention, basically, we've got to have a gimmick, and we've got to have giveaways. People love free stuff."

"Campaign bribes?" asks Ruthie, raising her eyebrows.

"Not bribes, exactly. It's . . . incentive. Like a bonus."

That sounds pretty good to me.

"Like candy or something," he continues. "Personalized Snickers bars!"

Ruthie shakes her head. "Justin did that already, remember?

Where are we going to get the money for that anyway? And again — what does that have to do with anything? Can we get away from image and get back to the message, the people?"

"Like you don't spend time on your image," Joe C. says. He points to her shirt that says AFRICA IS NOT A COUNTRY and the skirt she made out of a Jamaican flag. "Don't act like you don't care how you look."

"That's different," says Ruthie. "*I'm* different. I'm not trying to figure out how to be like everyone else."

"You're trying to be something, though," says Joe C.

"Can we get back to *me*, please?" I say. "I have to get home to help Pops with dinner."

"Oh, I forgot," says Ruthie. "I'm coming over to run lines with Monica. What are we having?"

"Mackerel rundown, I think," I say. "And green bananas. Maybe breadfruit too. But let's focus. You had a point with the giveaways. It doesn't have to be personalized Snickers, but . . . you know how people are."

Ruthie nods slowly. "I'll acknowledge that our generation is excessively materialistic and caught up in the tidal wave of consumerism. What about bookmarks? Though everyone threw Vicky's away."

"Why don't we just make a big sign that says 'Yes, I am a NERD'?" I say. Then I realize we probably don't need signs for that.

"Remember that girl who was all 'What are you gonna do for me?'" Joe C. says. "The reality is that people want to know what's in it for them. We have to figure out how to address that."

"By beating Justin at his own game," says George Henderson slowly. "You can be what people want. You can be the regular version of Justin."

Joe C. laughs. "What?"

George Henderson smiles. "Look, Reggie has an Everyman quality that can be exploited — he's more relatable, not so big-man-on-campus. All you have to do, Reggie, is spruce up your wardrobe, look mysterious, and charm the ladies. Be yourself, but act like Justin. It's not that hard; I think you can do it."

"That is laughable," Ruthie says flatly, and I glare at her.

"Go on," I say to George Henderson.

"Okay, tomorrow's rally. Just get up there, call some girls on stage for giveaways, tell a couple of jokes, lead people in a series of 'Woo hoos!' and you're good. Oh — can you put together a sound track real quick?"

"Are you kidding me?" says Ruthie.

"Sound track?" asks Joe C. "I might be able to work something out."

"What about Olive Branch?" I say. "It'll be a good opportunity to get the word out."

"You got the word out when you announced," says George Henderson. "Now you've got to get people to see how cool you are, and then you can say and do whatever you want, and they'll support you. They'll support the shelter," he adds quickly. "And that's the important thing, right? You beat the system at its own game, and then flip it so you can do what you want and people don't even know what hit them."

"You sound like me, sort of," says Ruthie. "And it's scary."

"But it's sort of true . . . I think," says Joe C. "People fall for anything you say if they think you're cool."

If they think you're cool.

"It would be kind of . . . subversive to knock Justin off his game a little," I say.

"I am really so sick of people misusing that word," says Ruthie.

We sit for a moment and I take a sip of banana-carrot Juiced! by mistake. After I come back from spitting it out, George Henderson asks, "What are you going to wear tomorrow? Can you get some new gear tonight?"

"Yeah, after my parents give me the million dollars they've been saving for just this purpose," I say. "Not happening."

"No offense, but you're not going to beat Justin on the visuals," says Joe C.

"He's right," says George Henderson, as though I wasn't there. "We've got to do more than just the cool stuff. We need to play up the regular guy angle . . . the little guy who brings big things to Clarke!"

"Like what?" I ask. "Quilted TP in the boys' bathroom?"

"Juiced! vending machines!" Joe C. chimes in.

"An eighth grade trip to Hawaii instead of Washington, D.C.!" If I could swing something like that, I'd be a big hit. The hero.

"What does any of that have to do with what you said in the cafeteria?" says Ruthie.

"Nothing," I say. "But it's the way to make what I said a reality. Let me get the votes first, and then I can get the work done. Everybody knows we can't really go to Hawaii, but . . ."

"But if we make them believe it for a while, do a whole feel-good campaign, they won't care," says George Henderson.

"I mean, everyone knows Justin's not really going to be able to get rid of grades and tests too," I say. Or could he? "But they cheer when he says that he will."

"Something to make people cheer!" says George Henderson. "I've got it — Reggie, can you climb the rope in the gym?"

"Not all the way to the top, but I can get close if I'm not being timed," I say. "Why?"

"You start climbing the rope, people will cheer you on, and we'll give out Twizzlers and shout 'Reggie McKnight, climbing the rope to success!' You sweating and working hard like that on camera, that's TV gold. Voters will remember that. And you don't have to get to the top. Just trying will be 'I think I can' enough to win people over."

"So it's all about the spectacle now?" Ruthie asks.

"With the Hawaii trip, you can give away leis, and maybe get some girls to wear coconut bras," says Joe C. "Can we get coconut bras by tomorrow?"

"I'm not listening to this," says Ruthie. "And I hope you aren't either, Reggie. Instead of fooling around, you should be fine-tuning your message. Tomorrow is a huge opportunity to call some attention to the shelter, to the homeless population in New York, to the inequality and disregard for basic humanity perpetuated by the West throughout the global diaspora —"

"You're right," I say. "I can't listen to this." My head hurts.

George Henderson picks up his briefcase. "I've got a LARPers meeting. Reggie, text me if you want help prepping for tomorrow. I'll be up, I'm writing a medieval version of *High School Musical* for English." He walks to the door. "I'll work on the rope-climbing concept. Remember, you don't even need to say actual words, just get the crowd going. Girls throwing candy into the bleachers. Lots of 'Woo hoos,' and you're set. See you."

He leaves, and we're quiet for a moment.

"Did they have high schools in medieval times?" asks Joe C.

"Despite the sexist tendencies, he seems like a nice guy," says Ruthie. "But this isn't just some show or something. The people are craving nutrients and he's telling you to give them junk food."

"Speaking of food —" I check my watch. "Ruthie . . . we've got to go." I look at Joe C., who's shuffling through his delivery-menu pile. "Do you want to come over for dinner?"

"Took you long enough," he says. "And speaking of long, did you know that Ashrita Furman of Jamaica, NY, pogo-jumped twenty-three miles in twelve and a half hours in 1997?" He grabs a Juiced! to bring along. "It's a world record."

I take the bottle out of his hand and toss it on the couch. "Kind of like how long you've been able to do this without your best friends murdering you?" I say. "We're only human, though. Don't push it."

Joe C. makes a move to get his Juiced! back, but Ruthie and I drag him outside.

"Let it go, Joe C.," I say. "You'll never know what the future holds until you do."

DECEMBER 1
12:01 A.M.

I run down from the bleachers, fist in the air, and . . . and . . .

Some of the girls are screaming so loud, their heads seem about to pop off, and . . .

Nothing. I keep squeezing my eyes shut so that I can slip into one of those "Reggie the superhero" fantasies that used to keep me occupied, but I'm wide awake. Might as well do more work on my speech. I get my new notebook out and put a towel over my lamp to keep the lights low. Mom would be screaming fire hazard if she saw, and for a second I wonder if a fire might be just the thing to stop this crazy ride. Maybe I want to get off.

No. That was the old Reggie. (And a somewhat psycho one.) I shake it off and write "NO I DON'T" in big block letters.

12:07 A.M.

Image counts. I mean, maybe if John the Baptist wasn't all crazy-looking and bug-eating, they wouldn't have paid attention to him. But maybe the people looked past the crazy-looking, bug-eating-ness because they were so into his message? I wonder if Dave would write me back if I e-mailed him.

12:10 A.M.

Did you have to think about eating bugs, Reggie? Note to self: When working on another presentation for the whole school, DON'T THINK OF THINGS THAT REMIND YOU OF PUKE.

12:23 A.M.

Justin doesn't even have a message! He's not all that. If I could just get some new clothes . . .

1:05 A.M.

Oops, Mom. She'll bust me for being up so late. And maybe I can just close my eyes for a minute.

4:30 A.M.

I wonder if George is awake right now. I wonder if George is alive right now. I picture him at a subway entrance, shivering in one of those donated coats.

4:45 A.M.

This wish list — tutoring, cleanup crew, textbooks, soap . . . somebody wants a cat! I bet it's Old Crump. That's easy, actually. We can just reach into a bodega for one. In fact, most of this stuff we can do. I know we can. Kind of nice to be a part of something I believe in.

4:47 A.M.

"sleepovrs at my Big Budees howss" — Charlie's handwriting is pretty good. That kid is something. Maybe I can bring Charlie up with me. The cute little kid factor will definitely get the girl vote! And I bet he would love to have the crowd cheering him on. I could let him try the rope a little. Should we wear the Dora shoes?

4:54 A.M.

Who am I kidding? It doesn't matter what I wear, I'm no Justin Walker.

4:58 A.M.

What made Mialonie start talking to me? And what's up with her and Justin?

5:05 A.M.

Justin's probably going to ride in on an elephant, and Vicky will somehow stir up a hurricane of hatred that will at least be memorable. . . . Even if I look like an idiot, the rope thing might be a good idea.

5:10 A.M.

How did I ever get myself into this?

5:12 A.M.

I should say something about extra credit for working at Olive Branch. Oh, wait — I forgot to ask Ruthie about that Effa Manley assignment. . . .

5:14 A.M.

I should ask Wilma if we can set up a bulletin board to display kids' artwork and papers and stuff.

5:15 A.M.

The extra-credit thing — is that too Vicky-esque?

5:30 A.M.

Got my spiel down. Looks good. Short, get the point across, get some cheers, and get out. Community service is feel-good, and the whole reward/extra-credit thing isn't too bad. . . . I bet people will have other ideas.

5:35 A.M.

Coconut bras might have been nice, but I'm not going out like that. That's not how I came in. And forget about the rope climbing too. I don't want to just put on a show.

5:40 A.M.

I still might bring Charlie up with me, though.

6:30 A.M.

Monica hits me with the phone before she hands it to me. My notebook falls to the floor as I sit up.

"You're supposed to be at the gym entrance by 7:45," Ruthie starts right in without saying hello.

I yawn. "Hi. How are you? Good, I'm fine," I say. "A little tired."

"Sorry. I'm just so proud of you, getting up in front of everyone like this." She pauses. "And I know you won't let me — or yourself — down."

"I think I'm good," I say. "I'm keeping it short and sweet. There will be some 'woo hoos,' but no ropes or coconuts. I'm staying on message."

"I know you will. You're going to be great. Just please, please, please don't be late. You know Blaylock will be freaking out because of the mayor and the TV cameras."

"I'll be there; I just have to stop at Olive Branch first. Okay, boss?" I say. "I'm going to talk about the wish list, and I want to run a few things by Wilma."

"All right," she says. "See you at school."

"Oh, and can you call Joe C.?" I ask. "I need you guys to pick up a couple of bags of mini candy bars. There will be *some* give-away madness. I'll give the people a little of what they need *and* a little of what they want."

"Compromise is a necessary . . . art," she says, and I can hear the smile in her voice. "Fine. Just don't be late." She hangs up.

I shower and dress in record time, and I don't look half-bad, if I do say so myself. And I do, twice, to my reflection in the mirror.

I'm grinning as I head out the door.

7:15 A.M.

Even though Mom loaded me down with a huge bag of clothes for the shelter, I get to the Olive Branch in record time. Before I can open with the fact that *I* didn't bring junky stuff, Wilma points me over to the donation corner. I set the bag down next to a pile of old clothes and glance around.

Charlie's sitting on the floor with a shoebox. His mom is asleep in a chair. I look at my watch; I know I'll be pushing it for the rally, but I plop down next to him and look into the box. It's full of a bunch of wooden train cars that look older than the ancient guy sitting in the corner. Most of them are peppered with teeth marks and they look pretty disgusting, but I pick one up.

"New train set?" I say. "You haven't come over to play with your Thomas trains in a while. . . ."

Charlie snatches the train out of my hand. "I didn't say you could touch that."

"Um, okay. Sorry," I mutter. "Hey, you want to walk to school with me? It's kind of late."

"I'm not going to school today," he says. "My mommy said I could have a vacation."

"Oh," I answer. "That sounds like fun, but . . . what about our deal? You come to school, we have lunch together? I'll miss you."

"I didn't say you could sit there either," he says.

What did *I* do? "Come on, we can walk together," I say. "You can tell me how things are going. It's getting late, and I've really got to go."

"Why don't you just go away?" he says, louder. A few people look over. "You always got to go. People leave all the time. Why don't you?"

I flinch. I want to get out of this place; I'll be late for the rally, and I can already picture Blaylock's glare at me while Justin takes a victory lap around the gym. I stand.

I should wake Charlie's mom up, tell her I'm leaving.

She just looks so tired.

And Charlie looks so sad.

I should tell him about bringing him up on stage at the pep rally. That'll put a smile on his face. He'll probably get all pumped up and we can get out of here together.

Or maybe not. He really looks so sad. And almost as tired as his mom.

Pay attention, smart boy.

If I run at top speed the whole way, I might be able to sneak into the gym while Blaylock does the intros. The mayor will probably blah blah blah too. I can make it if I leave now. I'll tell Charlie that I'll come here right after school. We can get ice cream.

Just pay attention.

If Charlie thinks everyone leaves . . . then that means what he really needs is someone to stay.

I take a deep breath. "Can I play for a few minutes?"

"No," he says.

"Fine. Can I just sit here with you for a minute?" I say.

After a long second, he shrugs.

"I'll take that as a yes," I say. And I sit there. And after a while, he starts playing, setting up those old beat-up trains in a line and making low train whistle sounds. He never looks at me, and I just keep sitting there, not saying anything. Just staying.

8:54 A.M.

"Principal Blaylock!" I'm out of breath. "I'm really sorry, I —"

"Reginald, nice of you to join us. Unfortunately, you should have joined us over an hour ago. You have missed the boat, the bus, and the point. A leader is responsible. A leader shows respect for Clarke and the electoral process."

"I can explain, I —"

"You owe the mayor here an apology as well," says Blaylock, turning to the man walking with him.

The mayor shakes his head at me. "You don't win elections by not showing up," he says. "Especially not in New York."

"Mr. Mayor, I apologize, it's just —"

They walk into Blaylock's office; Blaylock turns and closes the door in my face.

A few stragglers are coming down the hall, and I duck into a nearby doorway.

"Justin killed it," says an eighth grader. "He knows how to represent."

His friend nods. "Even Vicky Ross made me watch her, crazy as she is. That Pukey punk didn't even have the guts to show up."

"Someone should check the bathroom," says the first guy. "He might be having stomach issues."

I wait until they're out of sight before I head to class. And bump right into Donovan.

"Pukey!" he says. "What's up? Spilled your guts again so you didn't have any left to show up today?"

I say nothing, but I don't walk away either.

"You're a loser and a punk and that's all you'll ever be," he says. "And everyone realizes it now. Nice job, getting even the mayor to hate you. What kind of 'leader of tomorrow' doesn't even show up? You probably lost us that grant money too." He starts to push past me. "This is almost too easy." He walks off, and I force my mouth open.

"The name is Reggie," I say. Could I really have lost the money for Clarke?

"Where were you?" Ruthie whispers as I slide into my seat.

"I was at the shelter. Things . . . took longer than I expected."

"What is your problem? Why should we take this seriously if you don't? We went and bought your stupid candy and everything."

I look at Joe C., who shrugs.

"I'm *sorry*," I say. "What do you want from me?"

"Maybe more than you can give," Ruthie says. "Don't waste my time if you're not serious." She slams her notebook on her desk and everyone looks.

When class ends, I walk out with Joe C. "Listen, I *am* sorry. I just got tied up." He doesn't say anything. "So, what did I miss?"

"You know, whatever. Vicky was bumping her gums for like ten years. Justin's brother came again, they had music and did this whole call-and-response thing. Really got the crowd going. He had some sixth grade girls do a step show. Then he gave out Hershey's Kisses. Even the guys were grabbing them up."

"Oh," I say. "Not a big deal. Um, not gonna cost me the race, right?"

"Are you even running the race?" he says. "What's up?"

"Charlie was having a tough time, and I couldn't just leave him alone."

"I got you," Joe C. says. "It's just — you got us all fired up about this election."

"I know, and I'm sorry, but *I* got all fired up about this election thing because of Olive Branch, George, and Charlie."

"Yeah, but I thought the whole thing was that you were going to help the shelter by winning this election."

"I was! I am! I just — had to hang out with him this morning. It was important," I finish, and it sounds a little lame. When Charlie and I were heading to school, I was sure that I'd helped him, and I felt good. But now I wonder if I messed up . . . again.

I look at the hall clock, which may actually be right for once. "We're late already," I say. "See you."

I start jogging to class. Then I remember that Joe C. and I are going the same way, but when I turn around, he's gone.

7:15 P.M.

"I'm sorry I made you late for school," Charlie mumbles into the phone.

"That's okay," I say. "It was only a significant portion of my final grade."

"What?" he asks.

"Never mind." There's a pause, and I can hear his mother whispering on the other end of the phone.

"I'm sorry I was rude," he mumbles.

"No problem," I say.

"Are you coming back to see me?"

"Of course."

"My mommy says thank you for taking me to school. She said you were right that it's important to eat breakfast."

"Tell her she's welcome."

"I had fun on the bus," he says. "You tell good stories!"

"Thank you! So do you." This feels good. "You must have been like a lucky charm. There's usually no room on the bus, so I end up walking every day."

"Walking is good for you. You made me feel a lot better," he says. "Do you play with my trains when I'm not there?"

"Nope," I reply. "That's for us to do together. We're Buddies, right?"

There's a long pause and I wonder if he put the phone down or something.

"My pretend daddy left," he says. "I don't want you to leave too, cuz you're my pretend big brother." He starts to cry. "So I wanted to tell you to go *first*, before you left."

"Wait, George was your . . . Wait, *I'm* your pretend big brother?"

He sniffs; I hear his mom's voice, and then he speaks again. "My momma says you can't hear me nodding, so yes. Like a *real* one, but pretend."

I don't know if I'll ever be able to swallow the lump that's forming in my throat.

"Charlie, that's the biggest honor ever. I — thank you. And don't worry, I'm coming back. I'm sorry I haven't found George, but . . . I'm not running away. I'll be back."

DECEMBER 2
7:50 A.M.

The next day at school, Charlie runs up and hugs me in front of everyone.

I hug him back. "Good to see you," I say.

"Even though I know you're coming back," he says, "I wanted to come to school and see you first."

"Awwww," says Ruthie, as Charlie runs to class. "What was that about?"

"I told you," I say. "He was having a hard time yesterday, and he needed me. I'm sorry I missed the rally, but Charlie's more important to me."

Ruthie looks at me for a long time. "You're right. You did the right thing. I was wrong."

Joe C. and I pretend we've been knocked out.

"Did you hear that, Joe C.? Can you say that again, Ruthie?" I ask. "Maybe write it down too?"

Ruthie rolls her eyes and smiles.

"Charlie and his mom called me last night," I continue, "and it got me thinking about the campaign. I don't want to get the school all hyped up about nothing, or giveaways, or even winning money. I want my campaign to have substance, and that doesn't have to mean something big. Staying with Charlie was something that I could do for him, right then. And I think there's always something each one of us can do. It doesn't have to be spectacular or lead to loud cheers. But it matters."

"You did get people excited, though, when you jumped up on that table," Joe C. says. "And George Henderson and his friends, he told me they're down for the theater thing at the Olive Branch."

"See? And that would be great. That's exactly what I'm talking about. We can each contribute something small and make it count. What if more people started volunteering their talents at Olive Branch, sharing their skills and interests?"

"Like asking those girls if they want to start a step team at the shelter?" says Ruthie. "Interesting. Kind of a 'do unto others' approach."

"Do unto each other, I guess," I say. "What the Pledge is about. Sharing ourselves, in community. Listening first, and then acting accordingly." I'm warming up. "Why does it have to be either/or? Being involved in the shelter versus strengthening the school community? I want to bring the two together, like a mutual thing . . . a, a reciprocal relationship." I think for a minute. "I know we need help with the library and with painting at the shelter. Seems like we could get credit for those. We're all school nerds here, so academic credits are like cash money — scholarship money."

"Makes sense to me," says Joe C. as he takes notes. "I'll start working on posters."

"I tried to talk to Vicky about this once, and it sounds corny, but I was thinking about it some more last night. If this —

community service — is what Clarke is all about, then maybe it should be part of the core curriculum." I show them my notes from the night before. "Like, if we do a project, we talk about it in class, we write papers on it and stuff."

"We should come up with catchy slogans for this. Then we can hold our own rally or something," says Ruthie. "*That* would be subversive."

"Yeah, slogans," I say. "You're good at that kind of thing."

"I do have a way with words," she says. "I'll get on it."

"So we're talking about extra credit for helping at the shelter?" asks Joe C. "Vicky might even vote for you."

"I say even as part of the regular grades. Just part of the daily at Clarke, like pop quizzes and no toilet paper in the bathrooms," I say.

"Great idea," says Ruthie. "Reggie McKnight: bridging the gap between school and community. And then leading us over that bridge to a twenty-first century global community."

"I hope that's not for a poster," I say.

"Or for public consumption," says Joe C.

"And speaking of Vicky, her whole awards ceremony . . . we could have a small celebration —" I put my hand up as Ruthie starts to speak. "Wait, just listen. A small celebration, not to pat ourselves on the back or anything, but just to remind everyone that service is important."

Ruthie rolls her eyes, but she doesn't say anything.

"Co-opting opponents' ideas," says Joe C. "You really *are* becoming a politician."

I ignore that. "In the end, I'm sure people would rather hear that their work, no matter how small it is, is worth something, instead of how valuable Justin is."

"Or Vicky for that matter," adds Joe C. "She really is delusional."

"I threw up in my mouth a little while she was talking," says Ruthie. She looks at me. "I mean . . . sorry. Didn't mean to go there."

"That's okay," I say. "We all know I've been there."

She raises her eyebrows and turns to Joe C. "Did he just —" she begins.

"Yes, he did," Joe C. replies. "He joked about it."

"It sounds crazy to say that I'm proud of you for making a puke reference, but I am." She hugs me.

"So am I, my friend, so am I," adds Joe C., giving me a pound.

They leave, and as I head to class, I smile and say, "I'm Reggie McKnight and I'm running for president" to a couple of bored-looking seventh graders I pass by. And then I say it again.

3:03 P.M.

When I get to my locker at the end of the day, George Henderson is already there. He has silver dollars in his loafers and he's carrying a big black case that looks like an old-school doctor bag. He introduces me to the other LARPers, and we all head over to Fort Greene Park, right up the hill to the Prison Ships Martyrs' Monument. I think I'm the only one who's self-conscious; everyone else jumps right into some story that involves a lot of "hails" and swordplay. We take a break for snacks — bread, cheese, and cold sausage — and I think the fun of the whole thing makes the food taste even better. Someone's brought some fake "mulled mead," which tastes mostly like hot apple cider, and I'm happy for it since I can see my breath out here. A bunch of kids explain the complicated rules about magic and characters to me, and I really don't get it, and they can tell, but they're glad I'm there and keep trying to bring me in.

I'm having a good time, mostly just watching the action, and a couple of girls come over and ask me about Olive Branch and what it is.

"There are a lot of kids there," I start. "Whole families. I started going as part of a group project, but I think that we can do a lot more."

"Like what?" asks the one wearing fairy wings and carrying a light saber.

"Like tutoring after school, getting local businesses to donate stuff, just playing with the kids. George Henderson said some of you guys would be interested in starting a drama club." I think for a minute. "Making sure that they aren't 'they' anymore."

"I like that," says Warrior Fairy Girl. "I'll come check it out. Nice to see someone talking about something real when they're running for president. You've got my vote." She jumps up and joins a battle against a couple of dragons and a Stormtrooper. It's cool how this thing is so precious to them, and they want to share it with me. Usually it's the crappy stuff we want to give away.

DECEMBER 6
4:04 P.M.

When I stop by Olive Branch after school, people are like, "Hi, Reggie," in that easy way that says I'm a part of things, and it feels good. I look for George as soon as I walk into the shelter, and Wilma just looks at me and shakes her head. I make deals with God: *Bring George back and I'll pray every night. Bring George back and I'll keep my room spotless. If I win this election, You have to bring him back.* I am a little scared, trying to bargain with God, but He seems to be letting it slide. I talk to a couple of the kids; Charlie gives me a hug.

"Today is a good day," he says. "Really good, like when George used to live here."

"That's cool," I say.

"I hope when he comes back, he comes when you're here," he says. "Because he was always in a good mood after he saw you. Once he told me that we had to share you as our best friend."

I am happy and sad, and a little proud.

Wilma squeezes my shoulder and then points to a couple of boxes. "That must be some school you and your friends go to," she says.

"What friends?" I say.

"The other kids from your school," Wilma says. "Over there." She points to a group to her left, and marches away. I look over and see Vijay, Veronica, and James Kim, whose voice I've never actually heard. He's that kind of shy that teachers let slide, so they never call on him. I don't know if I'm more surprised to see them here, or to see them together. It looks like Vijay's teaching Veronica and James how to use his camcorder.

I feel weird about going over to them, but I do, and thank them for coming. Vijay doesn't even smirk once.

"I don't think I've ever seen you without that camera," I say to Vijay. "Sparrow works you hard."

"News flash: *Talkin' Trash* is not my life," he says. "I'm a serious filmmaker. I have a lot of short videos online. I just finished a series on Queens and all the different ethnic groups that live there."

"Really?" I say, surprised. "That sounds really cool."

"Thanks," he says. "So is what you're doing here."

I chat with him for a while, while Gabriella and Carmen lead James over to the library corner, which is looking pretty impressive. Veronica starts painting with Jeff and immediately ends up squealing about paint on her nose, but Wilma puts a stop to that fast and they get down to business. Veronica texts Josie, who shows up within minutes with three other girls; they all put on a bunch of old T-shirts and grab some paint rollers. Jeff mouths "thanks" to me with a big old cheesy grin.

Ruthie runs into the shelter for a quick meetup with her Listening Ears partner, and asks me to wait for her because she's coming over to run lines with Monica. Monica has really thrown herself into her role as Mama — she's even managed to glam Mama up a little so that she looks like Beyoncé's grandmother. As I wait for Ruthie to tear herself away from a gaggle of little girls, I hear her say "Philippians 4:13 — remember that!"

Ruthie and I head out.

"Did I see you having a conversation with James Kim?" she asks. "I thought I saw his mouth move."

"I did," I answer. "And he had a lot to say."

"Wow, Reggie, you really may be starting a revolution," she replies.

After we walk for a bit, I ask, "What was that Philippians 4:13 thing about?"

"You know, 'I can do all things through Him who strengthens me' . . . I'm thinking about starting a little girls' club and using that as the motto. The girls are so sweet — I'm going to see if my Little Buddy Jamila can join us."

"Sounds good," I say. "So . . . do you really believe that?"

"Believe what?"

"That 'I can do all things with God' stuff. Do you really believe that?"

She's quiet for a minute. "Yeah, sometimes I really do. If I don't think about it for too long but I think about it deep, you know what I mean?"

I look at her. "What do you think?"

She laughs. "Okay, yeah, that doesn't make any sense. What I mean is, if I think about it the same way I think about eating or studying for a math test, then it's hard for me to believe. But when I just feel it, like I feel heat from a rainbow or peace from watching a fountain, then I believe."

"I can't believe you just referenced hot rainbows," I say. "Do you believe in unicorns too?" She laughs again. "I want to believe in something," I continue, "but . . . I don't know."

"I think it's okay not to know. In fact, my mom always says that that's a sign of a true believer — knowing that you don't know it all."

"Hmmm . . . but then, how can you trust God, if you can't even figure Him out? Seems kind of unfair." I wonder if one of God's avenging angels is going to materialize and zap me away for saying that. "I've been trying to answer that question that Dave asked us way back: 'If God is so good, then why are things so bad?'"

"And?" asks Ruthie. "What answer did you come up with?"

"I didn't, that's what I'm saying." I glance at her. "What about you?"

"I just . . . Okay, remember how we were talking about the story of Peter in the boat in youth group a while back?" I nod. "And how when he kept his focus on Jesus, he was okay, but as soon as he didn't, he stumbled? I just go a step at a time, trust a little bit, and stumble a little bit too. I mean, I don't know about fair, but I believe that God is just. It'll all be right in the end. But I can work on making it as right as I can right now too."

"You're going to be Dave when you grow up, aren't you?" I say.

"I'm going to be whatever God has planned," she says, smiling. "And I'm convinced that He has something great in store for me."

"I wish I could be sure," I say. "I'm not trying to get struck down, but . . . I have questions all of the time."

"I don't think that's how He is," she answers. "I think God can take a few questions."

"I'm just gonna have to hope that some of whatever you've got rubs off on me."

"I don't know if I've 'got' anything, but you're welcome to hang around, even if you get on my nerves sometimes. I'm not going anywhere," she says. "And . . ." She stops.

"And what?" I say. "Come on, I bared my soul. No fair holding back."

She rolls her eyes. "I was just going to say that we can love each other through the doubts and questions and everything, but I didn't want you to take it the wrong way and get all weird on me. I mean 'love' in the holy sense."

"Like a nun and a priest getting with each other?" I say with a smirk. "That sounds like a movie I want to see!" She swings her bag at me and I jump out of the way, laughing. "Kidding, I'm kidding."

"I knew you wouldn't understand!" she screeches.

But I look at Ruthie a few times, with her Oxfam T-shirt and the bright yellow hat she knit herself, and I think I do understand.

8:40 P.M.

I've been reading the Black poetry book for the last hour instead of doing my homework. I really like "The White House" by Claude McKay. I wonder how it would go down if, instead of a big election-assembly speech, I said things like:

Your door is shut against my tightened face,
And I am sharp as steel with discontent;

But I possess the courage and the grace

To bear my anger proudly and unbent.

    I stand up in front of my mirror and practice saying the lines with different gestures and facial expressions. I almost believe myself; maybe Monica's not the only actor in the family. There's a knock on my door. I open it, and Monica peers into the room.

    "Who are you talking to?" she asks.

    "No one," I mutter. "We have to do, um, oral book reports tomorrow."

    "Whatever," she replies. "You have a phone call." She holds the phone out to me. "It's a girl," she says. "A *real* one, not just Ruthie. Oooh!" She makes kissy sounds and she is not covering the receiver, so whoever is on the phone can hear every word.

    I grab the phone. "Gimme that!" I whisper. "How would you like it if John Wilkins called and I did that to you?"

    She shoves me. "Rub it in, why don't you, Little Dumber Boy?" She stomps off.

    I sigh. So much for forging a new bond with my sister. For a second, I think about just hanging up the phone, but then I put the receiver to my ear. "Uh . . . hello?"

    "Hey, Reggie," says a voice so caramel it can only belong to one girl. Mialonie.

    "Hey! Hi! How! Are! You!" I sound like a male cheerleader.

    "Uh, not as good as you, I guess. You sound cheery," she says. "Are you pumped up?"

    "About what?" I ask.

    "The election? Hello, you're running for president."

    "Oh — yeah, I'm all pumped up," I say.

"I think you'd be great," she says. "And I wanted to know if you need any help."

"Help?"

"You know, with your campaign? It's too bad that you missed the rally," she says, and I hear the question in her voice, but I let it pass. "I noticed that you don't have any posters up or anything. We could have a poster party. Josie's a great artist, I'm sure I can get her to help out."

"Oh, yeah! Uh, sure!"

There's a pause.

"I was also thinking; remember that *Be Extra* book I have? I thought you might want to read it. Self-improvement from the outside in. I can take you shopping if you want. New gear, new you."

From the outside in? Whatever, I'm not going down that road again. "Well, that sounds . . . good, but I'm kind of focusing my campaign on getting the school involved at the shelter."

"I heard about that. What exactly are you doing?"

"Just hanging out with the people, I guess. That whole Listening Ears thing made me realize that just being there is important. I think. Not that I'm saying that *my* presence is so important, but all of us . . ." I'm lost. I wish I were tongue-tied — that would be better than this.

"I think it's so cool that you're doing that. That place is kind of depressing. I don't know if you remember my partner —"

"Miss Joycelyn," I say. "The quilter."

"Yeah," says Mialonie. "She told me that she prays hope into each one she makes. It's hard to believe that anyone can have hope in that place. Everyone there needs so much; I feel guilty."

"Yeah," I say, "but I feel like I need to be there too." My voice gets stronger. "It's not just a do-gooder thing, it's, um, reciprocal, you know? I get a lot from everyone there. It's even helping me with my homework!" I say, laughing. I'm laughing with Mialonie Davis, who looks like that girl on the video request show.

"You'll have to tell me more sometime," she says. "Just like you were supposed to tell me about Night Man."

"Yeah, well, I'm kind of done with that," I say. "But I can tell you about what I want to do at the shelter, if you want."

"Sure. And I've got an idea for the election. I can tell you this trick I learned from *Be Extra* about projection and portrayal. You portray and project a better version of yourself, and people can't resist it."

That sounds a little creepy to me, but Mialonie is into it, so maybe it's not that bad. Or maybe it really does work. Maybe I'm not talking to the real Mialonie, but a "better version."

"Are you going to the Holiday Jam?" she asks. "Or maybe you don't do school parties. I never saw you at any last year."

"Oh, um, no, I mean, yeah, I do. Go to parties, I mean." Back to blithering idiot in a single bound.

"Well, maybe we could meet up there and talk. Dance, even," she says with a smile in her voice.

Okay, Reggie, just play it cool and open your mouth and form words. Speak. Speak. Now!

"Um, that would be cool. I mean, yeah, I'd love to talk at the dance. And dance."

"Okay, great. We'll have fun. Listen, my sister is bugging me for the phone. I've gotta go, but we can talk more tomorrow." I almost drop the phone when she gives me her number.

"Sure, yeah, see you tomorrow . . . and, um, thank you."

She laughs. "Okay, you're welcome, I guess. Later." And she hangs up.

I do a dance from my room down to the kitchen and I don't even care when Monica sees.

DECEMBER 7
11:45 A.M.

"A poster party?! I suggested that a week ago!" says Ruthie, almost dropping her tomato and rice sandwich.

"You did? That's great, so we agree that it's a good idea. She's going to start doing some stuff at Olive Branch with us."

"I'm surprised she has time," says Ruthie, "what with all of the looking in the mirror she has to do." Hector walks over. "At least we have people like Hector who really want to work. And what's with her name? It's like fake Hawaiian or something. Did her parents make it up?" She gives Hector a tooth-whitener commercial smile.

"*Anyway*," I say, trying not to look at Hector, "did you come up with slogans and stuff for the posters?"

"Yes," she says, taking a sheet of paper out of her notebook. "Here are a few ideas. Remember, these are just, like, ideas . . . notes."

> *REGINALD GARVEY MCKNIGHT.*
> *FOR JUSTICE, FOR PEACE.*
>
> *VOTE INTEGRITY. VOTE FOR CHANGE.*
> *VOTE REGGIE.*

DISMANTLE THE POLITICAL MACHINE!
VOTE REGGIE FOR A NEW DEMOCRACY

"You've got to be kidding," I say. My voice is a little harder than I mean to sound. "Slogans are supposed to rhyme, they're supposed to be catchy. And what do you mean 'for peace'? We're not at war, we're at Clarke."

"I'm still working on them," she says, snatching back her sheet of paper. "I just wanted to show you the direction I'm going in."

"Well, right now it looks like the road to nowhere," I say.

"Why would you be going anywhere else?" asks a voice over my shoulder. I turn around to see Donovan cackling, Justin a little behind him, not smiling. A few kids stop talking and eating to watch what goes down.

"Shut up," I mutter.

"This is going to be so good," he says, snickering. "Only a loser like you could be this clueless about what a loser he is and try to run for office."

"Why are you so worried about it anyway?" asks Ruthie. "Scared that your candidate can't take the competition?"

"You guys are such bottom-feeders," Donovan says. "It's painfully pathetic." He starts off down the hall, laughing. Justin doesn't move for a few seconds, then he walks the other way. Donovan turns around — I know he's looking for Justin, but he tries to play it off. He looks at me and mouths "I hate you."

I turn back to the lunch table. "I'm sorry," I say to Ruthie. "I'm just stressed."

George Henderson appears with about a dozen LARPers carrying cardboard swords.

"How's it going?" he asks. "Thanks for coming to check us out the other day. We want to hand out flyers."

I give him a stack of the flyers I made and Ruthie puts an arm around him. That girl is just touchy-feely with the world these days.

"We really appreciate your help," she says.

"Yeah, we do," I say. "I just . . ." I feel like I need to be honest with them. "You know the LARPing may not really be my thing."

George Henderson looks at me. "It doesn't have to be. But you respected us, and we respect what you're doing."

A girl adds, "You got up on a table and made that speech, and you followed through. You're keeping it real, and we're impressed."

"You may have the makings of a LARPer yet," George says.

"Thank you, I guess," I say.

I impressed someone. I'm beginning to feel like a candidate.

DECEMBER 8
8:11 A.M.

When the theme music for *Talkin' Trash* starts up, people shut up right away. Vijay was everywhere with that camera of his; I have no idea how I'm going to look this time around.

"*Even if you are not ready for day,*" I mutter to myself as the music fades, "*it cannot always be night.*"

Sparrow chirps, "The race is ON!" There's a clip of Vicky running, I think it's to the bus stop to catch the B63, but it looks like she's literally running away from the election. Vicky's mug fills up the screen, and with a lot of head-tossing and glaring into the camera, she announces "that I have indefinitely suspended my Clarke campaign in order to embark on my quest to be Freshman representative on an as-yet-unnamed college campus."

"Can you confirm the reports that you are going down a shame spiral of humiliation and anxiety, barely clinging to the last vestiges of your sanity?" asks Sparrow.

"Of course not. What a joke. I've simply realized that my skill set is more suited to significant things, not the little eighth grade presidency."

"Aren't you worried about breaking the cycle of leadership in your family? Do you understand that you're a legacy? The voters, and your mom, want to know: Are you ready to be the first campaign quitter in the Ross family?"

"This interview is over," says Vicky, and the screen goes black for a minute. There's some whispering and giggling in class, but I don't dare look Vicky's way. Then the show cuts to the requisite Justin-can-do-no-wrong clips — dancing, shooting hoops, shaking Blaylock's hand, dancing some more, talking about opening a school store and improving school lunches, and dancing again.

But she ends with me, and it's not so bad. In fact, it's pretty good. "Reggie's generating some buzz," she chirps, and the corny bumblebee graphic doesn't take away from the fact that they open with a shot of me talking to the computer guys. On TV it comes off like I inspire them; you see me talk and then they high-five. There's a sound bite of me saying "the disenfranchised, the overlooked, the downtrodden," and maybe they did something to the audio, because I sound . . . *strong*. They cut right to a clip of Mialonie saying she wishes me the best; it's so fast that I'm sure it's very edited; she may have said the same thing about Justin, but who knows? There's a shot of me consulting with George Henderson, and since you can't see his Sacagawea loafers or his tie, we look serious and hardworking. Sparrow interviews Charlie, who calls me a "real-life superhero" (I hear a couple of "awwws" usually reserved for Justin on that one), and she talks about Olive Branch and my "pet project to help the homeless."

The show ends with me, Ruthie, and Joe C. walking down the hall in slow motion while they play music from this old boxing movie called *Rocky* that Mr. Castiglione always talks about. Sparrow finishes with, "A dark horse whose still waters run deeper than we thought — remember to judge a man by the content of his character, not the contents of his stomach!" Ouch. Then it ends.

Justin walks out of the class quickly, Donovan right behind him. Neither one is smiling.

"Don't worry about it," says Ruthie, coming up to me. "I know you're freaking out about that ending, but the rest of it was positive. Focus on that."

"I thought it was good too, until the Dr. King/puking reference," I say. "Do you really think it'll help?"

"Absolutely," says Ruthie, hugging me. "The overall message was that you're the guy to watch, the guy who's gonna make a difference. That you're the best man, and you're gonna win."

"Thanks," I say, thinking that I wouldn't mind another hug.

"I can't wait until your speech," she continues. "I can't wait until everyone sees what I already know."

The speech.

Is not something I can do.

"You can do the speech, Reggie," says Ruthie. "You're not going to puke, it was just stage fright. You're not that scared kid anymore." She squeezes my hand and goes up to talk to Ms. A about some extra credit.

Not that scared kid? Oh yes I am.

I'm not sure what people are going to say in the halls, but right away I hear a few people say "Hey, Reggie," and "Good luck." I'm late for math because two sixth grade girls come up to ask me about Olive Branch.

I see Vicky taking down "Vote Vicky!" posters. I feel like I should say something, but I don't.

Mialonie reminds me about the poster party and says we should do it soon.

Vijay has turned out to be a pretty cool guy. He sits at our lunch table, and Joe C. and I talk to him about making a documentary about Olive Branch. I'm thinking that we can get publicity from it, maybe even some news coverage.

Justin makes a big splash when he does a swing dancing routine on the basketball court with Audrey Glassman and a basketball as a demonstration of how well he works with others. I had no idea he was so dancy. I'm still a long shot; and I do wish that Ruthie didn't hand out recipe cards titled "Recipe for a Great President" with things like "2 cups kindness and 2 tablespoons conviction" typed on the back. Not when Justin is giving people mini Snickers bars that say "JW." But people call me "Reggie" at school. And I don't feel like everyone's laughing as soon as I pass by anymore.

Maybe I can take this thing.

DECEMBER 10
3:42 P.M.

Yesterday George Henderson and his friends busted into Olive Branch wearing fake armor and heavy cloaks and did some improvisational theater with a group of kids. Mialonie, Joelle, Cristina, and even Hector came by. Hector kind of took George's place in heading up the city construction, and I would never say this out loud, but he's doing a good job. The little kids don't talk about George, and at first that made me mad, because he did a lot for them. But Wilma said that these kids have been through a lot, and people come in and out of their lives all of the time. They're used to it, and they just "snatch at the bits of grace they can get."

When I get to the shelter this afternoon, there are some colored lights hanging from the ceiling for the holidays, and a big "Happy Whatever You Celebrate" sign over Wilma's desk. The place feels alive. I think people are bringing friends and family members; there are people working that I've never seen before. It reminds me of that first time I came in and saw George working with the kids, and there was that spark in the room. It's a full-fledged flame now, and a little part of me can't help but think, *I did this.*

I'm a leader. Me. Things really have changed.

Carmen comes over. "I told you," she says.

"What?"

"They're staying around, getting involved." She points to some of the teenagers painting with Jeff. "You brought them here."

"What school do they go to?" I ask.

She grins at me. "They live here, dummy," she says. I take a closer look. I can't tell them apart from the Clarke kids. "Since you stuck with us, and you haven't been acting all funny or stuck-up, they feel like they can be here with dignity. So, like I said: thanks." She hugs me and runs back to the library corner to take care of the people waiting to check out books.

"I can't stay long, I just came to find out about the next mural project," says Hector, breaking into my reverie. "I'm almost finished with the city. Soon I can show you how something else is done." Someone donated a bunch of boxes filled with packing peanuts. Hector looks to see if Ruthie's watching, and she's not, so he picks some up and tosses them at me.

"Thanks for the news flash," I say. He rolls his eyes. "Seriously, I appreciate your help. And I know Ruthie does too."

He smiles. "Yeah," he says. "I hate to tell you this, but you really are a fool for never getting with her. Oh, well, your lack of a brain is my gain." He lowers his voice. "I need some information, though. I want to get her something for the Holiday Jam. I was thinking a necklace or a bracelet. What do you think?"

"Why are you getting her a gift?" I ask.

"Because I'm smooth like that," he says, smirking. "When I

pick her up, I'll just flash the gems and she'll be like putty in my hands."

I stop what I'm doing and look at him. He laughs.

"I don't mean *that*, 'Dad,'" he says. "Maybe I was wrong about how you feel about her." He narrows his eyes. "Don't get any ideas, though. You missed your chance. If you ever even had one."

"I don't know what you're talking about," I say quickly. "I just didn't know you were picking her up, that's all. So, you guys are going together, like a date?"

"Yeah. Didn't you know?"

"Um, yeah, I just forgot is all. With all of this stuff here, and the campaign, I forgot all about the party." I pick up some packing peanuts and throw them in a garbage can. Ruthie is across the room; she looks over and smiles, but I can't tell if she's smiling at me or at Hector. I decide to leave early too.

6:00 P.M.

When I go in through the side door of the church, it feels like someone has just been there. I look around without moving too much; seems like the coast is clear, so I slip into the sanctuary. I do a quick bow/salute thing toward the altar and head for the pews.

"Hello, Reginald!" Reverend Coles. Again: Why can't there really be an invisibility cloak?

"Um, hi, Reverend . . . Coles," I say.

"Cools," he says, chuckling and snapping his fingers. He looks like he's in one of those old-school concerts my parents love that come on PBS during pledge time. "So I don't know if you've heard that we're losing Dave," he continues. He shakes his head. "We'll really miss him, won't we?"

I shrug; I seem to remember a period when Reverend Coles went to the bishop to complain about Dave holding youth group during the service.

"Well, I don't want you to worry," he says, patting me on the back. "I am going to pick up the slack while we work on a new plan."

I don't say anything. I wonder if he expects me to make a joyful noise or something, but I just can't.

"Actually," he says, looking away, "I was wondering if you might come talk to me about the youth group." He glances at me. "Tell me what you guys like about it, what I can do to keep things going."

Leave the ministry? I think, and then I immediately feel bad. He looks embarrassed and very, very tired. "Uh, sure, Rev. There's a lot going on right now, but, uh, maybe during winter break."

"Wonderful!" he bellows, back at full strength. "My door is always open." He pats me on the back again. "Did you come in for some reflection and prayer, son? Always a good thing. Seek, and ye shall find. Seek first His kingdom and His righteousness, and all these things shall be added unto you." I'm a little dazzled by the way he's able to turn this stuff on. He doesn't even stop to think. "He fills you when you're empty, with living water. God is good, all the time. Yes, He is. Rest in the Lord. I could use some of that myself." He sighs and walks away. I notice that he limps a little.

I take a deep breath and settle into a pew for some Deep Thoughts (I hope). Something shuffles behind me. I jump up; there's an old guy waking up a few rows back. He's either homeless or a fashion rebel — he's wearing a garbage bag with holes in it for a shirt and a bathrobe over it. His boots don't have laces.

"Got any change?" he asks.

I reach into my pocket for a dollar and give it to him. "Thanks," I mumble without thinking. "Have a good day."

He doesn't answer, and shuffles out of the sanctuary.

Please God, I hope that's not how George is doing now. If God has a plan for each of us, what's up with the raw deals? Sometimes I think life is like this big game, where we have just one opportunity to pick and there's a chance we end up losing it all. Was there something that I was supposed to do to help George, and I was so busy worrying about myself that I let it — let *him* — slide? Did I miss out on a chance with Ruthie before I even knew I wanted one? What about Pops and his job, how unfair that was? How does He expect us to deal with all of this?

I look around the church, and I realize it hasn't changed since I was a kid. The same statues that used to scare me a little, the bulletin board, the old organ, everything's been here since forever — through the big fire five years ago, the Easter extravaganzas, and the Christmas pageants. This place never changes.

But I have. And the older I get, the less I understand. I pick up a pew Bible, close my eyes, and open it. I look at the page; I'm in the book of Daniel, whom I never really liked. They were always holding him up to us in Sunday school — the guy who never doubted or even stumbled, who stood up for what was right even in the face of death, who didn't 'defile himself,' blah blah blah. I like the guys who messed up a little. But it's what I opened to, so I start reading. And when I get to the part where Shadrach, Meshach, and Abednego are in the fire together, I smile. Even if I go down in flames with this campaign thing, Ruthie and Joe C. are going to march around in the fire with me, and we'll stumble out, all singed and coughing, together. I know this. And just like that 'fourth man' who was like 'a son of the gods,' whatever or whoever it is that holds us together will be there too.

I read to the end, and then I take out my notebook. I'm going to try 'prayer journaling' like Dave used to talk about. I do some deep breathing and say Psalm 23, like Dave said he does. I write down some verses from what I just read, but then I forget about praying and start writing. Not *Night Man*, though. Something new. I'm not sure what it is, but it's something, so I'll just keep going.

7:19 P.M.

When I get home, Pops is watching the Food Network. I sit down next to him.

"Hey," he says.

"Hey, Pops," I say. We sit and watch a very excited team of people frost a cake. Pops is wearing sweats. Even when he's only making phone calls, he always puts on a suit. "Taking a day off?" I joke, pointing to his outfit.

He looks at me and I realize that it wasn't funny. "Sorry," I mutter.

The team is now very sad, because their cake fell. They are going to try to make another even though the announcer says there are only 18 minutes left.

"I can't play the game every day," Pops says. "It's a lot of work being non-threatening, yet professional and enthusiastic. Highly qualified, but not uppity." He sighs. "So yes, I'm taking a day off from the nonsense."

This is probably not a good time to mention that sometimes I wonder if we're going to be homeless. So I tell him something I meant to keep to myself.

"I'm running for president," I say.

He sits up. "What? What do you mean?"

"I announced it last week. Uh, it was kind of . . . sudden." I shrug. But he perked up, so I sit straighter too and clear my throat. "So, yeah, I'm running for president. I want to see some change at school, and I want to, to make things happen."

Pops is grinning like I already won the election. "That's the way to do it!" he says. "I'm proud of you." He's staring and smiling so hard, I'm embarrassed. I look at the TV, where Team Fallen Cake seems to be making a miraculous comeback. "Need any help with your campaign?" Pops asks. "When is the vote? You know, I was the first boy at St. Joseph's to be —"

"We vote right before break. I got this, Pops," I say. "But I'll let you know if I need anything. Thanks. Thanks for offering."

He grins again and stands up. "That's the way to do it," he says again, rubbing my head hard. He turns off the TV.

"Hey!" I say. "It was getting good."

"Please," he says. "We've got work to do. You've got an inaugural ceremony to prepare for and I've got résumés to send out.

Let's roll." He walks toward his study, and turns back and gives me another grin.

Let's roll? I grin back. That show made me hungry. I think Pops forgot about dinner. That's all right; I'll whip something up. I'm getting better and better at that.

DECEMBER 14
7:45 A.M.

"Give a little, get a lot," I say to a girl as I hand her my flyer. "If we demonstrate increased use of our school facilities by inviting the Olive Branchers here, we can make a strong case for additional funding for after-school programs, like a community step team." I can't help but think of Vicky as I add, "And in these competitive times, it does help to show a real commitment to public service on your Clarke Senior High application."

I've been doing this every morning as people walk into school. And it's working, I think. People keep coming to Olive Branch. Vijay's gotten some great footage of youth group kids and Clarke kids volunteering together at the shelter, and Blaylock is going to use it in the package he sends to the mayor's office to apply for that grant money. Blaylock's first reaction whenever he sees me is still a frown, but he doesn't ignore me anymore. And he remembers my name. We have a week till the election.

In homeroom we watch *Talkin' Trash* — a "Special Election Report," according to Sparrow, who's perched on the edge of her seat like she's ready to jump up and accept her Emmy award. Onscreen, she turns to the camera. "This is Erica Barrow, and today *Talkin' Trash* is conducting Man-on-the-Street interviews, impromptu, unedited, and uncut. We want to know what YOU think." The camera zooms in on Vicky, walking down the hall as though she has someplace way more important than eighth grade to be. "Vicky!" Sparrow screams. "Are you ready to comment on your former campaign manager's ascendancy? Was he planning it all along? Do you feel betrayed?"

I hold my breath.

"As you may know, I am now suspending my college freshman representative campaign to be the voice of reason here at Clarke," starts Vicky, with that nightmare smile. "I *have* heard that he's stolen some of my own ideas about community service, but Pukey doesn't understand the most important part — preparing ourselves to serve well, not just doing a bunch of stuff to make us look good."

I'm pretty sure I don't have to feel bad anymore.

"But," presses Sparrow, "your former campaign manager deserting you and then launching a splashy campaign himself — it is a deathblow to your spirit, isn't it?"

"I would have to care more to feel betrayed," says Vicky. "And as for the corruption claims surrounding Pukey's campaign . . . he probably isn't involved." She pauses. "As far as I know."

No she did not just do that.

Then Sparrow flashes her big teeth and chirps, "Mialonie! A few questions . . ." We get to watch Sparrow run down the hall in her really short skirt, and it's not a treat. "Mialonie, I understand that you've been volunteering at Olive Branch Shelter. Does that constitute your endorsement of, um, Reggie McKnight's campaign?"

She said my name! Not Pukey! My actual name on camera!

"I support Reggie and the work that he's doing there," says Mialonie. "People should check it out."

"How do you respond to claims that he is using the homeless as a political opportunity?" says Sparrow.

What?

Vicky comes into the frame and whispers into Sparrow's ear.

"And," says Sparrow, "this just in: He may also be pocketing donations to the shelter."

WHAT?!?!

"Who's making those claims?" asks Mialonie.

"I can't reveal my sources," says Sparrow, and you can tell she's been waiting to say that one.

"Whatever," says Mialonie. "Reggie was down with the shelter way before he entered the race. He has a lot of potential, and an open mind, which is more than I can say for some people."

Sparrow pushes the mic a little closer. "So you're actively campaigning against your ex-boyfriend, front-runner Justin Walker?"

She didn't have to say front-runner.

Mialonie gives Sparrow a look that should have withered her, but Sparrow is inhuman, and just stands there ready to chirp something inane. When Mialonie walks away, Sparrow turns to the camera.

"There you have it, people. Nothing like a woman scorned. Wonder what Justin could have done to inspire such womanly wrath? Maybe he just didn't understand 'a woman's worth.' Clearly, Mialonie is an independent woman, and —"

I tune out. Sparrow has an amazing ability to latch on to a

word and use it until she's wrung every last bit of meaning out of it. I don't want to hear the word "woman" ever again.

Justin is the first to leave class; he's not smiling. Donovan scurries out behind him. I look at Joe C. "That wasn't too bad, huh?" I say. "Except for that part about me pocketing donations. I mean, no one's going to believe that, right? We don't even ask for money."

He grins. "Come on, Vicky was so obvious about her Machiavellianness that it's not very Machiavellian. I think that segment was sweet. Justin has some competition . . . and you have some Mialonie!"

We smile and punch each other's arms, pretending that we're the kind of guys who joke like this every day. A couple of people say "Hey, Reggie," as we walk down the hall.

"Should be a good poster party," says Joe C. "Maria might stop by too."

If she can leave that alternate universe she exists in, I think. But I don't say anything. I'll leave Joe C. to his fantasy life. Mine's on its way to becoming reality.

11:47 A.M.

Ruthie is kind of quiet at lunch, spending most of her time talking to Cristina and Joelle (who sits with us every day now). I don't look over at Justin and Donovan's table. I don't have time really; people are coming up to ask me about Olive Branch and the campaign. My talking points seem to have caught on. I did a Clarke wish list too, and make sure that people know that I'm ready to fight for the elimination of tuna tacos and an increase in the bathroom paper products supply. I don't go as far as promising to eliminate tests, but I do promise to create an "Assessment for the Real World" Task Force that will work with the administration on alternative grading systems and test prep classes that emphasize stress relief.

George Henderson stops by the table. "We should hold a rally right after school," he says, "to capitalize on this *Talkin' Trash* momentum. What do you think?"

"I think I'll give it a try," I say.

He gathers Ruthie and Joe C. for a quick conference, and when lunch is over, they tell me to meet them at the front door right after school. I don't know what they've got planned, and *I* definitely don't have a plan, but I'm ready.

"Thanks, guys," I say. "Let's do this." I'm feeling reckless. Justin brushes by me; he turns and gives me a quick nod.

That's right, I think. *It's me. Watch out.*

3:03 P.M.

> *"Two, four, six, eight!*
> *Clarke students are really great!*
> *Reg McKnight can sure relate*
> *To what real people want and need*
> *And take us to a higher level*
> *So come on out and join the revel!"*

"*Reg* McKnight?" I mutter to no one in particular. Ruthie is jumping up and down on the steps shouting this "rhyme." Her exuberance seems to be drawing a few people over, and I can't help but think that she looks . . . cute. Hector is standing next to her like a bodyguard, which mars the image a little, but George Henderson convinced her that pom-poms would look more supportive than demeaning, especially since she has on one of her DON'T MESS WITH ME, I'M A REAL LADY T-shirts and a miniskirt with STRONG BLACK WOMAN on it. Her voice is getting hoarse, which is kind of sexy.

I shake myself a little. Focus, Reggie. George Henderson said it would be a good idea to make a little speech ("a rallying cry, har har" he called it), and I still have no idea what I'm going to say. I tried to make some notes during study hall, but ever since the Sharpie incident, Mr. Carter walks up and down the aisles to make sure we're actually doing schoolwork.

Joe C. is sitting off to the side, scribbling, and I'm hoping he's writing another cheer. Ruthie winds up with a shout of *"La Luta Continua!"* which I don't really get, but whatever. The little crowd yells it back. Hector hands her a bottle of water, and she comes over to me.

"I'm not going back out there alone," she says. "Joe C., you're gonna have to cheer with me for the next round. I know what you said, but this is too borderline stereotypical cheerleader. Next time I'm playing my banjo. I've been songwriting."

"Deal," I say, grinning.

"You guys can work out the details and the longing looks later," Joe C. says. He nudges me forward before I can even say anything about "longing looks."

It's just the front steps. It's not a stage. I'm outside, and I'm not Pukey.

I'm me.

"Uh, hello," I say to the crowd.

"We can't hear you!" yells someone.

"President Pukey is making an address!" screams someone else.

I close my eyes for a minute. Then I open them and start again, louder.

"I'm Reggie McKnight and I'm running for president." A couple of whoops and scattered claps. "Basically, uh, I'm running to show that this election can mean something. Volunteering at Olive Branch has shown me that we can do more than just the usual school candy sale or competing with one another." I'm warming up. "Or be negative. We can help others and ourselves by getting past surface issues and making positive changes." I look back at my friends, and they both smile at me. "You may have seen my flyer." I hold it up and start reading. "Academic credit for doing the right thing. A literacy program at Olive Branch, with tutoring and storytimes. Walking partners to and from school for the little kids. Babysitting. After-school activities, like chess, drama, basketball . . . And here at Clarke, um, funding for school sports teams, cleaner bathrooms . . ." The crowd that came to see Ruthie is starting to drift away, so I skip the rest and shout, "Join us, the People's Party, at Olive Branch and beyond! Let's change the world, starting right here, right now!"

A few people clap, maybe half of them, and I take a bow and move off to the side. Joe C. grabs Ruthie and starts a new cheer:

"Get up! Stand up!
Stand up for your rights!
Get up, stand up!

Let's unite and fight!
For community service!
Don't be nervous!
You can help the nabe thrive!
And for A's still strive!
It's not about you,
It's not about me;
It's working together
In unity!"

They finish with a flourish: Ruthie lifts Joe C. high into the air, and that gets the most cheers yet. We're all laughing, and I feel like myself and it's good.

DECEMBER 16
4:30 P.M.

With less than a week until the election assembly, I'm still trying to get my speech together. My new notebook is almost full. I look at the stuff I started writing in the church sanctuary a week ago, the stuff I wrote down the night before the Step Up And Lead rally, and realize that there's something there. Not *Night Man*, but something different. The transcripts are in, and I'm finished with my Listening Ears work, but I'm still listening for stories. And seeing them too — James and Veronica together at Olive Branch, the painting, the library corner, Wilma sorting through all of those donations and wrapping them up with dignity . . . I need to talk to Vijay about our documentary. I can see the tagline: "Ordinary People Who Do Extraordinary Things." It needs work, but I like the concept. I think about showing this notebook to Ruthie; maybe it'll convince her to take my writing seriously. I don't know why that matters to me so much.

What I'd really like to do is talk to Dave about it, but since I can't, I open my Bible to the book of James, since that was the last part he talked to me about. It's kind of confusing — like it says you can't have faith without "works," but I remember all the times Reverend Coles warned us not to think we could do anything to earn salvation. Of course, he made a crack about the Pope on the one day Joe C. visited.

Okay, got to focus on my speech. Who would've thought I'd have this many chances to reinvent myself? Center stage again. This time's going to be different.

There's a knock; Pops sticks his head in. "Working on the big campaign?" he asks.

I nod. "Um, sort of, Pops."

"I know, I know, I'm not supposed to talk about it, but . . . just let me know if you need some help." He comes in and walks over to my desk. He picks up the Black poetry book. "Have you looked at any of these?" he asks.

"Yeah," I say, glad that I'm not lying. "They're pretty good."

"This was one of my favorites," he says, and then clears his throat.

"If we must die, O let us nobly die,
So that our precious blood may not be shed
In vain; then even the monsters we defy
Shall be constrained to honor us though dead!"

"Oh, and the ending —" He continues:

"Like men we'll face the murderous, cowardly pack,
Pressed to the wall, dying, but fighting back!"

"Claude McKay doesn't get enough recognition," he mutters. "The Jamaican literary tradition doesn't get enough recognition."

I try not to roll my eyes. "So Pops, what is he saying? Fight even though you know you're going to lose?"

"Well," he says. "Why not go down fighting? You'd feel better about yourself."

"But you'd still be a loser," I say. "So what's the point?"

He yawns. "I guess it depends on how you define loser," he says. He puts the book back on the desk. "Do you want some mint tea?"

"No thanks, Pops," I say. "But I appreciate it." He stands there for another minute, then leaves.

There's another knock. Monica comes in before I even say that she can. She's holding the phone. "For you. Some guy named Justin."

I take the phone and wait until she leaves.

"Hello?" I say.

"Hey," he says. "Reggie? What's up?"

I clear my throat. "Yeah. What's up?"

"So you've been really holding it down at that homeless shelter," he says. "People are talking about you all over school, how you're spreading positivity and all that."

"Something like that," I say.

"So, I was thinking . . . Do you want to just work together on this?"

"What do you mean?" I ask.

"The election. Do you want to run together, as a ticket?"

"Clarke's never had a VP spot," I say. "It's just the president."

"I can get the rules changed," he says.

I bet you can. Now that would shoot me into the social stratosphere. Hanging out with Justin, being his running mate —

"Wait, who would be who?" I ask.

"Huh?" he says. "Oh, yeah. Well. I mean, I guess it would make sense for me to run as president. . . . Blaylock's been, uh, giving me a lot of advice, and, well, it just seems like it might be smoother."

Of course. I can be the sidekick.

"I can talk to the TV people who covered that rally you missed. If we teamed up, I could probably get us some news coverage."

"I can't imagine Donovan liking this idea," I say slowly. And that, I realize, is a very attractive part of Justin's proposal.

"Donovan will get with the program. I don't like a lot of things he does anyway," says Justin. "And I need to let him know it."

It's tempting. I could be redeemed. I could finally be That Guy I've always wanted to be. Or at least That Guy's Friend.

"Um," I say.

"This way we can both be winners," he says. "And not just . . . one of us."

I know he was going to say "and not just me." There's a pause. It would be so easy to say yes and walk into school tomorrow under a Justin cloak of cool. And the thought of how mad it would make Donovan to see me take his place, be the guy who talks to the pretty girl's best friend, the guy who's protected and popular by virtue of association, no matter what. And vice president is nothing to sneeze at. I could still do the Olive Branch stuff, and I'd probably get more attention with the Golden Boy's light reflecting off of me. It's almost enough for me to agree.

This little light of mine, I'm gonna let it shine.

"I'm sorry, Justin. I'm going to stay in the race. You know, finish what I started and all. But thanks."

"No problem," he says. I wonder if Justin *has* problems.

"We could still talk about the TV coverage though," I say. "If you still want to."

"Sure," he says. "After the election is over, let's talk."

"Thanks for calling," I say. "I appreciate it." And I do. The guy's popular for a reason. Okay, lots of reasons, but I guess his basic decency is a big part of it.

"I'll see you at school," he says. "And at the O.B."

"See you," I say, and hang up.

While I'm still standing there, the phone rings again. It's Ruthie.

"What's up?" she asks.

I don't want to talk about Justin's call yet. I'm not sure what just happened.

"Nothing," I say. "I was doing some writing, thinking about the O.B. — I mean, the shelter."

"I thought you were done with that comic book thing," she says. "Oh! Were you working on your speech?"

"I'm just . . . writing, don't worry about it," I say. "So, you never told me that you're going to the dance with Hector."

"Well, I mean . . . we're not going *together*, we're just kind of walking there side by side, and then entering the building in unison. . . ."

"Uh-huh. So, he's, like, your boyfriend now?"

"Don't be crazy! My parents would kill me."

"But what if your parents wouldn't kill you?" I say in a low voice.

Another pause.

"Can we talk about this seriously, after the dance and the election and everything is over?" I ask.

"Yes," she says. "We can always talk." We stay on the phone for a while, not saying much, until we make a pact to hang up at the same time.

I slip out of the house and head to the Q train. I'll catch heat for being late for dinner, but I go to Union Square anyway, and I'm not disappointed. He's there, and he's finally in season, banging out those Christmas songs on his battered old steel drums. I walk right up and he hands me the mallets like he's been waiting for me. This time, when I finish playing, I don't even wait for applause. I drop my allowance in the bucket, thank him, and go back home. I sing under my breath the whole way.

DECEMBER 17
6:03 P.M.

"Come *on*!" bellows Monica. "I can't be late." She's standing by the door, holding the "Mama" shoes that she got from Auntie Joyce to wear in the play tonight. She got a standing ovation opening night, and I have to say that I'd probably go see her again even if my parents weren't making me.

"Monica Angelica Una McKnight," says Mom calmly as she walks down the stairs. "You must be a real lionheart gal to be talking to me like this."

"Sorry," mumbles Monica.

Mom wraps her arms around Monica. "It's okay. I know you're nervous. And I know you're going to be fabulous. You look" — she glances down at Monica's short dress and slips a grandma sweater over her shoulders — "beautiful."

Let's not get carried away, Mom.

Pops comes out of the kitchen. "Son! I've been thinking about your campaign, and —"

"This is *Monica's* night!" Monica, Mom, and I say in unison. We all laugh.

"You're right," says Pops. "I apologize. And Monica, I'm proud of you." He whips out a bouquet of flowers from behind his back. It's the third one in three days.

It's probably a light trick or something, but my sister is glowing. She and Mom hold hands as they stand in the foyer; Mom kisses her forehead and tugs the dress down a little more.

As we head out, Pops whispers, "I have an idea for your speech. You'll love it. It's exactly like what I did when Dexter Robertson tried to undermine my second term as Head Boy. We'll talk later."

DECEMBER 20
7:47 A.M.

I almost walk right into Mialonie, who's waiting at my locker when I get to school.

"Hey, Reggie," she says. "I wanted to tell you that Josie and I are thinking about doing a recipe book with the Olive Branch seniors. My mom said she could get her sorority sisters to help us out."

"That sounds good," I say.

"I'm glad you talked me into sticking with it. Remember when Dave first told us about it? That seems like a lifetime ago."

I still haven't spoken to Dave since I stormed out of the library. I'm not even mad at him anymore, but I don't know how to tell him that.

"Yeah," I say. "Things are completely different."

"You must be really excited about the election. Seems like it's gonna be a close race."

"You think so?" I say. "I mean, I know how I compare to Justin."

Mialonie sighs. "I still have that book . . . You've got a lot of potential, you know. I can take you shopping, did I tell you that? You could wow everyone by becoming a whole new guy."

Just when I'm getting comfortable being Reggie. I change the subject. "Didn't you used to go out with Justin?"

"Why do you ask?" she says, a definite chill in her voice. When people answer a question with a question, they don't want to answer.

I sigh. "No reason. Stupid question. Forget it."

"Are you okay?" she asks.

"Just tired," I say. "And I have to work on my speech for the assembly."

"Well, then you'll be fresh and spontaneous," she says.

"Yeah, being an eleventh-hour candidate has its advantages," I say. "I hope."

She laughs. "Well, the bell's about to ring," I say. "I'll see you at the poster party."

"See you," she says. I stuff my backpack in my locker and grab my books. I don't watch her walk away.

4:24 P.M.

I can't believe this turnout. Even though everyone is scrambling to get term papers done before the break, a bunch of people have shown up for the poster party at Joe C.'s. Not only are Mialonie and Josie actually here, but Cristina, Joelle, Vijay, James Kim, and George Henderson and his LARPing crew came too. And Hector. The election is in two days, and we are focused.

"Slogans, people!" Joe C. calls out. "We need catchphrases!"

"The winds of change," says Josie. "Or just wind of change, I guess."

"Meh," says Joe C., and Josie frowns. She's not used to a luke-warm reception.

"Too strong to stop," says James Kim, in a surprisingly deep voice. Josie turns away from Joe C. and looks at James with interest. She whispers something to Mialonie.

"Yeah, that's cool," says Hector. "But use the number 2, instead of words." I'm impressed, but then he adds, "Number 2 . . ." and starts giggling.

"Vote McKnight to fight for right," says Joelle in a soft voice. She still looks down when she talks, but I think she knows that we're all friends here. Even Mrs. C.'s dogs seem to be on my side. They're not slobbering on everyone and jumping around; Joe C. just put on the Food Channel, and they're all lined up on the couch watching this Tyler Florence guy. I feel like offering them a bowl of popcorn.

Ruthie sits next to me. "It's a regular Rainbow Coalition in here, it's fantastic!" she whispers.

"Huh?" I ask. "What's that?"

"Don't you ever talk to your parents?" She shakes her head. "It was a civil rights organization, big in the eighties, all about people of all races working together. It's still going strong. Never mind. Oh, and it's also a political party in Kenya. But I'm sure you knew that."

"Yeah, fill me in later," I say as she stands to go.

George Henderson comes over. "This is great!" he stage-whispers. "People are coming out to support you! I know a winner when I see one."

I wonder if he's ever actually looked at Justin. I still haven't mentioned Justin's offer to anyone.

Joe C. walks up and pats me on the back. "This place is buzzing. We're almost there!" He walks away humming something. I think he thinks it's "Hail to the Chief," but I'm pretty sure it's the 1812 Overture. I'm smiling to myself when I notice Ruthie touch Hector's arm, and I can't help myself; I walk over there and grab hers.

"Ow!"

"Sorry," I say. "Joe C.'s busy — can you help me get some more food?"

"Sure," she says, and follows me to the kitchen.

Mrs. C. may not be around much, but she keeps the place well stocked with snack food. Ruthie and I start grabbing bags of chips and stuff from the cabinet. I rip open a bag and down a few.

"I think Joe C. has some big musical plans for your victory party," Ruthie says. "Can you make sure it's not all Bob Marley? He means well, but I think he's trying to be authentic and everything."

"Bob Marley *is* authentic," I say. "But I know what you mean. I'm on it." I swallow my mouthful of chips. "So." I clear my throat. "My mom went to Mile Gully Primary School."

"Uh-huh," she says, raising her eyebrows.

"And I was thinking that maybe Clarke could do some sort of partnership thing with them, or another school in Jamaica — maybe an exchange or a fund-raiser or something. And maybe you could help me; you're like the global girl of the campaign. . . ." I trail off, and she hugs me.

"Reggie! Going global! I'm so excited! Oh, I have so many ideas —"

"If I win, I'll need you to keep me on track," I say. "And thanks for the rally. I know it wasn't exactly your style."

"Rah rah," she says, smiling. We stand there for a minute. I wonder if my breath is offensive. At least it's not onion and garlic. She smells good.

I lean toward her. . . .

Mialonie pops her head in. "Reggie!" she calls. "We need your opinion."

Ruthie picks up a couple of bags and heads out. "I'll take these," she says softly. "Aloha."

Mialonie comes into the kitchen. "These are the slogans we have so far — I kind of like this Dark McKnight idea on the list."

"That was Ruthie's idea," I say. "I sort of shot it down before. I guess I was wrong."

"Oh, I didn't know she came up with that," she says. "She's into comics?"

"No," I say. "She was just trying to come up with something that related to me. She knows the stuff I like." I smile.

"What's so funny?" she asks.

"Uh, nothing," I say, trying to look casual. And powerful. And serious. And taller. I'm always trying to be someone else around Mialonie. It's kind of exhausting.

"Oh, we need more dog treats too. A commercial for some show called *Barefoot Contessa* came on and the dogs started barking at the TV. Joe C. said you know where everything is."

I go over to the cabinet under the sink and pull out a bag of dog treats. "Here you go," I say. "And, um, Mialonie, I really appreciate you coming out like this. Thanks."

She grins. "It's all good. I think you're going to win this thing."

I wonder if she really thinks so. I wonder if I really think so. Then I remember Sparrow's "woman scorned" commentary.

"I haven't told anyone this," I say. "But Justin asked me if I wanted to run with him. As a ticket. Together."

"What about The Weasel?"

"Who?" I say.

"Donovan," she says, like I should know. And I do, but I didn't realize *she* did.

"Yeah, that's what I wondered. But he sounded kind of over Donovan. Anyway, I turned him down."

I don't know if I want her to be impressed by the fact that Justin asked or by the fact that I turned him down. Both, I think. Is she impressed? I lean against the counter and try to look like a maverick.

"It figures," she says, rolling her eyes. "Justin's always in the market for a sidekick. It's like oxygen to him. He thinks he's such a big dog."

"So, what were you? To him, I mean," I blurt out.

She shrugs. "It was no big thing. And it was like a hundred years ago, the beginning of sixth grade." And I can tell that I really shouldn't bring it up again. "I'm nobody's sidekick, though," she says, laughing a little. "That's for sure. And you can be a big dog too, with some help. You should go the whole superhero route. Posters with you wearing a cape, emphasize how you saved the O.B. kids."

"I didn't 'save' anybody," I say. "And that's not really me."

She leans over a little, and I look into her eyes.

"It could be," she whispers.

"I used to take piano lessons with Ruthie," I say. *Where did that come from?*

She looks confused, and then says, "Uh, really? That's very nice." She moves away, and I'm . . . relieved?

"Yeah," I go on, "for a long time. Well, she still does, but I don't anymore." Dear God, please zap my mouth now.

Mialonie turns to close the cabinet door. "Um, okay," she says. "I'd better get these out there, before the dogs start howling." She pauses for a minute, and then she leaves.

I want to bang my head against the refrigerator but instead I slam my fist on the counter. "OW!" I yelp.

Joe C. pops his head in. "You okay?" he says. I shake out my hand and nod. He grins. "You were in here for a long time, playa." He wiggles his eyebrows. "What happened?"

"Nothing," I say. "And don't say 'playa,'" I add, taking a sponge out of the sink and throwing it at him.

He dodges the sponge and it hits the wall. "Gross," he says. "You're going to have to wipe that up."

I do, and then without looking at him, I say, "I still don't know if I can do it."

Joe C. knows exactly what I mean. "It's just a speech. You've got this. Anyway, you've been speechifying for, like, two weeks now."

"But . . . me, on that stage again?"

He's quiet for a minute. "Well, you *could* do a stunt or something, or do your speech in Pig Latin, like —"

"No, it's not a joke, or some silly thing anymore. I can't do that to the shelter, or people here who care. Or myself." I toss the sponge back into the sink and wash my hands. "Where's Maria?" I ask.

"Oh, she just texted me," he replies, looking all sad, and I feel like a jerk. "She can't make it. And she was going to bring zeppoles too."

For a second I picture Maria in some kind of ruffly old-fashioned dress with red-and-white checks, throwing a pizza up into the air and saying *"Mamma mia!* That's *amore!"* I laugh.

"What's so funny?" Joe C. asks.

"Nothing," I say. "She'll bring them next time, right?"

"Right," he says, and we walk into the living room together. I've got to keep believing in second chances.

DECEMBER 21
8:08 A.M.

I'm like a boxer before the title fight. Except I'm not in the ring. I'm in the auditorium. About to be front and center stage again. And the fight is against my own stomach.

"You have your talking points, right?" asks Joe C. "Do you want to go over them again?"

I hold up the two sheets of paper. "One: Clarke was built on a mission and a message. Two: We have not fulfilled them. Three —"

"You're not going to just read the list like that, right?" Joe C. interrupts. "Start with the 'We Can Do It' stuff."

"I thought the list sounded more take-charge," I say. "You told me I sounded like an infomercial before." I'm sweating. I was going to go without eating anything this morning, but my mom wasn't having it and made me have a bowl of cereal. Ever wonder what partially digested oat flakes taste like? Because I can tell you.

"Leave him alone, Joe C.," whispers Ruthie. "But Reggie, you have to make eye contact with the audience. Show your personality. You're reading too much. You know this. You've got this."

Was the milk sour? I think the milk was sour.

Blaylock walks over and grumbles, "You're up first, Reginald. Five minutes. Keep it . . . clean." He's wearing sneakers.

"You guys should go," I say. "Thanks for everything." Joe C. pounds me on the back, Ruthie hugs me, and then they're gone.

I'm alone. Justin must have some big entrance planned; I've seen a bunch of kids wearing matching sweatshirts and holding "JW'S HOUSE" posters, but I haven't seen The Man himself yet.

I look at my speech again. "I'm Reggie, and I believe in myself, and I believe in you. We are the future; let me lead the way."

Wait, did I actually write that? I think back to all the reading and writing I did at church and at home. It can't come down to Vicky-esque clichés.

"Let me give you a few reasons why you should vote for me. *One: Clarke was built on a mission and a message. Two: We have not fulfilled them. . . .*"

Maybe Joe C.'s right, that's too negative. Should I start off with *Seventeen: Olive Branch provides shelter and care to over one hundred families a month. We can help*? Is it too late for me to go get Charlie?

"Keep up the bad work, Pukey," says Donovan, emerging from the shadows like in some Batman comic.

Don't answer. Don't listen. *Twenty-Three: We have the talent and resources to share.*

"Is that your little speech, Pukey?" he continues. "Why don't you save it, because nothing can save you. How will it feel to be known not only as the guy who thought he could beat Justin

Walker, but the guy who puked twice in the same year in front of the whole school?"

I swallow.

"Because you will. I can tell you're about to do it now. You want to puke, don't you? There's bile tickling your belly and climbing up your throat like a snake. Do you feel it? Are you scared?"

"Shouldn't you be with your candidate?" I say, and I hope he can't hear my voice trembling. "Or maybe he doesn't even want you around."

"I've seen you trying to talk to Mialonie Davis. You know you're her latest makeover project, right?" he says, as though I haven't spoken. "Usually she picks some ugly girl, but this year . . . this year, you were so pathetic and ridiculous that she chose you. Congratulations, son. So maybe you should try to at least keep us in suspense, choke a few words out before you do the Technicolor yawn all over the stage. Again. Your Whiteboy boyfriend can comfort you with his wannabe rhymes. Hey, maybe you can hit your girl Ruthie with it. Covering her in yak would be an improvement —"

I lunge, and even as he steps aside to let me trip and fall, I see the fear in his eyes. I see it. I hit the floor, breathing hard. My speech pages are scattered, and I hear Blaylock introduce me as I pull myself up.

"The first candidate up will be Reginald McKnight," Blaylock intones, turning toward me.

I brush past Donovan as I head onstage.

"You forgot your speech, punk," he mutters.

I don't even look at him. "No I didn't."

8:23 A.M.

"So, uh, hello. I'm Reggie — Reginald Garvey McKnight, and I'm running for president. . . . Thank you. . . . A couple weeks ago I got up on a table in the cafeteria, and, uh, and made my big announcement. And it felt pretty good, standing up there and being the center of attention.

"But, um, there are times when being the center of attention hasn't felt so good. Yeah, I guess you remember. . . . See, I thought that you'd never forget it, and it looks like I was right. . . .

"But then I got involved with the Listening Ears Project, and the Big Buddy program (hi, Charlie), and I stopped thinking about myself so much. I know adults think that's all we do, think about ourselves, but that's not always true. You've proven that over the last couple weeks by getting involved with Olive Branch. And I'm proud of you. And I want to thank you, because I've learned some lessons.

"Anyway, I was talking about never forgetting it. I realize that the thing is, I was the one who couldn't let it go, the whole . . . Pukey thing. Yeah, I said it. I let it define me.

"I wanted to be a leader so that you guys would see me in a new way, so that I could have a new image. Image is so important to us, isn't it? Most of us don't want to be weird or even just a little different. We just want to fit in. But what I've learned is that there are more important things than fitting in. That being true to yourself — even when sometimes you can't figure out who you are — will last a lot longer than being popular. That it's really hard to help anyone else when you're focused on yourself. I needed to see myself in a new way first. I learned a lot and was given a lot by getting involved with the Olive Branch. It's been humbling; I was just a small part of things. And that's okay. I'm the little guy. There's room for the little guy — there's a need for the little guy.

"So I can't say that I'll be the most charismatic leader Clarke has ever had. That's not me. My opponent is a good guy, and he's a popular guy, and if you choose to elect him, I'm sure he'll do a good job.

"But I'm sure I'll do a good job too, if you elect me. We can work together to bring the Clarke principles to life, just like I said.

"The activist Cesar Chavez said, and I memorized it because it's so true, 'We cannot seek achievement for ourselves and forget about progress and prosperity for our community. . . . Our ambitions must be broad enough to include the aspirations and needs of others, for their sakes and for our own.' *For their sakes and for our own.* Clarke is already making a difference at the Olive Branch, and I think the Olive Branch is making a difference at Clarke. People are stepping outside of their circles to work together. And there's so much more that we can do together. We can start in little ways, by being kinder to one another, by welcoming strangers, and by leaving each other room to grow and change.

"We can make a difference.

"I know that usually that means something big and flashy and, um, newsworthy, but just saying hi to someone you've never spoken to before makes a difference. Sitting at a different lunch table sometimes makes a difference. Remembering to, um, love the people who love you makes a difference. So, uh, maybe that made no sense at all. I'm still trying to figure things out myself — I'm a work in progress.

"I want to say some words that I, uh, didn't get to say on the first day of school: 'We, the Clarke family, refuse to wallow in miseducation, but will fully participate in the teaching and learning of one another. We have an abundance of smart, art, and heart to create the community of service that our ancestors dreamed of.'

"Think about it. You don't have to do something BIG. Just something right. And when you do something wrong, that's not the end of it; you can step up again and still do something right. We can build up without tearing down, even if it's only in baby steps. I had this fantasy of winning big in this election; I've learned that sometimes winning big really means living small.

"Um, thank you."

DECEMBER 22
6:47 P.M.

I put on too much of this stupid body spray and now it's too late to take another shower. I brush my teeth for the fifth time, check my nose for boogers, and look at my watch; okay, now I really have to go. I don't want to get to the Holiday Jam too early and stand around getting stale, but I don't want to get there too late and have everyone turn to look at me as I walk in. Besides, they're going to announce the election results right in the middle of the party; I can't miss that.

At first I thought I'd completely messed up on the speech. My voice was all thin and mumbly half the time, and that was probably a good thing because I don't think I made any sense. I was close, I think. I feel like when I was little and we'd rent a car to go to Sesame Place and I couldn't wait to get there, and every time I'd ask, Mom would say, "We're almost there, honey." I think I'm almost there. I can be there in time to make a good president; I believe that. But I'm not sure who else does. There were some giggles, especially when I talked about love and when I brought up the Pukey thing, but afterward a lot of people said "Good luck, Reggie," in the hall, and a few even came to my locker to ask about Olive Branch and tell me some of their ideas.

Before the polls had even closed yesterday, Ruthie changed the New World Order Collective to a club called Agents of Positive Change; she asked me if I wanted to be copresident, but she's meant to lead that one. I'm going to work with Vijay and Joe C. on making this documentary about people at places like Olive Branch, sort of like a visual Listening Ears Project. I really have a lot to thank Dave for. I should have called him, or at least e-mailed him; I'll see him tonight at the dance and I don't know what I'm going to say. I'll just wing it and pray for mercy. Story of my life these days, but it's working out okay.

I try to sneak out without anybody noticing, but the creaky step gives me away and Mom, Pops, and Monica all rush out of the kitchen and go "awwww" and take pictures and hug me. (Monica kind of gives me a shake and makes a big show of sniffing.) I can't believe Mom made it home this early; she must have really zipped out of there. She's treating Monica to a movie, and Monica seems real enthusiastic about it even though Mom has already made her change her outfit twice. Pops pulls me aside and gives me a little extra cash; I don't know why, the party is at school right down the street, but I'm not going to complain.

I get out of the house in one piece (barely) and walk/run to school. I stop to catch my breath, and there's a tug on my sweater. It's Charlie.

"Hey, Charlie!" I say. "What are you doing out so late?" I look around and see his mom a few feet away. She smiles and waves.

"I'm going home. I had a playdate with Anndalisa," he says. Then he lowers his voice. "We're getting married."

I am proud of myself for keeping a straight face. "Really? Uh, congratulations!"

"Do you want to be my best man?" he asks. "I was thinking that we could wear superhero costumes."

Okay, so I smile a little this time. "I'd love to be your best man," I say. "But I think we should wear our regular clothes."

"But I want to be a superhero!" he says.

"You are, all by yourself," I say. "I was so proud when you told me you apologized to Anndalisa. That was the superheroiest thing ever!" He makes muscle arms, and I laugh.

"Charlie!" his mom calls. "We need to go. And Reggie looks like he's on his way to something important."

"No problem, Mrs. Calloway," I say. I lean down a little to whisper to Charlie. "Listen. I'm starting a new project. About a guy in eighth grade and his friend in kindergarten and all of the different people they meet who help other people."

"Yeah?" he asks. "Can I see it one day?"

"Absolutely," I say. "And not only that, it's a movie, and you can help me make it. We'll be partners and make my house our studio. I'll give you a key."

The look on his face is so good.

"If you're going someplace important," he says, "how come you're not wearing your shoes?"

Oh, no. God, please don't make me have to wear those tonight. "Remember, we're superheroes all by ourselves, no matter what we wear," I say quickly.

He nods. "Yeah. It's who we are inside that counts." He smiles. "And what we are is brothers for real!"

We part ways, and by the time I get to the school doors, I'm cheesing like a fool. I walk in, buy a ticket, and go over to the lockers to wait for Joe C. Donovan strolls over to me, alone.

"Hey, loser," he says. I ignore him.

"You know you hear me," he says. "You're such a punk."

I look at him. Right at him. "I don't have anything to say to you, Donovan. And it seems like you can't think of anything to say to me, since you just say the same things over and over. Why don't we agree to just stay out of each other's way?" I keep my eyes on his. I will not look away first.

"You're gonna lose the election, you know," he says, sneering. "Bad. I don't know why you want to humiliate yourself all of the time."

I just shrug, and look beyond him for Joe C.

"You think you're better than me," he says suddenly. "You always did. But I saw you that day, watching us throw spitballs at Vicky." He narrows his eyes. "You were just glad it wasn't you. Punk."

He's right, and that memory will always make my stomach hurt a little. I know what I did — or didn't do — and I can't change that. But I also know what I *will* do, who I *will* be from now on.

"The difference is that I won't do anything like that again," I say. *So help me God, okay?* "I don't have the same confidence in you."

"You pretended to be my friend because your parents made you, but you never liked me."

I start to say something, but I don't. Because it's true. I never really liked Donovan.

"Yeah," he says, nodding. "Who cares? It's a privilege not to be liked by a loser. That's why I dropped you after you got with your new boyfriend. I could see it."

If this were *Night Man*, Donovan would be getting smaller and smaller with every word, until he was just a speck. And then I would stomp him. But it's not *Night Man*. I remember the promise I made to Charlie. "Listen," I begin. "Or don't. I want to say I'm sorry for the things I said to you that day with the shoes."

"Like I ever cared," he says. "Whatever, freak. Your jokes were weak anyway. You probably got them out of a book."

How does he do that? He sees that he's got me, and smiles. "You're pathetic," he says. "Wait till everyone hears that one."

For a second, I panic. Then I wonder who he's really going to tell. Justin? Sean? I think about the Donovan on the basketball court, the one that I'd be friends with. I know that I'm glad to have the friends that I have, the love that I have in my life, and I almost feel sorry for Donovan because he doesn't.

Almost. I'm not that Christian yet.

"It doesn't matter what you say, Donovan," I say. "It really doesn't."

He just keeps standing there for a while, and I stand and look back at him, right in the eye. I can hear the music from the party, and more and more voices. Sounds like it's filling up.

"Why am I wasting time with you, loser?" he says. He turns and walks off with quick, short steps — the way I walked when I felt exposed and stupid and just wanted to be invisible.

I look at my watch. Where is Joe C.? I wonder if I should just go in and look for him.

"Hello . . . Reggie?"

I turn toward a soft voice. It's a girl with a huge pile of curly black hair and a body like Barbie's. She can't go to this school; I would have noticed her before.

"I'm Maria," she says, smiling. "Maria Salvucci? Joe C.'s friend?"

Maria Salvucci. In the flesh. I smile and put out my hand.

"It's really, really good to meet you," I say. "Finally."

She smiles again. "Joe C. wanted me to come and get you. He's inside, doing the music. He was supposed to just do a couple of mixes, but it looks like they're trying to get him to DJ the whole party."

We go inside, and the cafeteria has been transformed. For a minute it does feel like we're in a teen movie. Joe C. is up on a platform; he sees us come in and he waves, then he goes back to whatever DJs do with all of that equipment. The place is packed. A few people nod, and I nod back. Some of them shout "Good luck!" over the music. Maria goes over to sit next to Joe C. More than a few people's mouths drop open as they stare, and I'm happy for Joe C. I need to remember to tell him that.

There's a group of adults standing in a corner smiling at the kids. Mrs. Lowenstein goes over and inserts herself between Vijay and Veronica, who have melded into one person on the dance floor. I see Dave, and I take a deep breath and walk over.

"Hi, Dave," I say.

"Hey, Reggie," he says. He sounds pretty cheery, and I get the feeling that we could just talk and go on like nothing happened, but I know that I can't do that.

"Dave," I start. "I'm sorry. I, uh . . ." I'm not sure what to say after that.

"It's okay, Reggie," he says. "But thanks, I appreciate the apology."

"Thanks for the second chance," I say.

"I learned from the best," he replies, smiling. "Gotta give as good as I get."

I stand next to him for a while. He's nodding his head to the music. "That's your friend, right?" he asks, pointing to Joe C., and I nod. "He's a star. Shouldn't you be doing eighth grade things like shaking your booty with the ladies? And I know there's a big announcement you're waiting for."

So he does know; Dave probably knows the whole story. Ruthie. Oh, well, I don't mind.

"I've gotta admit, this politics thing is a surprise from you," says Dave. "You're a good guy, Reggie. Politics isn't for the good guys."

"'Why do you call me good?'" I say. "'No one is good but God alone.' Book of Luke . . . I think." I made a Bible joke! Maybe *I'm* going to be Dave when I grow up.

Dave laughs, loud and hard. "Touché," he says.

"I've been hitting the Book," I say.

"Yeah?" he says. "And?"

"And I have a lot of questions," I say. "Enough to want to read more. And maybe e-mail you about it, if that's okay."

"Of course it is," says Dave. "Always."

"I mean, I still don't get why we have wars, why hurricanes demolish whole neighborhoods, why babies go hungry," *and why people are homeless*, I want to add, but I don't. "But I guess I have to do something in spite of that. It's worse if I'm not getting it and doing nothing too. I mean, I can do something about the parts that I do get, right?"

Dave smiles. "You *were* paying attention!"

Paying attention. What if George could see me now? It's weird how someone could have been in my life for such a short time but have changed it so much.

Maria takes over the DJ booth; about half the people on the dance floor stop and stare when she kisses Joe C.

Dave wanders off to talk to Ms. A. I try to scope out the room without looking like I'm doing it. Mialonie materializes right in front of me. She's wearing something gold and glittery, and looks like that girl who hosts the *Top 20 Video Countdown*.

"Hey," she says. "How is it so far?"

I shrug, trying to play it cool. "It's all right. You know, just a middle school party."

She raises her eyebrows. "Oh, you're too cool for that too?"

I start laughing. "Come on, Mialonie. We both know that I'm not too cool for anything." She laughs with me.

"I have to go find Josie," she says, "and then maybe we'll dance?"

"Maybe," I say. She leaves, and as I watch her go I wonder if we're destined for eternal banter.

Ruthie and Hector walk up; Hector's fly is open. I'm not going to tell him. I look at Ruthie and it's like I have super-powered specs on. I can see all of the Ruthies that I know, the Ruthie that punched me in kindergarten and the Ruthie that held my head after I got hit in dodgeball. The Ruthie that talks about the future of the UN because she really cares, and the Ruthie that believes in God, and me. The Ruthie that knows me, really knows me, and sticks by me anyway. The Ruthie standing in front of me who looks shiny and pretty and *good*. The Ruthie who is not like anyone else in this world. Right this second I wouldn't mind being that superhero who sweeps the smart-mouthed heroine off her feet, bends her back for one of those big movie kisses just before the credits roll. But I'm just me; I take a deep breath.

"Hey!" Ruthie says. "I've been wondering when you were going to get here. Isn't this nice?"

"Yeah." I nod. "You look nice."

"Thank you," she says.

"Let's dance," Hector says to her. She looks at me.

"It's funny, I don't remember giving you the Cesar quote," she says. "But I'm glad you could use it in your speech."

"You didn't," I say. "Sometimes I learn things from other sources." She hits my shoulder; a love tap, really, and I grin.

"Where's Mialonie?" she asks.

I shrug. "She's probably around. You guys go ahead, I'll see you on the dance floor."

"Save one for me," she says. "We haven't danced together since the African dance recital when we were seven. Remember? You were the only guy and had to dance with all of us."

"I didn't know how good I had it," I say. We laugh, and they go. Hector steps on her feet right away, and I smile.

I sit down in a folding chair against the wall. A few more people say "Good luck" as they pass by. Sparrow and Vijay wander over, equipment in hand.

"Reggie!" yells Sparrow. "Reggie McKnight! Any final words of wisdom before we get the results?"

"Words of wisdom?" I repeat. "I don't know about all that. . . . Um, it's all good." I give the camera a thumbs-up. Sparrow shrugs and slides away in her high heels.

"You're pretty cool about the whole thing," says Vijay, putting the camera down. "I'd be nervous. Or excited. Or something." I just smile and try to lean back in my chair, but I almost tip over. "I bet that footage we gave Blaylock put us over the edge to win that grant money."

"I hope so. You did a good job," I say. I'm sure Blaylock will blame me into eternity if we don't win that money. And I'm not Brian Allerton; my family can't send me to private school.

"Hey, you want to meet during the break to work on the documentary proposal?"

"Yeah, let's do that," I say. "Joe C.'s already got some good ideas for the sound track too. I told him the theme is everyday heroes of New York City."

"Yeah, that's cool." Vijay points to Joe C. on stage. "He's good." Veronica walks by. "Later, dude," says Vijay, following her.

"Reggie? Are you okay?" I look up. It's George Henderson. He's wearing a velvet tux.

"Oh, hi, George. Just daydreaming. Are you having a good time?"

He nods. "Absolutely. And I've got my real outfit ready too. I'm waiting for the rest of the LARPers to get here." Blaylock is walking up to the microphone. "Hey, it must be time to announce the results. I think you really have a shot — I'm proud to have been a part of your campaign."

"Thank you," I say. "You helped out a lot."

"People paid attention to you," he says. "I think you're gonna win."

"Either way, we've got a lot of work ahead of us," I say. "I'm glad to have you on the team."

Blaylock gets up to the microphone. "Young ladies and gentlemen, I want to thank all of you for making this year's election a success. I am proud of the way that *most* of the candidates comported themselves. Your campaigns exemplified the principles of civic responsibility and community service that we hold dear here at Clarke. I am pleased to see our student body take an interest in —"

"Just get to the results!" shouts Ms. A.

Blaylock frowns. "Without any further ado, the new president of Clarke Junior School is . . ."

Joe C. turns on an electronic drumroll. Ruthie blows me a kiss. Mialonie is dragging Josie over to me and smiling.

I look up and say a quick prayer. I guess it can't hurt.

DECEMBER 23
5:48 P.M.

"You don't need me to tell you some crap about how even though you lost, you really won, right?" Joe C. is storyboarding opening scenes for the documentary. Mom and Pops are in the kitchen making dinner together. Joe C. brought Juiced! for everyone. Ruthie's late.

"No, especially since you make it sound so good." I look at him. "But don't you have any inappropriate facts or weird trivia to distract me from the fact that Justin crushed me?"

"No, I'm done with that for good," he says. "Maria made me quit."

"How'd she do that?" I ask. "She must be a miracle worker."

"She threatened to start inundating me with nineties boy band trivia," he says.

"Ooh, that's cold," I say, laughing.

"Sucks that Justin will get to be the one accepting that giant check for the grant money from the mayor," says Joe C. I shrug as the doorbell rings.

"That's probably Ruthie," I say.

"I'll go down with you," he says, smirking. "Unless you want a minute alone together first."

I start to tell him to come on, and then I think about it.

"You've got a point," I say.

When I get downstairs, Ruthie is standing there, smiling at me and holding a bag of Doritos and a thick book that looks like a scrapbook. "Merry Christmas," she says.

"What's this?" I ask, taking the book.

"Joe C. gave me all of your *Night Man* outlines and his drawings, and I had them bound," she says. "I read them — I hope you don't mind. It's so good. You write a good story, and it . . . has truth. I should have known."

I flip through the book. It's beautiful. She's beautiful. I set it down on the steps.

"It kind of trails off, though," she says. "You have to finish it. How does it end?"

I couldn't have written myself a better opening.

I grab her and bend her backward until we're both almost horizontal. She drops the Doritos. Before she can say anything else, and before we both fall, I kiss her.

I'm not going to get all sappy and soft, and say anything like Ruthie's lips are unbelievably sweet.

I'll just say that it's good. Very, very good. And I'm pretty smooth, if I do say so myself.

I guess it's a good time to roll the credits.

But this is only the beginning.

Acknowledgments

To the Tara Belle Girls, The Take Charge/Be Somebody kids, The Peace of My Mind crew, and all of the young people I've known — your stories are precious and powerful.

To the YaYaYas (Kate M. division), Paula's Kids, The Debs, Tenners, and all of you wonderfully supportive folk of the kidlit community.

To The Incomparable Editrix, Cheryl Klein, for wading through the slush and lavishing Reggie with the love and respect he deserved all along.

To my extraordinary friend and agent Erin Murphy, who is always on my side.

To my dear friend Paula, whose boundless love and generosity of spirit is everlasting, and Madeleine for the perfect writing advice.

To my awesome Writer Buddy who knows good pizza, good books, and is truly good people.

To Yumi Glassman, my amazing gift of a friend and little sister, who never got the manuscript but gets me like no one else.

To the ladies of BSF; Linda, an original "agent of positive change"; Pamela; Ki; Thal; Nantz, who walks every little step with me; Black Ev the Ghostface Killah and true superhero; prayer warriors and lifelong soul sisters Mel-ski-rock and Wend2xBass; David, who put on that bandanna and helped me through those hardest days; Kate, Mama P, Auntie Xie Xie and all of my "other mothers": You restore me, and for you I give thanks.

To my family: my daughter, the most wonderful storyteller I know, who inspires me daily; my sister, my lifelong cheerleader, ever-willing reader, and incredible survivor; my huge-hearted husband, who laughs in the face of irascibility, and never doubts that all will be well, and my parents, who knew I could do it, and loved me through it, no matter what it was. (Thank you, Mommy, for telling me to talk back.) No words can express my love for you all.

To the Author, whose grace allows me to revise every day, and whose unconditional love gives me life.

Thank you.

AFTER WORDS™

OLUGBEMISOLA RHUDAY-PERKOVICH'S

Eighth-Grade Superzero

CONTENTS

About the Author

Olugbemisola Rhuday-Perkovich is often asked about her name, which is pronounced just like it's spelled. She is the daughter of a Nigerian father and a Jamaican mother, and is married to a man of Croatian descent. She was born in New York City, and has lived in the United States, Nigeria, and Kenya. She says, "I spent a number of my younger years traveling to and living in different places. I attended public, private, 'international,' and religious schools. Much of my childhood was spent at a different school for every grade, and each move brought with it opportunities and challenges around identity" — experiences that play into *Eighth-Grade Superzero*.

As an adult, Olugbemisola has worked as a publicist, youth group leader, educational consultant, and freelance writer. She also studied writing with Paula Danziger and Madeleine L'Engle. She now lives with her family in Brooklyn, New York, where she loves to cook, bake, sew, knit, and make a mess with just about any craft form. Please visit her website at www.olugbemisola.com.

Q&A with Olugbemisola Rhuday-Perkovich

Q: *Where did* Eighth-Grade Superzero *start for you?*

A: The seed of the book was an image that popped into my mind one day, of a ten-year-old boy in his bed in the middle of the night, with the covers pulled over his head because there were bugs loose in his room and he was terrified that one would crawl into his mouth—and it was secretly being filmed for a school-TV reality show. At the same time, I also had the idea of this boy throwing up in the cafeteria on the first day of school because of a prank played on him by his older sister. Much later on, as I began to seek out the heart of Reggie's story, I was inspired by people and moments in my life, and by some of the teens that I taught and worked with—particularly their desire to tackle big questions, to be thoughtful, and to be activists in many different ways.

Q: *Which characters were easiest to write? Which ones were the most challenging?*

A: Reggie was not an easy character to write. It took me a long time to love him; he seemed so whiny at first! It was important for me to go back and rediscover his lovable moments and his positive qualities and revise with those things in mind, to add dimension and depth. I can't write without really loving my main character—I may not like them sometimes, and they may do, say, and think things that make me crazy, but they're like family, and I have to love them and want to wade through their lives with them in order to make a story work.

I love Ruthie. I wish I'd been as bold as Ruthie when I was in eighth grade! But even though I was extremely self-conscious, I did try to step outside of myself. Academically and do-it-yourself fashion-wise: Like Ruthie, I was very much into expressing myself that way. My mother always encouraged us to be engaged with more than our personal issues, and to make larger issues personal; we did a lot of rallying, demonstrating, going to vigils, etc. She set a marvelous example that I try to remember as a mother myself now.

I know that I used to get frustrated with a lot of the female characters I read as a teen, and I think that part of why Ruthie developed the way that she did was because of my desire to read about a strong girl who loved herself, who was confident without being conceited, who wasn't self-absorbed and self-pitying, and who woke up every day knowing that she could do something to make the world a better place. A lot of times there were characters in books that I strongly identified with, but I wouldn't have necessarily wanted to hang out with them. I would have liked to have been friends with Ruthie.

Q: *What were YOU like in eighth grade? Did you ever run for school office?*
A: I think I was trying to set a record for number of after-school activities. Obsessed with A+s. Tired of people suggesting that I change my name to something easier when I got older. Certain I'd be a playwright and live in a very

modern Central Park West apartment with lots of windows and stainless steel appliances. I wore lots of neon, rubber bracelets, large and mismatched earrings, off-the-shoulder fashions, miniskirts, and patterned tights. I was an enthusiastic participant in lip-sync competitions, and a member of the (very small, but mighty!) math and debate teams. I was a voracious reader and painfully earnest journal-writer who desperately wished someone would know that I was a "true princess," and a dreamer who was never quite able to mask just how out of place I felt. I did run for office more than once. We'd moved around a lot in my childhood, and I soon found that running for office was a way to navigate the social landscape at all of my different schools.

Q: *The relationship between Reggie and Monica seems especially rich and real. Do you have any brothers or sisters? How did you get along with them when you were kids?*

A: I loved writing the family scenes, and had a lot more that just couldn't fit. Monica and Reggie were just so much fun to write. In the earliest incarnations, Monica was even more of an antagonist—she and Donovan teamed up a couple of times! I really loved exploring how both siblings struggled with image and identity, and how they bonded in that struggle, while always remaining wholly themselves (I hope). Growing up, my younger sister and I didn't have the kind of relationship Reggie and Monica had. (I was pretty bossy, though.) I have a couple of friends, sisters who were much more at odds with each other—when they fought, my sister and I would pretend it was pro wrestling, and say "And in this corner . . ."

Q: *What's next for Reggie, Ruthie, and Joe C. — both in their lives and in your writing?*
A: I don't know if Reggie, Ruthie, and Joe C. will show up on the printed page again, but I do have fun imagining their lives through adulthood. Reggie and Joe C. will probably drift apart for a while; the tension in their relationship will grow, but I'm confident that they will end up stronger friends in the end. When Ruthie's fifteen, she spends a summer in Jamaica, reconnecting with her family and her cultural roots, and she realizes that she's not as connected as she'd thought she was. And Ruthie and Reggie, the couple? They'll have their ups and downs!

Q: *What do you hope your readers will get out of* Eighth-Grade Superzero?
A: My own teen years were some of the richest for me as a reader. I got so many gifts that I'd love to give back in some way. Books were a place of respite for me during a tough time; they gave me a space to work out who I was, even try on different identities at times. My teen reading years were also a period when I learned to read critically.

I hope that readers connect with the idea that there are many different kinds of "heroes," many ways to be an activist—the small things matter, and not everything that we say, do, and think needs to be for public consumption or for some sort of recognition. And I hope they see there is always room for mercy, redemption, and growth.

Q: *What advice would you give to somebody in a situation similar to Reggie's at the beginning? Or to middle school students in general?*
A: We don't have to let others define us. Let's look for the humanity in each other—not get stuck on type and stereotype, and the fear that leads us to be exclusionary. The club doesn't get any cooler when you don't let others in. It's just smaller, in a lot of ways.

Don't let the "tyranny of the urgent" overpower the "urgency of the important." (Those terms are not my own—they're from a book by Charles E. Hummel.)

Sometimes things seem huge—an argument, an embarrassing incident, who's popular and who's not—and they obscure real, precious opportunities in our lives to make change and be transformed.

Keep words like respect, dignity, and compassion in your mental pocket.

Keep a notebook (a real pen-and-paper kind, that no one else sees). Pay attention, and write things down. Even though I cringe at some of the ridiculous and pompous stuff I've written over the years, I think the writing down, the processing, was important. And for me, writing things down, like quotes or passages by others that inspire or provoke me, helps me to remember and use them in real ways in my daily life.

Ask questions. Listen to the answers. Realize that there is often not just one right answer; sometimes there isn't one at all—especially for the "Why?" questions, but you should still ask those a lot.

Make things without worrying about being good at it.

Challenge yourself. Be uncomfortable regularly.

Smile.

And read stories.

Ruthie's Apple-Broccoli Muffins

A message from Ruthie: "Mr. Cutler, the school custodian, wasn't impressed with my first try, so I worked on the recipe. These really are tasty! You can make them yourself, but be sure to ask an adult to help you!"

Ingredients (Makes about 12 muffins)

1 cup all-purpose flour
1 cup yellow cornmeal
3 to 4 tablespoons sugar (raw turbinado sugar is best)
$2\frac{1}{2}$ teaspoons baking powder
$\frac{1}{2}$ teaspoon baking soda
$\frac{1}{2}$ teaspoon salt
2 eggs, beaten
$1\frac{1}{2}$ cups plain whole milk yogurt
$\frac{1}{4}$ cup melted butter
$\frac{1}{4}$ to $\frac{1}{3}$ cup finely chopped broccoli tops (just the "flowers" at the very top—the result will be almost like poppy seeds)
$1\frac{1}{2}$ cups chopped apples

Instructions

Preheat the oven to 425 degrees, and grease muffin tins with butter.

In a medium bowl, whisk the dry ingredients. Then, in a larger bowl, stir together the egg, yogurt, and butter. Add the dry ingredient mixture, and stir just enough to moisten. Mix in the broccoli and apples. Drop the mixture into greased muffin tins, filling them about halfway, and bake for 15-20 minutes.

Additional Notes

- If you're short on time, you can start with any corn muffin or corn bread mix, follow the directions on the box, and then add the apples and broccoli.
- If you'd like a more savory muffin, eliminate the sugar, use $1/3$ cup of broccoli, and add 1 to 2 cups of shredded sharp cheddar cheese.

Adapted from the corn bread recipe in *Spoonbread & Strawberry Wine: Recipes and Reminiscences of a Family*, by Norma Jean and Carole Darden (Clarkson Potter, 1994).

Making a Difference, *Eighth-Grade Superzero* Style

Do you see someone in need, or something you'd like to change? Would you just like to be more involved in your own community, or do something to change the world? Here are some ways to get started as an "Agent of Positive Change":

1. ***Read*** about inspiring real-life kids who made a difference:
   - Neha Gupta, founder of Empower Orphans. She got the idea to help orphans when she was nine years old: http://www.empowerorphans.org/founder*
   - William Kamkwamba, "The Boy Who Harnessed the Wind," who started building windmills and more in Malawi at age fourteen: http://www.williamkamkwamba.typepad.com/
   - Breaking the Chain, a literacy organization founded by teen author Riley Carney when she was fourteen years old: http://www.linkbylink.org/
   - The winners of the Clifford the Big Red Dog® "Be Big in Your Community" Contest: http://www.scholastic.com/cliffordbebig/contest
   - Ari, also known as "Miss Attitude," describes herself as an "Afro-Latina who loves to read and speak her mind." She started her book blog, Reading in Color (http://www.blackteensread2.blogspot.com), to spotlight literature by and about people of color. Ari reads and writes the world, coordinating numerous advocacy

campaigns, because ". . . I want all teens of color out there to see themselves in books."

2. ***Pay Attention*** to things that you care about, issues that are important to you. These can be questions at home, at school, in the larger world — wherever. What do you notice? Who can you help?

3. ***Write.*** Carry a notebook and a pen or pencil wherever you go — you never know when you might notice something you want to think about further, or when your superpower will inspire you!

4. ***Imagine.*** What's your idea of a wonderful world? Picture yourself doing something to bring about the change you want to see. Envision the setting; the people, animals, or things around you; body movements; and dialogue.

5. ***Choose*** three things you'd like to focus on. Write down what you want to do, why you want to do it, why it's important to you, how you think you can best do it, and who is involved. Oh, and when? That part's easy! NOW. Start small.

6. ***Write More.*** Write a letter to your "audience." Who are you writing to? Your friend? Parent? Teacher? Sibling? Community leader? The president? Yourself? Would you like someone to join you in your efforts? Are you asking them to make a change? Think about: What's the most important part of your message? These are some helpful phrases to use in persuasive writing: "This is important because . . ."; "Another reason is . . ."; and "This might remind you of . . ." You can use this letter as a reference for yourself, or . . . send it out!

7. **Talk** to your friends, family, teachers, and community members. Discuss possible ways to take action— letter-writing, petitions, starting a club, making an effort to say hi to people you don't know, asking someone how they're doing, or giving your sibling a random hug. Maybe it's a personal, inner change you'd like to make—it all matters!

8. **Think** for yourself. Reggie had a lot to figure out, and a lot of people telling him what he should do and who he should be. Don't only pay attention to what other people tell you to pay attention to—think for yourself. That doesn't mean you dismiss people who think differently—it's important to listen, to pay attention, and to let others help you develop your ideas. Keep digging for information. Your brain is one of your biggest superpowers—use it!

9. **Get Started** and don't give up! Change doesn't always happen quickly. Sometimes it takes a long time. But YOU can always be a part of bringing about change in your community and beyond. For some ideas, check out the Oxfam Activist Guides: http://www.oxfam.org.uk/get_involved/campaign/activist/guides.html

Many organizations offer tips and resources for kids who want to be changemakers:

- Global Youth Service Day: http://www.gysd.org/resources
- PeaceJam: http://www.peacejam.org/

- Do Something: http://www.dosomething.org/
- Yes! Magazine: http://www.yesmagazine.org/

Some organizations doing great work for and with children around the world:

- Heifer International: http://www.heifer.org/
- Craft Hope: http://www.crafthope.com/
- Girl Up: http://www.girlup.org/
- Rocking the Boat: http://www.rockingtheboat.org/
- Cooking up Change for Healthy Schools: http://www.healthyschoolscampaign.org/event/cookingupchange/
- Teaching for Change: http://www.teachingforchange.org/
- Teaching Tolerance: http://www.tolerance.org/

You can do it!

*All online resources cited in this section were available at the time of publication.

Meet Night Man

Olugbemisola Rhuday-Perkovich says, "I asked my sister, Kikelomo Amusa-Shonubi, to draw these pictures of Night Man for me, and told her to do whatever she thought after reading the book. I think he's perfect! She got the tough/tender thing just right; he looks like he's *lived*, and will use his power and knowledge for good."

Art © 2009 by Kikelomo Amusa-Shonubi

Art © 2009 by Kikelomo Amusa-Shonubi

Also from Arthur A. Levine Books

By Sara Lewis Holmes   ## By David LaRochelle

By Lisa Yee